OFRA

THE CONCUBINE ON THE HILL

Gad Ohana

TotalRecall Publications, Inc.
1103 Middlecreek
Friendswood, Texas 77546
281-992-3131 TL
www.TotalRecallPress.com

FIRST EDITION

1   2   3   4   5   6   7   8   9   10

To my parents,
whose love guided me.

Author(s) BIO:

Gad Ohana. Born in Morocco and raised in Israel. After serving in the Israeli army, he pursued studies in Hebrew, Political science, and music in Miami, Florida. Writing this book was a labor of love. Gad was intrigued by the controversial saga and the taboo affiliation of this biblical story from over 3,000 years ago.

In addition to writing this epic novel, he wrote the libretto and composed the music for "Ofra the Opera," based on the same narrative.

Gad lives in West Palm Beach, Florida.

Editor(s) BIO

Sigrid Macdonald is the owner of Book Magic, a company that provides manuscript evaluations, copyediting, and proofreading.

Acknowledgment

I want to thank the staff of the Jerusalem University library. I would not be able to get my work done without Miss Loren Schissel. For her devotion and assistance. To Mrs. Sigrid Macdonald, from Proofreading, and who introduced me to my Editor/Publisher, Mr Bruce from Total Recall Publishing, who enabled me to reach you, the reader, my daughter, Yael, Deborah, and Liorah, whose presence brought meaning and inspiration to my life.

Prologue

Three thousand years have passed since fifteen-year-old Ofra, a beautiful Judean maiden, walked in the streets of Bethlehem. "Ofra" is a breathtaking story about the monumental mission of introducing the first seeds of an abstract and universal concept of the invisible God.

Young Ofra is mesmerized by Gershon the Levite, her teacher and flutist. They are both sons and daughters of slaves. She is particularly drawn to him when he speaks with passion about his new God in heaven. This is where our story begins.

The twelve tribes, all former slaves and known as Hebrews, returned to their ancestors' homeland, and were called Israelites among their neighbors. In those days, toward the end of the Bronze and the beginning of the Iron Age, the pagan gods Baal and Asherah were the mascots of the land. The Hebrews settled throughout the land and relocated a simple wooden acacia box containing segments of stones engraved with the Ten Commandments. It was their only tangible evidence connecting them to their invisible God, which they used to resist the pagan gods.

The Israelites developed a phobia toward the ruling kings, understanding the dictatorial and corrupt nature of god-kings and pagan priests. They were hopeful, believing that sooner or later, the pagans living among them would follow. The Hebrews chose not to appoint a king in the land of Canaan, which was known as the "Levant," encompassing Syria, Jordan, and Lebanon. The Israelites began to govern themselves through a system based on personal choice, but had to make adjustments to living with complete independence. This form of ruling was managed by elders, judges, and the priesthood. For three hundred years, they would maintain a liberalism rooted in freedom.

Our story mirrors the pioneering struggles and dilemmas faced by the early Hebrew tribes as they sought to establish their identity, especially among the Tribe of Benjamin. The aristocratic younger Benjamin tribe, brother to Joseph, the prince of Egypt, challenged the Priesthood for their leadership of the young nation in Israel. The Benjamins wanted to preserve their aristocratic customs from back in Egypt, including practicing homosexuality as a privilege. They insisted on imposing that privilege on men from other tribes entering their territory. A brotherly feud led to the first recorded civil war in history, sparked by disputes over morality, self-expression, unity, and individual freedom.

Greece, two thousand miles away, was recuperating from its cruel and vicious Trojan war. Ofra, the concubine in Bethlehem, and Helen of Troy in Greece both ignited brutal sagas. These two beautiful women are symbols of different ideologies that forged their way forward into history, each in a distinct direction. In Greece, it was to glorify and expand the powers of the king and the pagan gods. In Judea, the challenge was to plant the first seeds of a universal God concept while preserving unity based on logical, rational, and moral principles. This was opposed to the mythological and pagan spirit that prevailed in that era.

What caused the Hebrews, a small group of people, a drop in the ocean among nations, to march against the pluralistic majority? Like a river that refuses to join the sea. They regarded themselves as a bright meteor slamming into the darkness of paganism, which might have carried with it, on their part, a sense of intellectual arrogance. The Hebrews realized that freedom enhances logic and reason. Did their own truth and worldview trap them? I use historical fiction as a vehicle to walk hand in hand with the biblical storyteller, trying to answer the question that might shed some light on today's reality.

Finally, a woman's pain is never too old to be told or retold. Ofra, the concubine in this saga, is worthy of having a name, voice, burial, and a closure. Ofra deserves to be added to the long list of women's suffrage throughout history.

About the Book

"Ofra, The Concubine on the Hill" is an epic saga inspired by events that took place in the biblical land of Canaan during the Bronze Age, approximately 13th century B.C., thirty years into the Israelites' return to their ancestral land. The first challenge the young tribal nation, led by the young priesthood, encountered was how to keep unity among the twelve tribes under the banner of the new Hebrew code, the Holy Ark of the Ten Commandments. Friction arose when the Tribe of Benjamin, fixated on the past, felt entitled to live by their own ways.

The Benjamin tribe was insistent on keeping the Holy Ark in their territory. At the same time, there was a consensus among the other tribes and the priesthood that a central location was necessary for the Ark to be easily accessible to all the tribes. It was accomplished by selecting Shiloh to serve as a "worship anchor" in the northern part of the country. The tribe of Benjamin vehemently opposed the move. They also wanted to preserve their aristocratic elite customs from back in Egypt, from the times of Joseph, the Prince of Egypt, when they practiced homosexuality as a privilege.

The story revolves around Gershon, a member of the Levite tribe, a teacher, and a keeper of the holy tent. While conducting classes under the sycamore tree, he is lured by the youthful charm and beauty of Ofra. She is captivated by his passion as he expresses his complete devotion to his new God in heaven and to his people. Ofra's father, a wealthy Amorite merchant who had now become a widower after marrying Ofra's mother, a Hebrew, instilled in his daughter a sense of justice and anti-pagan sentiments. Ofra joins Gershon the Levite in his missionary endeavor and moves with him to the Triangle. She soon realizes that a Levite's wife's life is not an easy one, abandons their home, and returns to her father's house. Gershon, unable to live without his beloved Ofra, convinces her lovingly to come home. On their travels back to the Levite's house, their short-lived contentment is abruptly severed. While pausing for the night, they are not welcomed in the Benjamin territory, their brethren's domain, which leads to tragic events, and a civil war ensues.

Chapter 1
"Ascending"

On a day chosen by heaven in the year 1238 B.C., a young Judean woman was set free at dawn in the tribe of the Benjamin territory. She was raped and savagely abused all night long by three men from the Benjamin tribe. She stared at Yarikh (Yarai-ak) the moon god and pleaded for mercy. Her tormented screams were carried away by the summer wind whispering among a big family of pine trees. But Yarikh was deaf and mute, as was the stillness of the night. The three men dragged her breathless body closer to a stone house and left her motionless body at the door. She knew the laws of the land prevailed over a women's pain, and no matter what, the house door will only be opened when Shemesh the sun god appears.

She tried not to look back at the bloody trail. She coughed up blood, spat up mud, and switched to the other elbow, but quickly muffled her screams because she was afraid those horrific men might return. Her frozen arm muscle trapped in midair, was unable to pull down her torn black linen dress. "My husband cannot see me this way," she mumbled. The unbearable sharp pain persisted inside her fragile soft young body like a dagger and yet she managed to cover her naked bleeding body.

"Mother in heaven" she sputtered "what have I done to deserve such a punishment? My father always insisted that I concentrate on El, Jehovah, the only true God, and it's true I was always fascinated with the neighbor's gods and goddesses, but I never worshiped them or even took part in their rituals, as my friends did. Am I being cursed by the gods?' she continued to contemplate. "Maybe because I deserted my husband? Am I being punished by Jehovah, the God of Moses, the Hebrew God? Or maybe it's because my thoughts were not always occupied with his name?" She took a deep breath, her body shivered down to her broken ribs. She didn't know she was being used as a messenger. Her desecrated raped body was a message directed toward her husband, the priest, the Levite. Her head was spinning. She did not shed tears in her early childhood, because growing up she was a happy child, but last night she cried and screamed until her voice was extinguished, and the well of tears dried out.

Her spirit hovered like a bird in the sky, on its journey to heaven, the same way the Egyptians believe when we die, we become a soul. "What is happening to me?" She looked down at the Ephraim mountains. She gazed at the land of Canaan, her birthplace, with its red soil and sharp limestone rocks which exposed their crowns like white eggshells among the sea of trees. She recognized the tiny squares below which were connected with one another. "That is my settlement down there on the mountain slope" her fatigued mind continued its passage. The soft and gentle illuminating rays were barely peeking over the Judean Mountains at dawn, and yet the smallest hint of daylight hurt her bloody swollen eyes. Her mind froze the second she saw the yard and the house; it all looked so serene and peaceful as if Shemesh, cleansed away the horrible events which took place last night in this very place. "My painful screams and were lost among the evergreens" she muttered while her tongue wiped salty tears from her torn lips.

El in heaven witnessed the unspeakable events she suffered. Like Nanna the goddess, El was silent and voiceless. She heard upsetting stories from her father, like the one about the Priest who tore a daughter away from her mother's hands only to be sold to another Priest. She never imagined she could encounter a fate like the one she endured from those horrifying men violating her during the night. "Why are the Gods not listening?" Now at this very moment she was silently screaming "Why are the Gods silent? Why am I being deserted by the Gods?" How can this be?" she murmured while struggling to breathe.

Ofra is the concubine on the hill, as she is called and labeled by others. Though furthest from the truth, she is often called the harlot. She saved her husband, the priesthood, and their honor! Even if El was silent, she could still be proud of her pure naïve self. She had no way of knowing if her Gershon survived last night's terrifying ordeal. She tried to concentrate her swollen eyes on the wooden door. This is the same place where the night before, the city people swarmed the yard. They were shouting to get "the man" out of the house, because they wanted to "know him." They yelled and hollered and demandingly insisted to see him. The man they wanted was Gershon, her husband, the Levite, the servant of the new emerging priesthood.

The sun's warm rays caused the tall Judean pines to shed their melted dew in the morning breeze. It caressed young Ofra's inflamed face and broken body. She licked the droplets with her parched tongue. Although it is not customary for a guest to take it upon himself to open the door to his host's house, at last, the old man's door was opened by her husband, Gershon. She knew very well what these sickening men were capable of, but so glad to see her husband alive. Gershon did not wait for the old man, and he opened the door before the first light hoping to see Ofra approaching the house. He also wanted to leave early to avoid the townspeople before they awoke and brutally confronted him.

"I knew Gershon would not abandon me," she reasoned lying on the steps. Gershon, having not slept for a solitary minute, prayed, and expected the best outcome as he opened the door.

Her blurry eyesight followed his movements as she was drifting into a complete unconsciousness and began connecting with her transcendence. She wanted to linger a moment longer to take a last glimpse at Gershon and express her suppressed rage in that last moment. Believing Ofra simply fell asleep on the steps, Gershon's stern controlled voice faded into her decimated hearing capacity. "Get up and let's go. Quickly!" He stood with his back to her at a measured distance and didn't notice her bloodied body. He looked fatigued in her dimming eyesight with his wide shoulders slumped inward. He had the appearance of a man who had been up all night. "Get up and let's go. Quickly," he repeated. The words sounded so distant, like a voice which persists, bouncing back and forth, dissipating into nothingness. Gershon is clearly naïve as he had no idea what the Benjamin's were capable of doing to Ofra. In her fatigued state, she tried to scream but couldn't even move her lips. "I was tortured and brutally beaten and raped by three men! How can I stand up?" She was motionless. As young as she was, she had grown sufficiently to understand the Levite's words and actions. She was not surprised to hear him say "Get up! Let's go!" because she knew that Gershon couldn't possibly believe that something so appalling as murdering a woman can take place among his brothers. Gershon possessed the kind of ignorance which only a true believer in his new God can possess. She knew he was capable of twisting his own perception and reality. To believe that the Benjamin's, might be the kind of people to rape and act like animals, and have the capacity to torture and brutally beat a young innocent woman, was beyond his understanding. This kind of violence and cruelty existed in the lives of slaves, who lived by the mercy, or the lack of it, by their masters, not amongst the Benjamins who Gershon regarded as his brothers and his countrymen. It is exactly what made her fall in love with Gershon, follow him and agree to marry him and become capable of surrendering herself. It was his capacity to see no evil, pure and clear as the notes she heard from his flute. She was young, but for the short time she was with Gershon, she accepted his world views and embraced all that made him unique. She understood his way of thinking, and realized, too late, that her father's words had now become a reality when he said, "The present must be taken seriously Ofra. Be aware of what is happening around you." The old lady echoed her father's words interpreting reality in her own way, by saying "A fistful of lentils a woman can cook, is worth more than the sweet words in your ear."

Ofra knows now that her father's teachings were correct. "You cannot disregard reality Ofra, and if you do you will suffer the consequences."

Sadly, Gershon lives in his own reality which brought them to this tragic moment. Ofra's exhausted mind continued drifting toward the end.

When he realized she wasn't responding, he leaned closer to her, and shouted in a trembling voice "Boy, bring the donkey, fast!"

She saw his agonizing look, full of pain, while he approached her on the rocky ground. He carried and laid her down on the donkey sideways, legs and arms dangling to the ground. Frantically, he rushed toward home, running as fast as he could from the Benjamin territory. Gershon, in front, pulled the donkey behind him with a rope. The boy ran after them with her blood dripping to the ground through her fingertips. "Master, Master, Blood!" The boy screamed while wiping the red drops with his fingers each time the breeze blew them on his face. His master turned and nodded his head, looking at the boy while prodding the Donkey's lower belly in a frenzy with his sandaled foot.

Gershon, shocked and bewildered, was praying she would make it home alive. Ofra, the victim of the feud between Benjamin against Judah and the priesthood was ascending to heaven without knowing the aftermath.

"My father warned me! The Priesthood has many enemies!"

As they reached the Levites house, Gershon's tears turned into relentless sobbing as he laid her on the table. He was fearing the worst.

Chapter 2
"The Amorite"

Bethlehem Judea was a small enclave where the descendent of Judah, the fourth son of twelve brothers, pitched his tent, and named it after himself. It has been almost four hundred seventy years since his ancestors arrived back into this land and passed through this crossroad town. They were slaves for so long, and now, thirty years into the land of their forefathers, the Hebrews, the ex-slaves, began to experience freedom. Everyone carried the word freedom on their lips and in their hearts. They were enchanted, and at times provoked by their newfound independence. Often times they were fooled by the autonomy of their choices and began acting irresponsibly.

As the saying went in those days 'freedom will do that to you brother. Don't stress the bow too hard, it might break, and your arrow will go nowhere.' They needed to keep their actions in balance and learned to govern themselves. There was no king in the land, each tribe managed their own territory, and every man was a master in his own home.

Ofra lived in this Judean enclave with her father, a wealthy merchant. They lived next to descendants of Shelma, and the Caleb family, a branch of the Judean tribe. They were poets and writers living next to dairy farmers, merchants and ranchers. They all had one thing in common, they were all ex-slaves and sons and daughters of slaves. According to rumors in those days, Ataniel Ben Kenaz lived there, the man who stood against Nechushtan, the wicked Canaanite ruler, whom for eight years imposed heavy tax and extorted the poor. Next to the gated entrance to the enclave stood the building housing the Priesthood, the Levites and the Cohens. The structure was a combination of mudstone and logs. It housed the archives including writings on papyrus, clay, animal skin and stone tablets. These were engravings which they brought back from Egypt. The Levites and the Cohens brought them from the land of Goshen. The priesthood, comprised of Cohens and Levites, headed the Jehovah deity, which continued to gain power around the territories of the twelve tribes.

The people said that Ofra's father helped to bring a good part of the archives across the desert. The people knew that Ofra's father was blessed with the qualities displaying honesty and sincerity enabling him to overcome the Egyptian borders and the scrutiny of the harsh inspectors. They examined the load of papyrus papers and tablets which were written in very early Hebrew letters. They characterized it as insignificant Canaanite writings. They considered it to be the language of the farmers, the poor, the slaves, and the shepherds, all of whom the Egyptians disliked and deemed inferior and useless. The abundant natural waters of the Nile, the big river, the Iteru, as it was called, was considered a sign, a gift, a blessing from the gods to the Egyptian people. Adversely, the hot steamy Sinai desert was considered to be 'the curse' to the Egyptians.

Ofra's father, better known as the Amorite, was a well skilled merchant, as he traveled from Egypt to Judea on only one prior occasion. He received clear passage at the borders with a hearty smile and by handing a small clay dish with honey to the inspectors. "It's from Jericho the great oasis" he stated with a cheery smile and a convincing voice. But he knew that a dish of honey and a convincing smile would not get him over the next border with Pharaoh's stringent avaricious army of inspectors. This Amorite merchant, an experienced trader, knew when to change his tactics, when dealing with the harsh and cunning officers. He started his winning sales pitch, by glorifying the great Pharaoh, proclaiming praise in a deep quasi showy voice. "The great one, master of the world, heaven and earth!" When he addressed the chief Egyptian border guard, Ofra's father concluded his art of negotiation and persuasion by presenting a jewel. "This is a small token for you, honorable inspector. If your heart is bewitched by a woman you desire to conquer, here is something special you might want to accept." He handed the officer a turquoise stone. "I've yet to meet a woman who can resist this precious and expensive gem. It's from the Sinai mines" he whispered in the officer's ear, while he switched into a hearty glorified laughter. It worked. One of the wooden wagons being pulled by two mules, full of inscriptions of the twelve tribes and four hundred years in the Egyptian diaspora, was now free passage through the grueling desert to Judea. The other wagons behind them were comprised of small groups of families who didn't make it in the exodus seventy years earlier. They were from the tribes of the Benjamin's, Judeans, and Levites, who like many others, were being forced to run from King Ramses' decrees. Similar to the many refugees before them, the land of Canaan became their safe haven and future home.

"Where did you learn how to bargain your way through guards?" the Benjamin asked the Amorite. "Oh" answered Ofra's father. "A Hebrew merchant once taught me that the art of persuasion begins with praising the almighty Pharaoh. The rest is easy."

"And the gem, the turquoise, where did that come from?" another Benjamin inquired. "That's from the Judean Caleb family who is supporting this mission." Ofra's father responded.

Ofra's father was deeply proud of himself. The multitude of Hebrews who ran away with Moses in a massive rush, left behind significant writings. Some people believed that the writings were destined to be part of the holy works of Moses, and he promised Ofra's mother that one day he would bring these "treasures" (meaning the writings) to the new land.

He managed to obtain the manuscripts which many believed included the Hebrew alphabet the slaves used to communicate among themselves which later became the Hebrew language.

The Goshen Center in Judean Bethlehem was named for the land of Goshen in Egypt as a remembrance of where they came from. The main structure made of mud and stone housed the writings brought in by the tribes from around the young nation. A collection from the twelve tribes, having been four hundred years in Egypt, was now retained in this structure. It had slowly become the central archive of the nation. The Priests and the Levites occasionally slept in the main building when needed and conducted classes for the Goshen School. The entire Center was comprised of five huts made out of tree trunks and covered annually with fresh palm branches. They always began to turn yellow brown with the emerging Judean summer sun. The huts served as outdoor classrooms where students sat on olive tree stumps. There were other wood chairs, Egyptian style, with their original greenish stain, which somehow survived the trip from Egypt arriving on camels and donkeys.

The Judean's gathered in a celebration the day Ofra's father arrived back from his treacherous passage across the desert from

Egypt with the manuscripts from their forefathers. It was a joyful procession on that Thursday afternoon especially for Ofra who had been waiting impatiently for her father's return. She knew he would have a special present for her and having lost her mother too young she depended on his guidance and protection. He adored Ofra and showered her with his love.

Chapter 3
"Intrigue"

Heading towards the Goshen Center, Ofra walked brushing the tree trunks along her way as a form of amusement. She passed by the Goshen School, which was quite a distance from her house hoping to get a glimpse of Gershon, a teacher at the school. Ofra did not attend classes at the Goshen School and her father did not like her going that far unescorted. Her classes assembled under the shade of the trees in the vicinity of her house not far from the grove. Gershon the Levite, the teacher at the Goshen School, was on her mind. Under one of the fading green huts, she hoped with anticipation to catch a glimpse of Gershon while he was conducting a class. Fourteen-year-old Ofra was intrigued by Gershon, who was almost twice her age. Gershon was a member of the Levite tribe. They were poets, musicians, teachers, and more than anything else guardians of the holy tent. They were followers of Jehovah and the ten commandments. Their mission was to spread the word of Moses, of God in Heaven, under the supervision of the Cohens.

Gershon's wide shoulders and strong frame always grabbed her attention. He was out in the yard with the company of four other men. They noticed Ofra waving her hand in genuine happiness, and they squeezed Gershon's back. It signaled him to nod in Ofra's direction. He waved back with a brief acknowledgment. She inhaled a double dose of the cool fragrant Judean Mountain air and continued walking.

Outspoken Rachel, Ofra's best friend and classmate freely gave her opinions often. Rachels words were echoing in her head *"I would never get married as a concubine! Only as a first wife! A man gives respect to his first wife!"*

Safta, the caring old lady at home who has been with the family through Ofra's mother's illness and death, voiced her opinion, *"My dear Ofra, it is not true what Rachel says. A man gives love to the one he loves. It does not matter if she is a concubine or a first wife."* Ofra contemplated these thoughts as she promenaded past the Center.

"Isn't he the most handsome of the bunch?" she fantasized with a smile, her body slightly shivering. She walked all the way here just to take a glimpse of the man to whom she was enchanted and then began to ramble home.

Passing the olive grove, Ofra was singing her favorite song 'Its harvest time'. She hurried her steps because evening arrives early in Bethlehem. The mountains shield the falling rays, causing darkness to overwhelm the land.

She entered her father's house, a one-story stone house with six interior stairs leading to the roof. The elaborate olive wood entry door revealed that the house inhabitants were affluent. The stone and mud walls were professionally chiseled making the house appear especially prominent. The house next door resembled a cave, carved in the mountain, with the limestone walls in varying sizes. Several houses were randomly attached, and their doors were made of ordinary pine wood. Unlike Ofra's father's house with its exquisite wood door, the neighbor's homes were common and lacking any artistic characteristics. All of the homes were surrounded by a stone wall serving as its security safeguard.

"Ofra, you are quite late arriving home," he said lovingly.

Ignoring her father's complaint, she diverts into a subject she has been pondering. "Abba, if the land of Egypt you left, was so beautiful, why did the people choose to suffer so much in the desert to come here?"

Abba, in his late sixties, was a chubby, cheerful and generous man. A caring and kind father who was attentive to his daughter's inquisitiveness and marvel. He loved life and shared his positive outlook with Ofra.

"My Ofra always likes to ask grown-up questions" he smiled. "Well, the class is going to gather tomorrow under the mulberry tree, and I want to be prepared when the Levite discusses the subject about the Exodus from Egypt." Ofra's voice was full of excitement. Her father stopped rolling the colorful linen garments he bought from a well-known merchant.

"Let's start with Abraham the Amorite leaving his father's house" he said in a calm voice. "Ofra, do you remember the other day, I showed you Abraham's resting place? We had such a nice day riding to Hebron and saw our ancestral fathers and mothers."

"Yes father, but you did not tell me why Abraham had to leave his father's house." Her bantering tone was full of curiosity. Her Abba was accustomed to his daughter's yearning to get to the bottom of everything.

"All I know is that Abraham was not happy with the way the Priesthood of Nanna treated the people, especially when justice had to be served in the land of Ur. Abraham was a man who valued honesty and integrity." Ofra's father continued, "they say that one day Abraham saw a Priest of Nanna separate a mother from her beautiful, magnificent daughter, to be sold as a slave to his friend, another Priest."

The father imitating the Priest during this horrific exchange said, "It is the will of Nanna the moon god. It has been told that Abraham heard the mothers' scream, which had never been erased from his memory, nor his heart." Ofra's father articulated the events of this sad story to his young maturing daughter as clearly and concisely as he could. A story from more than 700 years earlier.

"Well, this is all I know from the stories I've been told. Perhaps, the Levite will have more insight and I'm sure he will give you a better perspective."

"Yes daughter," the old lady threw herself into the conversation, "sometimes beauty is a burden." "Why didn't Nanna the moon god of laws and Ningal his wife, take the girl away from the priests' hands?" persisted Ofra in a sorrowful voice. "In the land of Ur, the priests spoke on behalf of the Gods, and sometimes even the king could not override the decisions made by the priests." "Oh father, the priests have more power than the king?" Ofra said while shifting into a high-pitched voice.

"Yes daughter, and the people aligned their beliefs with the Priests and the Priesthood." "But why? Aren't the people on the side of the King?" "Not always daughter, but the Priesthood considered themselves as the messengers of the gods. It was always that way. The kings didn't dare to question the gods, in order not to upset the people." "Oh!" Ofra jumping into another topic remembered what happened a few days earlier when she heard the loud voices of the Benjamins who rode into town demanding to speak to the high Priest. She continued "The other day the Benjamin's demanded to speak to the high Priest at the Goshen Center."

"What were you doing at the Goshen Center?" her father said in surprise while he was organizing the linens, not noticing the exchange of looks between Ofra and Safta.

"Oh, I'm sure Ofra was just dropping off the fresh baked breads we made for the teachers."

Ofra, saved by the old lady, ran to her room.

Chapter 4
"Assimilate"

The next morning Ofra and her Abba traveled a short distance to the old market. Ofra rode her trusted donkey holding the yellow rope she and Safta twisted into a braid year back. It matched the yellow blanket she sat on, side-saddle, and was trailing her father. They stopped at three stores made of brick and mud and supported by cylindrical logs. He delivered his linens, then loaded their two donkeys with bread, vegetables, honey, pomegranate, and grape wine. Ofra waited patiently until her father completed buying the provisions then she said with a voice full of excitement, "Abba please, I want to see the face of Nanna and Ningal and ask them why they didn't save the girl from the bad Priest." Her father scratched his head, looked at the perishables that were piled on their animals but went along with Ofra's request as he had so many times before. She was his baby and clearly his favorite and he enjoyed indulging her whims. They went into the figurine store. At the center of the store on a wooden chair sat an old blind man. They all greeted each other upon entering, with the words "peace be on you." "Show me, Ningal and Nanna" said Ofra excitedly addressing the owner who was standing toward the rear of the store.

"You want to go that far back into the land of Ur? Aren't you too young for that?" the store owner grinned. Ofra smiled back rapidly nodding her head. "Yes!" He walked over to the shelf and then put the figurines in the hands of the blind man. "This is

Nanna, the moon god and this is his wife Ningal" said the store owner. The blind man then placed the Ningal beside him.

"Nanna the moon god, with the crescent moon above him, is the rider of the winged bull. He is the night illuminator of wisdom, the reader of the past and the future. He is the gift giver." The blind man ran his fingers through the figurine and paused. "Now you can pass me a beer" he said accustomed to being compensated for his recitations.

Ofra's father bought him a beer, a mixture of boiled water, and some grains floating in a clay cup. The blind man reached down to pick up the figurine of Ningal and brushed his fingers mostly on the figurines eyes and then continued. "Ah the eyes of Ningal! The gods are watching us. The great lady, the honeymooner, the lover, the wife to Nanna. Ah Ningal, the mark of water and fish. Womb mother to Shemesh, goddess of the sun." Then the blind man pulling two new figurines from behind him said "This is the Baal which brings rain on this land, and his wife Ashrah, who bless children. All young girls worship Ashrah, wishing one day they will marry and be fertile. Now if you have a wish daughter, whisper it to Ashrah, open your heart to all of the gods and the goddesses and your prayers will be received."

Ofra's father, disturbed, looked at the store owner. It was revealed by the exchange of his glance, that there will be no more beer for the blind man. One was more than sufficient for his services. The blind man was steering young Ofra into another direction. He was probably bribed by the Baal and the Ashura priests who were roaming the streets of the market converting people to their beliefs.

"Come daughter we are running late, and we must take our food home." He said while exiting the store.

"… but father the blind man still did not tell me why the beautiful lady was separated from her daughter by Nanna." Ofra professed following him out.

While untying the donkeys Ofra's father spoke softly. "That's why Abraham left the land of Ur daughter, in search for justice and the true God. Carry God in your heart and mind daughter. Now I'm not saying you have to discard your figurines and charms in your olive box, but what I am saying is, in time, you will find out that the one true God is living and breathing in you. You know you are at peace when you carry God in your heart, and in your mind, not in your olive box." They started their walk home.

Ofra loved growing up in Judean Bethlehem. She listened to stories being told and retold from travelers and merchants visiting her father's house. He was loved by the Judeans and the people in the old part of town. She and her father would walk into a store, she would sit on a small wooden chair or a stone, while her father would talk and talk, until he made the sale. Her favorite store was the store with the figurines, masks, and household goods. She identified all the figurines and knew what each represented. Ofra could never comprehend if the goddess Anat, the sister to Baal, was good or bad. Anat possessed love and hate, fertility and was a virgin, all in one. That was a mystery to young Ofra. She knew the names of all the deities by heart. She loved going to the market with her Abba and enjoyed the excitement of the carriers rushing through the narrow aisles, moving big white and yellow chunks of salt to the main road for pickup and transport. From the candy store, she would leave with her favorite honey sticks. In the scarf store, after her father would conclude his negotiations, Ofra would receive a gift from the store owner. This went on and on each visit to the market and when she was back at home, she had amassed a big collection of scarves and trinkets. Friends would joke that when her father was searching for a particular item for a store owner, they would find it among Ofra's enormous collections.

Her father was a master in hospitality, a very kind-hearted man and honest in his dealings. One day she asked her father a question, but his usual smile turned serious. She never saw him this way before. He pulled out a chair and asked her to sit down.

"My daughter, you ask me why people address you as the daughter of the Amorite, while others are referred to as the daughter of the Caleb family, or the son of the Gidoni family. My daughter, the people respect me for my dedication to your mother and her beliefs. They did not forget about my journey back to Egypt and how I returned home with the writings and transcripts that were left behind. The daughter of the Amorite is an honor and I want you to be proud to be my daughter."

Ofra closed her eyes and filled her heart and lungs with the deepest love for her father and the mother (Emma pronounced Eema) she never met.

"I always believe that you can tell a man by the God he chooses, And, even though I was born an Amorite, I chose to believe in the God of Abraham as my El, and I chose to follow your mothers' beliefs. El is not a Priest, El is not a King, El is our God and allows us to make our own choices."

"And my Emma? Tell me more about her?"

"Emma was part Judean and part Nubian" her father lifting his head, looked at a fixed point in the sky and continued. "We met in Egypt. I was an Amorite. We could have stayed in Egypt and enjoy a better status. And I can't say that the Amorites enjoyed a better status because they didn't. The Egyptians didn't like the farmers or people like us from the mountains. But, … we weren't slaves."

"What is a status, Abba?" she inquired. "Ah! How can I explain status? Ok, rich is a status and poor is a status. A slave is a status, and a free person has the best status." "And my Emma? Did she have a good status?" "My daughter, it's sad to say, but your mother was a slave. The powerful tend to slave the weak and the Hebrews like your mother did not assimilate."

"What is assimilate Abba?" "Oh, that's a hard one. Let's see." Her father paused to think of an example.

"I know! You like white flowers daughter, right?" "Yes, I do Abba." "Imagine you have five red flowers, one is white. You are told you can bring them to the king as a gift, but also told that the king *only* likes red flowers. Now what would you have done, daughter?" Ofra thinks about this dilemma. "Oh hmm. If I take the white flower out, I will please the king, but I will not be happy because I like white flowers."

"Now imagine that the white flower is your voice, your opinion, your belief. Now what does that signify? Is the king concerned about your white flower, your opinion, or your voice or your belief?"

"No Abba." "So, what are you going to do?" "I will not like that."

"Well, people who recognized King Pharaoh as being a god, and accepted his words and orders without question, were called assimilated. The others like your Emma were forced to be slaves because she did not assimilate. Your mother and the others like her did not believe that Pharaoh was a god. The Egyptians put them in together in one place in order to use them as workers and slaves."

"Oh no" Ofra sighed.

"The Egyptians abhorred the slaves and their inability to accept Pharaoh as a God. But the Egyptian Priests told the King that they knew the Hebrews would never accept him as their God. '*They already have their God, the God of Abraham in heaven. You'll never convince them that you are a God. If they did not assimilate after four hundred years in our kingdom, they never will. Let them go,*" her Abba was imitating the Egyptians.

He took a pause and continued. "As time went by, I adopted her God, El in heaven and I grew to love her more and more and we ran away to a faraway land."

"Like Abraham did?" Ofra recalled the story about Abraham leaving the land of Ur in search for justice and the true God?"

"Exactly daughter."

Chapter 5
"School"

Ofra was almost fourteen years old and possessed the kind of beauty which stirred a man's attention. Her eyes were luminous, and her shiny black hair would twirl down her back. Her body was narrow from the waist up, curvy from the hip down and she had a long, towering neck. Her face sparkled with the kind of allure that could mellow a man's heart or ignite his wrath.

"My Ofra, you can tam a mule with your stubbornness" her father would say. "My father, you can force a snake to abandon his nest" she would joke back.

She was quick with her tongue, yet shy. She possessed unique and desirable qualities for such a young woman coming into her own.

"I will walk with you to your class" the old lady noted Ofra's happy mood.

"Thank you, Safta; we are going to meet under the mulberry tree today."

"Good, its closer to the house. Come daughter, let's go, I can tell you are looking forward to those lessons. It is written all over your glowing face" the old lady smiled enjoying Ofra's infatuation. "I like to listen to stories, Safta." "Hmmm, you are a story listener, and Gershon is storyteller. That's a match!" The old lady giggled as they walked the short distance. "Don't forget to let father come for me when I'm done." "Don't worry about that, you know your father will be on time."

It was the beginning of summer. The fruit on the mulberry tree did not ripen staining the ground with its succulent fruit. Thirty years into the land, the broad mulberry leaves shaded the class of 1235 B.C.

Ofra knew that Rebecca, her classmate, would arrive early, as usual, and before the boys had a chance, would be the first one to ask the opening question in the class. The students were fortunate to attend these classes requiring a fee and Ofra's father was gratified that his daughter was acquiring a passageway to knowledge. Rachel, her closest friend, just arrived and she slid down from the donkey in a graceful and respectful manner. She arrived with her regal air, like a princess, denoting her majestic arrival. Because education was a man's domain, Zilpa, an only child, was dressed like a boy upon her father's insistence despite her feminine ways. Back in Egypt, there was a practice from the land of Goshen, where women taught their children in hiding when the men were absent. There were four fortunate girls, the rest of the class were all boys. Reuben was the helper, Dan was very shy, and Ariel wrestled the meaning of each story with Gershon, the storyteller, the Levite, their teacher. The girls sat downwind on the left side of the ground forming a half-moon. The breeze brought the light perfume scent of jasmine from the girl's side. The lovely fragrance barely masked the robust sheep odor from the boy's side.

Gershon left his donkey in the shade and greeted everyone "peace be on you my youthful cheery bunch." Humming, he removed the linen cloth protecting his wooden flute and began to play. He moved his body to the rhythm of the flute and when the pitch was higher, he stretched his body forward. He walked backward with the lower notes. People on donkeys and camels passed by and some stopped to watch the swaying storyteller and his jubilant privileged students. Ofra moved her body to the music each time he hit a high note. All of her concentration was on her teacher. She did not hide her eyes from Gershon, on the contrary, she was hoping to steal as many glances as she could before the lesson began, but to no avail.

When he stopped, he rolled the flute back into the cloth, and said "Last time we talked about sacrificing to one god or sacrificing to many gods."

Ofra evaluated each one of his moves. She sat close and followed Gershon with her eyes while he finished wrapping his flute. She was seated crossed legged on the ground, elbows on her knees and supporting her chin with her palms. All of her focus was on her teacher. The lesson progressed with many exchanges amongst the group and Gershon was pleased with their thoughtful discussions as he led them to think about Moses and the Ten Commandments. As time was running short, they concluded their dialogs.

"And why must we pray to all the gods? Rebecca announced in a loud voice.

"My father said in Egypt the big river had enough water for everyone. But here, people pray to Baal to bring us rain" Ofra responded.

"I don't know why everyone in town thinks my father is a crazy man. My father said to me, lift your head to the sky, your eyes and mind will open, do not occupy your mind with the Baal and the Ashra like others do. There is God, just because we don't see him it doesn't mean he's not there" Rebecca said adamantly.

"My father says that in the old days, the elders said we don't have to believe in Nanna, the moon god, because their priests judged and gave verdicts to the people as they wished. My father says, there was no justice," Reuben spoke decisively.

"Yes!" said Ofra, "that's what my father says too. That is the reason why Abraham left the land of the big rivers because there was no justice by Nanna."

This open discussion continued for a long while until Gershon concluded the session. "Well, I guess your fathers are all wise men. Now, we need to expand on the subject about Moses and the Ten Commandments. You all have been memorizing the Commandments so our next lesson we are going to expand our discussion" said Gershon.

With the conclusion of their lesson, each student brought their fee. Ofra looked at Gershon, he returned her glance, and she quickly lowered her eyes. Ofra and Rebecca started gathering the donations and placed them next to the tree. Some brought a small dish of honey, others a dish of lentils, and others, figs. Upon turning, Ofra bumped sideways with Gershon. Her body jerked and then she froze. Her cheeks reddened. Her brown eyes opened in surprise and her arched black eyebrows lifted. She made an inaudible noise in a low voice and Gershon smiled. She ran toward her father who had just arrived to walk her home. He had his usual smile lifting his round cheeks. She adjusted her step to stand next to him. Gershon thanked her father for the honey.

Walking away Gershon could hear Ofra telling her father about the day's lesson. "You were right Abba. Abraham left his father's house because the Priest didn't judge right."

They walked on the dirt track crossing through the small olive grove, and she touched the olive trees with the palm of her hand. Gershon came alive in her young mind. They entered the neighborhood with homes of two and four rooms, built in clusters with mountain stones. The poorer families didn't have the carved stones, their homes were built with round limestone, pasty mud and layered with pine logs. These homes resembled mountain caves with a curvy structural look. The prosperous families had homes with chiseled stones and oak logs. The house doors were all similar except the affluent homes were carved intricately. Ofra's father's house was notable. It had an open roof which made it higher than the other houses. The house walls were made with beautifully shaped stones. The backyard was full of unchiseled stones on display for sale along with logs piled up on the ground and branches in their natural fork formation used for building huts. Ofra's father, the Amorite, sold various types of merchandise including building materials. He was well respected, a fair tradesman, and generous with his hospitality.

Ofra grew up contented in this comfortable house, in her father's domain where his guests were graciously fed on the long wooden table. Bread, honey and wine were always served to his guests and friends.

Chapter 6
"Contentment"

Today Ofra promised her friends to help gather the olives in the orchard, the last day of a weeklong harvest. The ancient olive grove in the Judean enclave was located just across the main road where the fruit and vegetable merchants displayed their crops. It was mild and sunny in Judean Bethlehem, just the right kind of day for the gathering. Ofra went up to the roof and looked in the direction of the grove. She heard the familiar singing and some of the noisy merriment. She loved the music and the cheery atmosphere. She was most excited because she thought there was a chance to see Gershon and the look in his eyes when he played a tune and how her heart would beat faster when he came close to her. Ofra told the old woman that the Levite plays the flute like a shepherd. Then the old lady told Ofra that the Priests in Egypt were all trained in music. They were taught how to play the flute and the harp especially for the new year celebrations and the Opet festival celebrating the marriage between the great Pharaoh and the Gods. Ofra heard about the golden boats serving the gods on that festival from one of the guests from Egypt who came to visit and sell goods to her Abba. She overheard him say that Pharaoh, Ramses the second, that awful slave owner, sacrificed 1300 rams in his celebration of his marriage to the Gods.

She hurried downstairs and out to the street and ran the short distance towards the increasing laughter which was becoming more inviting.

"Ofra, Ofra! Come! Give us a hand." the girls chanted in unison.

Ofra hurrying, leaned down gently, placed half of a fiery red pomegranate at the foot of the Ashra statue at the entrance of the grove and then joined her friends who were circling a tree. A group of men were shaking the branches releasing the olives of varied shades of green. Some as colorful as the fresh grape leaves of the valley and others as dark as the midnight sky. The girls were gathering the falling ripe olives filling their raised skirts laughing loudly and singing joyfully. The townspeople across the small village joined in when they heard the girls singing their favorite song 'It's Harvest Time'.

"🎵 It's harvest time. Let us sing a song of love and praise, its harvest time let us rise and meet the sun, we fear no sweat, no matter how hard it will be, we'll tame the land, until it bears all the fruit it can 🎵"

Coming down the road riding his donkey and playing the flute, Gershon, the Levite, looked delighted and joyful as he was approaching the frenzy of jubilation. He came to deliver the blessing.

"Look! Gershon, the Priest is coming" said one of the men. "You mean the inspector? The crazy missionary?"

Gershon descended and left his donkey to rest in the shade. Still springing to the trotting motion, he was whirling to the rhythm of the melodic 'harvest time' as he approached the grove owner. The two men began rubbing the oil of the olives with both hands and discussed the improved quality of the color this year versus the past year's bounty. Then as Gershon gave his blessing for an even more prosperous outcome for the next season, he turned slightly and noticed Ofra standing amongst her peers. An awkward feeling overcame him in the nicest way. He gave her an ambiguous nod. The singing finished on a high note because the harvest was fruitful and about to end. Ofra fulfilled her third and last task of gathering the ripe olives as she looked in Gershon's direction. When they spotted each other at the far end of the grove, she was able to examine his features in a different manner. She noticed that he was broad shouldered and slender, and his skin was bronzed. All too often he carried the ark of the covenant in the scorching sun. All Levites grew a beard, but Gershon's was incredibly short, and his curly black hair barely brushed his strong shoulders. He was wearing a white cotton top that touched his knees and was held by a flax rope around his waist. Her eyes followed his fast movements and his muscular legs. He was in his late twenties, the average age of the new Priests.

Ofra wore her favorite linen garden dress with a fiery red lining, the type that she wrapped tightly around her body. With her right hand, and grabbing a corner of the linen, she would drape the fabric starting from the upper left shoulder rotating over her belly and around her back, and then back around, tucking the last corner into her waist and tying it off with a braided golden cord. The perfect dress with enough cloth to catch the small green fruits.

As she dropped her last batch of olives into the basket, she was close to Gershon who was walking through the field back in the direction of his resting donkey.

Ofra suddenly addressed Gershon blurting out a juvenile question "What is your favorite God?" She blushed and felt embarrassed as soon as she heard those ridiculous words coming out of her mouth.

Caught up in surprise with that kind of question, Gershon replied "Well, I am a Priest from the Levite tribe. I serve the house of Aaron upon command, and I believe in Jehovah, El, the master of all in heaven."

Ofra was relieved that he gently avoided admonishing her folly and wanted to extend the interaction, so she asked another question.

"Why do you need to inspect the fields for each harvest?" "Just to make sure we are sorting the good and bad fruits" he paused and then continued. "And to give a blessing."

Ofra was alluring him and enjoying this attention and said, "You learned to play the flute so *b e a u t i f u l l y* Gershon" accentuating *beautifully* as she pursed her mouth. "Thank you" he replied with a smile and couldn't help but notice her plump lips. "The soft sounds of the flute are especially pleasant to my ears. I taught myself how to play and it allows me to partake on the holy days and during harvest season."

"Where do you live?" she was inquisitively wondering.

"In the triangle, among the tribes of Judah, Ephraim and Benjamin."

She plucked a fig while talking and did not realize she was squashing the poor fruit with her fingers and spraying Gershon's face with its milky white juice. He laughed, then attempted to wipe the moisture with the back of his hand. He hurried to his donkey and quickly brought the leather pouch filled with water and sprayed her palms. She rubbed her hands joyfully and embarrassingly laughed out loud. He too rinsed his hands and face.

"Why do you enter the class singing?" asked Ofra hoping to prolong their chit-chat as they reached the donkey tied to the tree.

"To remind the town that I'm on my way and that I have arrived. And most importantly to get the class ready and prepare your ears to be receptive to listening."

"Come, let me walk you to your house" he said.

"Hmm, my father would not approve" she muffled.

"On the contrary, I'm not sure. I think he will be pleased knowing you are with me. I think he will be proud of you." Gershon with an assured posture pulled the donkey behind him with his right hand as Ofra walked next to him.

"Tell me more about the triangle Gershon? Is it like Bethlehem? Does it have a big, beautiful market like we do? Is it scary?" she asked curiously.

"I live in the Ephraim mountains, on the hill slope, which is surrounded by a lot of trees." Gershon was curious and continued "And why are you asking me all of these questions?" he said, with a big smile. "Because I never get the chance under the mulberry and the fig trees" she said smiling.

As Gershon and Ofra were walking off the fields, the harvesters were drinking sweet wine and placing their fruit offerings at the feet of Baal, the god of rain and his wife Ashrah the god of fertility. They were chanting their blessing as if it was a new moon thanking you Baal and Ashrah for the rain, enabling a good harvest.

Several of the men watched as Gershon walked out of the gate with Ofra toward her home.

"The Levite is doing well, that's what people are saying" said one man.

"He has enemies! Inspect this! Inspect that! You know not everyone embraces the new Laws of the priesthood, especially not the Benjamin's."

"The work of the Levite's is very important, and I also heard he's a good teacher."

"I like that girl" whispered one of the harvesters pointing at Ofra.

"I think it's too late. It looks like the Levite likes her! I think she might be spoken for. Anyway, you can't afford a concubine, you can hardly afford what you got!" They both laughed.

Chapter 7
"Classmates"

A week passed and Ofra waited full of anticipation for the next class gathering. The old lady noticed Ofra's excitement, it showed all over her face. Acknowledging the mood, the old lady smiled not unlike a jester. While Ofra's father was away, Ezer, who was highly trusted, watched over the house. He walked Ofra to her class convened under the fig tree. Zilpa was there, dressed as a boy, as usual. Ofra and her friends speculated that Zilpa probably possessed a unique beauty under her clothes because not only did she have a big, beautiful smile, but she had sparkling smiling eyes. To remind the late comers to hurry up and move to class timely, Gershon announced his arrival playing the flute. Ofra noticed that Gershon's bouncy notes signaled that he was in a cheerful mood as well. Ofra wore her preferred white dress with one of her prettiest scarves. Ofra arrived as Rachel was dismounting her donkey in that unique dignified way. Ofra was always amused by her routine of sliding down gently with her legs tightly closed like a proper lady. Rachel sat on the floor next to Ofra.

Full of emotion, the students, as the people in Bethlehem Judea, were still talking about that cold afternoon of the eclipse in the winter month of Tevet. Although it was several months earlier, they were fixated on the darkness that covered the land after the event. They watched how Yarkh (Yareyak) the moon god, and Shemesh the sun goddess wrestled each other. Shemesh with its red rays began hiding behind Yarikh's white face. The orange and red radiance filtered to earth in magnificent colors. Then the daughter and son of the almighty El spread darkness on the land, creating panic, and they all ran like a frenzy of lambs fleeing from a jackal.

Across from the girls, the boys were laughing and talking boisterously, and they watched Rueben impersonating his grandfather, his Saba. It appeared that Rueben, once again, was echoing the stories his Saba repeated frequently. They heard Rueben's loud voice. "My grandfather was there when this happened a long time ago when Joshua saw Yarikh and Shemesh wrestling each other" said Reuben recalling the story they all heard before. "My Saba said it is to remind us of the brave days of Joshua in Givon years ago when there was an eclipse during the war and the soldiers were afraid that the Gods brought this strange and frightening darkness upon them" Rueben said in one long breath. He continued impersonating his grandfather's low deep voice like a tuba marking its conclusion. "Joshua shouted, I'm *the man, your leader, do not be afraid, follow me to victory.*" Rueben's Saba, having fought with Joshua, had firsthand experience, knowing that this eclipse was not a mythological interference as the other soldiers believed.

"And my father too, thinks like Joshua and my Saba. He does not believe in Yarikh and Shemesh as the gods. He believes only in the God of Moses." Rueben concluded.

"No!" Rachel challenged. "Yarikh, Shemesh and Anat are the gods and goddesses! They are our friends. They protect every girl and woman!"

She then stood up and in a theatrical style like a prima ballerina declared "Go out, mothers and daughters, bathe in the moonlight, purify yourself, it is a big occasion!" Rachel knew all about the illuminations of the gods from the fascinating stories her mother and all the women before her conveyed.

"I remember!" Zilpa added with a voice full of enthusiasm "I saw the people from every roof, they danced, some naked! They spun in the silvery moonlight and like Shemesh, they twirled their hands and bodies like we do" she demonstrated by gently weaving her fingers high above the head like a dancer with both arms outstretched. "Yes." she said "Yarikh tried very hard to escape Shemesh's embrace." Confidently Zilpa added "They didn't last together."

"Yes, in the end, Yarikh abandoned Shemesh" Ofra stated in an authoritative manner. "She tried to keep him, but she couldn't" she said loudly shrugging her shoulders.

Ofra looked at Gershon, awaiting his reaction to see if he was drawn into the intimate atmosphere her phrase was suggesting. Their eyes locked into one another, Ofra staring dreamily and Gershon distractedly, while all the class noticed. Ofra felt uncomfortably embarrassed by her spontaneous assertiveness. She blushed and continued talking. "My father says, in the land of Goshen in Egypt, no one was allowed to speak about the Gods and Goddesses, only about Jehovah, El, the God of Abraham, and Moses."

"Why?" Reuben was quick to question.

Gershon quickly responded "Because Reuben, it is one of the Ten Commandments given by our liberator Moses. We believe and worship in one God in heaven."

"Oh, but El is boring to look at with that beard and always so serious," insisted Rachel.

"Daughters and sons of Hebrews, God in heaven makes you think" Gershon spoke. "And how does heaven make you think?"

inquired Ariel. Stroking his beard with the fingers of his right hand, Gershon replied "By questioning and marveling, my young Ariel." "Oooooh" they all said, extending the oooooh.

"You speak like my father" Ofra addressed Gershon.

Ofra once again adds, "Anat the courageous warrior, the Goddess of love and war, is the sister to Baal who brings us rain and prosperity."

She took a second to pause and continued in a spontaneous playful dialect, "A-n-a-a-a-t the f e r o c i o u s and the L-O-V-V-V-E-R." She said this sweetly and mischievously stressing the word lover while eyeing Gershon's reaction. "She, Anat, challenged El and threatened to pull him down by his beard to the mud."

"Oh" said Gershon acting startled. "Ofra knows much about the gods and the goddesses. But you left out the part about Anat and how cruel and how fast she runs to spill blood. Does it go together with love?" Gershon asked. "And how about mercy?" Gershon quickly changed the subject and guided the class in another direction. "Mercy is a weakness! That is what my father taught me." declared the newest boy in the class. "Is feeding the sick and the poor a weakness?" said Gershon "Ben Ari is my name" said the handsome young boy ignoring Gershon's comment. "I'm passing through from the tribe of Benjamin. My father talked about mercy as a weakness in the battlefield."

Ofra sensed that these two were heading for a challenge, so she jumped into the conversation. "Brother Ben Ari, Anat spills a lot of blood in her wars."

"I didn't speak about Anat" Ben Ari responded with an air of arrogance and confusion.

Ofra contemplated the idea of Anat the ferocious also being a lover and completely ignoring Ben Ari's comment, continued her rhetoric in a sweet and soft voice, "Love is sweet like honey, like the love of Jacob for Rachel."

Ben Ari gave Ofra an exasperated glare.

Gershon realized he was once again being drawn into Ofra's youthful agenda and her very skillful web, but he went along with it anyway. "Let us all keep our hearts and minds in a balance, like a merchant weighs his grain." Gershon concluded the class and Ofra helped gather the donations.

"Ofra? Are you going to the grape harvest on Sunday? You know, the big one next to the city gate?" Rachel asked before they all went home. "My father doesn't allow me to go that far by myself." "The nice-looking boys are going to be there, and maybe Gershon too." Rachel said coyishly. "I want to go!" said Ofra, her face glowing like a torch when she walked toward Ezer the stone chiseler. He brought Ofra's donkey with him to escort her home. She looked back before she left because she felt as though Gershon's eyes were following her, behind her, but a crossing camel disturbed the moment and Ofra and Ezer made their way home. "Mother" she said as she entered the house, "Please speak to father. I must go to the harvest on Sunday. The one by the gate."

The old lady stared at Ofra's eyes smiling "Let me guess? Gershon?" Ofra smiled back and sashayed thrillingly to her room humming, 'It's harvest time ...'

Ofra's excitement was flooding through her body, as her movements, entranced in the melody was like a colorful peacock augmenting its feathers.

Chapter 8
"Gripes"

"The Benjamin's are here! Make way! … and they don't look happy. By the expression on their faces, they look as irritated as a hungry wolf who has just lost its prey" the bystander at the Goshen gate announced vociferously.

The twelve riders got off their horses in a unified well-trained manner. Arad the Benjamin officer in charge, said to his assistant "I hope the high Priest is here." Anticipating their arrival, the assistant Priest stepped out to the front yard.

"Welcome to Goshen Brothers Benjamin. Judah and I were awaiting your arrival. Water your horses and feel comfortable cooling down, Brothers. When you are ready, seat yourself at the table over there" the Priest said pointing to the long pine table where Ada was pouring water into two dozen clay cups.

Moments later, the Benjamins walked over to the meeting. "We are all ready to listen and talk" the Priest motioned with his right hand. In no time the front yard leading to the road filled with a crowd. They were all concerned to hear and understand the growing dissent between the Benjamin's, Judah, and the priesthood. The Benjamin's who always chose to sit on the left, seated themselves, while the Judeans sat on the right. The Cohens sat on either side of high Priest at the head of the table. Arad, a first-generation into the land, was a tall, copper skinned young man with wavy black hair. He looked like an Egyptian soldier with his determined stern air on his face.

Arad looked straight at Judah and said in a forceful voice "Are we being ignored by the Priesthood and the Judeans? Are we intentionally being left out of the decisions regarding the Ark?"

"Before you continue" interrupted the elder Benjamin man in a whisper. "Hold on brother Arad. Let me do the talking as we agreed." Arad acquiesced.

The old man addressed the high priest. "The talk among the people is that the Judeans, the Simonies and the priesthood are united. It looks like they are making the rules for the rest of the nine tribes. For example, Brothers, the holy Ark has not passed in our territory for some time now. And when it does, it only goes as far as Kiriat Yarim which is located next door in the Judean territory. Are you crowning Shiloh as the holy Ark's permanent home? Have you abandoned Bet-El in the Benjamin territory where the shekinah dwells?"

"I gave the order" announced the High Priest who was joining a tad late but was listening as he approached the table.

"And why is that?" Arad asked confrontationally.

"Brother Arad, we know that the Shekinah, the divine spirit, dwells in the Benjamin territory in Bet El from the time of Jacob. No one is doubting that. But half of the tribe's dwell north. We feel that Shiloh is located at the center of the land. It's accessible to all the tribes."

"As Benjamin's, we have our God given responsibility to keep the Ark in Bet-El" the elder Benjamin shouted, and his clan raised their fists in endorsement. The Benjamins assembled and came to air their grievances. And there were many.

As old as he might have been, this prompted the elder Benjamin to jump out of his chair and unravel a goat skin for all to see. It had sketches on it. "Look here, brother Judah, look at these nations. Ur, Assyria, Egypt, Kush, Babylonia and Mesopotamia. If we don't build an army and train our sons to fight and teach them to ride a horse in battle, we will become a nation of slaves again!"

The High Priest realizes he needs to calm this emotional outburst understanding that the Benjamin's have several gripes that might be valid. It was clear that they came with different ambitions. They are sounding the alarm to the young nation's vulnerabilities and want a nation protected by the sword. The Priest recognizes he must show the Benjamins they have to trust the might of the Hebrew God and the Ten Commandments. The nations presented on their goat skin have been living by false Gods and their Hebrew brothers and sisters are unfortunately following in this misguided direction. The Priest knew he must immediately demonstrate to the Benjamins the core differences in a drastic way.

"I hear you, brother Benjamin," the High Priest responds and immediately diverts the direction of the meeting. "Look at the face of this Baal and the Ashrah. Do you want the people to believe in this?" The High Priest took the statues and threw them forcefully against the stone wall. The statues were crushed into smithereens.

The crowd erupted in shock, and many moved their heads to avoid looking at the shards and fragments fearing that the gods are now provoked and might retaliate.

"Ah, it's just a stone brother," added a Cohen. "We agree! The stones are not Gods. But the Holy Ark will stay in its lawful and rightful place. God ordered it from the time of Jacob" the elder Benjamin banged the table with contempt not allowing the Priest to divert the issue.

The Benjamins continued to hold fast to their convictions about the location of the Ark and their ambition to turn the future of the nation to be like the other nations. The Priests countered using the disagreement about the other nations believing in false Kings and false Gods. The Benjamins wanted the Ark in Bet-El for economic reasons, but the Priests wanted the Ark in Shiloh for centralization. There was no meeting of the minds.

"My brother Benjamin" continued one of the priests. "You know it is not about God, it is more about who is not God." He took a pause and continued. "We all know those pieces of stone are not God. A wise man can see the difference brother." The Priest took a long breath, lowered his voice and continued. "Brother Benjamins, these days, everyone appoints himself a God. We just left one in Egypt. As we are now speaking, Ramses is marrying the Gods. He is crowning himself as the 'God of Gods' at the Opet festival. Do you remember when our people were slaves and we heard about the Pharaoh who sacrificed one thousand three hundred rams to crown himself as the 'God of the Gods'? I wonder how many of our people broke their backs mining and covering the boats with layers of gold for the procession on the Yeor, the big river. Or the Itero, as the Egyptians called it. We call it the red bloody river because our babies were thrown alive to the crocodile infested water to satisfy Sobek the crocodile God. It still brings tears to my eyes."

Another priest joined the heated discussion. "Are we now going to substitute the Pharaohs ram horns with the Gods of the countries you are showing us? Ashrah, Ishtar and the ancient Bulls of Heaven of the east? You want us to resemble those nations on your map?"

"They will take your heart brother, and they will feed it to the vultures" said another Cohen in a serious tone. "That is penned in their writings."

"Oh brother Benjamins, you talk to us of Ur? You sound like their kings, the Gilgamesh and Murdoch from the far past who believed they were two thirds God and one third man, justifying mingling with humans and stealing the dignity from the noble men by taking their wives. They lied and manipulated their own people."

"The time has arrived brother Benjamin to open your eyes and mind to the written words of the God of Moses. Teach the children the distinction between heaven (Shamaiym), and earth (Eratz). This way the children will look up in wonder as our father Abraham did." "He was an Amorite" somebody shouted from the crowd. "No! He was a Hebrew" yelled another person. "And what is the difference?" the High Priest turned around and addressed the crowd. "Most important is your vision, your mind, and your perception." "Yes! Yes! Shamaiym and Eratz" some of the crowd repeated the Priests words.

The priest continued to address the Benjamins "Is it possible that you, brother Benjamins, prefer that our people believe in those pieces of stone?" He said pointing at the broken pieces of the Ashrah and the Baal. "Is that which dwells in the holy Ark not stone?" the Benjamin stated in anger.

The high Priests face turned red, but he held his breath and maintained his composure, and lowered his voice. "There is a big difference brother Benjamin. Believing in a statue serves as a tool in the hand of kings, rulers and so-called Gods, like the Pharaoh. When you believe in a written word by God, it makes you think, feel and act in a godly way. And the Ten Commandments are godly."

"Yes! Yes! The Priest is right" someone shouted from the crowd.

The elder Benjamin continued. "Isn't Judah now acting like a king? Supported by you! The priesthood! What is the difference between Pharaoh and his army of priests in Egypt and you the Priesthood and Judah? It surely looks like the same direction."

"Are you comparing the priesthood in Judea to the priesthood of Egypt? How dare you, Benjamin?" the Cohen spewed. Ada rushed as she poured fresh water into the clay cup for the Priest. He cleared his throat and continued talking in a relaxed voice. "The Priesthood, the house of Aaron, regards Jehovah in heaven as our El. The Ten Commandments of Moses are our laws that teach us how to live and conduct our lives in a moral and ethical way. We have been abiding to these laws since the days of Joseph, since the days of slavery, and they are our laws now today as free people."

The Benjamin responded. "Well brother Cohen, we the Hebrews are shepherds, sons and daughters of slaves." And before he continued, he began vigorously shaking the goat skin map, "THEY are the almighty powerful empires." "Yes, brother Benjamin, you are right. They are almighty powerful. Are you eager to establish a kingdom like all their Kingdoms and Empires? Is it possible brother I don't hear a voice of reason, but a thirst for power?" the Priest looked up and continued. "Not long ago we were slaves. Our hearts are still bitter and fatigued. Forty years wandering in the desert and thirty years into the land is not enough time to heal our wounds. We have no king now. Each man can do what he thinks is right in his eyes or the eyes of God. ... and in his mind and in his heart. Freedom must be the prerequisite for all of our teaching and learning. Let us experience it. It takes time to adjust. A man's freedom is our best remedy."

"My brother, the Priest! Is not Judah acting like a king now?" the Benjamin insisted.

"And in what way brother Benjamin? Looks like you are building an army, I don't see Judah doing that?" the Priest responded. "Of course we're building an army. We border with the hostile Cheshbon nation" Arad quickly snaps back.

Eraz the top Judean officer comments. "Yes, we all, and by that, I mean, our entire nation is threatened by the Cheshbon nation and others. But we must be a nation following God and the Ten Commandments."

The High Priest silently and attentively listens to this rhetoric going around and around for two hours, recognizing the stale mate and the escalating tension between Judah and the Benjamins. He knew that the Benjamin's snubbed and kept their distance from the other tribes because back in Egypt the Benjamins benefited from their privileged status. Benjamin and Joseph, the prince, were brothers from the same mother. They were more aware and informed about the political events in Egypt and in the Mediterranean basin. They adopted the Egyptian ways of physical and military training and the practice of homosexuality as an entitlement.

"I don't think Judah, and the rest of the tribes including the priesthood, will rush and come to our rescue if we are attacked by the Cheshbonites" Arad the Benjamin's top officer rebuked.

The Priest countered "Benjamin, you have to trust. I understand being a member of the elite kept you far from your brothers, and I don't blame you for that. But you are still a Hebrew. The Pharaohs realized that. That is why you were driven out of Egypt, like the rest of us. Times have changed, embrace it brother. What makes you think that Judah and the rest of the tribes will abandon our youngest brothers when facing the enemy? Shed your tough Egyptian skin, Benjamin. Clear the arrogance you adopted in those privileged golden days when you were with the elite in Egypt. Put trust in your brothers. We are no longer in Egypt."

Arad exasperated, upset, and feeling betrayed that the tribes are uniting and making decisions without them turned toward the Priest and said, "Judah is building an alliance with you, and the Simon's as well."

"The priesthood aligns with whoever follows El, Jehovah, God of Moses. We are the voice of logic and reason and live by a strong moral code. Join us Brother Benjamins in this alliance" the elder Priest stated pragmatically with conviction. Judah waited while Arad, the Benjamin's top officer, stood up, walked ten steps to the water jar in the shade of the sycamore tree and filled his cup. When he returned, Judah, in a soft calm voice and capturing the acute attention of everyone at the table, said "Join us in this alliance, with God of Moses."

Arad spoke. "We must live and protect ourselves by the sword. If we will not defend ourselves, then we will cease to exist and ultimately perish. We will be slaughtered like cattle. Let us build armies and prepare and train our children on how to defend themselves. The bronze swords are now being replaced by iron swords. They are ten times stronger and deadlier. And we don't want to be slaughtered by iron swords." Arad's stern voice was escalating as he spoke.

Another Benjamin officer stood up "Yes! Arad speaks the truth. The Philistines, the sea people, are invading with greater numbers and competing with us for ownership of our land. They are looking for a new place to call home. They are settling in the lowlands along the coastline, as we speak, and preying on the merchant ships in the big sea. It is only a question of time when we will have to face them in a battle. The nations around us are learning the iron sword. We must be ready."

"Is this a prophecy my brother Benjamin?" "No, my brother, this is reality." The High Priest who had been silent during these fiery conversations, stood up, raised his arms and head up to heaven and said in an emotional, passionate, and commanding voice "Our God in heaven, the God of Moses will protect us and will fight our wars. And we will bring the message of the Ten Commandments into the heart of every nation."

The Benjamins were completely agitated from what seemed like complete absurdity of the Priests words. Holding their heads and rolling their eyes they began standing up. It was incomprehensible to believe that the Cohens could be so out of touch with this dire situation, and it was inexplicable to believe that their young nation would continue to exist in their spiritual and utopian naiveté.

In the eyes of the Cohens, the rest of the nation dwelled in a religious mythological abyss, and their people disconnected from reality. The Cohens believed that the people of those nations were manipulated by the hands of power-hungry kings, and rulers. Both were competing among themselves for world superiority and domination. The sounds of the Trojan war, fifty years earlier, still echoed in the Mediterranean. Some of the elders of the Benjamin's still remembered its ripples in the land of Cannan.

Arad climbing his horse was furious as he spoke. "NO! Let us put our trust in the sword to protect us. High Priest, with all due respect, and brother Judah, we are committed to save this young tribal nation. Please join us Judean brothers. I hope the day will not come when we will have to divide and follow our own way. We will not be vulnerable, and we will not get slaughtered by the Philistines with only the Ten Commandments to protect us. High Priest, your words will not protect us! Your words will not protect our land, son of Aaron! Your hands will be filled with the blood of our unprotected woman and children."

With that, the twelve Benjamins mounted their horses, fuming with disdain for their brother's misjudgment.

"Rule by the sword or perish!" Arad's final words echoed as they rode east to their territory.

Chapter 9
"Harvest"

Sunday was only three days away. Ofra was waiting eagerly to find out if she would be granted permission to attend the harvest. Her father would be arriving home soon and was afraid he would object to her meeting her friends that far from the house. She was making a list of all the reasons to convince him without divulging her true intentions. She was hoping Safta would help her win her case because she knew her father would not permit this kind of encounter. Ofra was not in the mood for any confrontations. She climbed to the roof, frenetically pacing, and rehearsing her speech audibly while intently watching for his arrival. She finally spots him in the distance, his donkey loaded with all the usual provisions he stores in the house for his friends and guests. He was greeting and talking to the neighbors as they were all carrying food for Shabbat. This new day of observance was becoming a day of rest for many in the tribes. Ofra was becoming increasingly impatient and wanted to greet him as soon as he walked in the door.

It was right at dusk when her father arrived home with the food for tomorrow's special meal. She flew down the steps with more momentum than usual and was unable to contain her excitement. After her father handed the baskets to the old woman, whom Ofra always called grandmother, Safta, he noticed that his daughter was overly exuberant. Raising his eyebrows, he inquired with a smile "Did something happen today, Ofra?" The father noticed the two woman exchanging glances, with the young one giggling and the older one with a beaming smile.

Ofra, spurted in a crying voice "There's a big festival on Sunday and I promised all of my friends that I would be there." Her father looked at her in surprise and she didn't love this look. Safta saw Ofra's disappointed expression and jumped to her rescue. After listening to the old lady conveying all the reasons why it would be a good idea to allow her to attend the festival and reassuring him that his daughter would not get involved with the foolery that occurs in the evening, he finally agrees. He knew his daughter would be leaving at dawn and returning at dusk, and for Ofra's security, he insisted that Ezer his worker, accompany her to the harvest and back. Ofra's jovial Amorite father knew he wouldn't be a suitable escort because of a possible forthcoming hangover from the wine complimenting the Shabbat meal. Early morning on Sunday, the two rode off, Ofra on her donkey and Ezer on his mule. Ofra looked around until she spotted Rachel standing with their other friends. Her eyes began wandering the grounds three hundred sixty degrees looking for Gershon who hopefully would be conducting the inspection and reciting the blessing. Panicking she thought "The Cohen's will send another Levite! And not Gershon? How ridiculous! But maybe he won't be here. Is he thinking like me? Is he hoping *will Ofra be there*?" Interrupting her own internal conversation, she picked up a weaved basket from under the fig tree and caught up with Rachel and her friends.

With the help of the young boys and girls, the farmers worked intensely the entire season to reach this well-awaited moment, reaping their anticipated rewards.

Some of the girls came with other intentions; to find a future husband. Certain girls stayed the night hoping to 'force' a marriage promise, especially when the men got drunk, but they all came to enjoy the fun while earning their day's work.

Ofra and Rachel managed to fill up their basket, both girls helping each other, and each holding their side of the overflowing grapes. The moment she heard the flute playing *'It's harvest time'* her heart began racing. The morning breeze cooled the light sweat created by the weight of the grapes and her nervous excitement. By now everyone was singing, she lowered her lids when his piercing eyes met hers

but she quickly starred back at him in time to see him mouth the words "I knew you were going to be here." Gershon chuckled as she lowered her head shyly powerless to hold in the overwhelming unfamiliar feelings she was experiencing. Unprepared to examine his own romantic feelings for Ofra, he walked toward the grove owner to inspect the harvest and recite the blessing.

Ofra ran to the long-necked water jar under the fig tree. Filling her ceramic cup, she drank more than usual to satisfy her parched lips, and then with the remaining few sips splashed her neck and face. She walked over to a shady spot and sat under the tree for quite a while. She was incapable of identifying these strong emotions as she has never been exposed to a romantic love. She spent enough time recuperating and wanted to join her friends in the celebration. She stood up rested one foot on the tree trunk, looked left and right, pulled up the side of her dress exposing her upper leg, took out her painted clay bottle with two of the tiniest handles, no larger than a thimble, that had been tied around her thigh with a leather cord. She poured the scented oil into her left palm, began dabbing her neck and arms rapidly, immediately tied the vessel back around her leg and straightened her dress quickly. Just as she finished, Gershon showed up, still wearing the radiant fascination shimmering on his face. She was taken by surprise and glowed with a rosy blush. "A fig tree with a scent of cinnamon oil?" He said teasingly She smiled like a mischievous child caught in the middle of doing something provocative.

"Hebrew girl, you're pouring your charm on me."

"But Gershon all my friends know about you."

"Yes, Ofra, the whole town knows! You ride all the way here to wave at me each time you pass the Goshen center. I think everyone notices." "You do not want me to wave at you any more Gershon?" She answered in a childish manner.

With a serious attitude encircling his upright posture, Gershon said in one breath, "I am Levite! A follower of Jehovah, the God of Moses. A missionary. I devote my life to El."

Ofra, disappointed, doesn't know how the conversation turned around so quickly and drastically. She was hoping for words of affirmation, but unexpectantly and with her arms crossed says "I know who you are!"

Gershon was now the one caught off guard by Ofra's obstinate words and her capacity to slice right into his serious demeanor. And although he quickly realized he should say something sweet; he chose to continue this important and sincere exchange. He needed to make sure young beautiful Ofra understood his devotion to God.

"Ofra in what do you believe more, Jehovah, God of Moses, or the Baal and the Ashrah?"

"The Baal gives us rain; I really like that. But mostly I like the Ashrah, the goddess of fertility, because …" Ofra moves her head away from Gershon in a taunting manner, "… one day I will marry, and I will have a child." Tenaciously, she turns back to look directly into Gershon's eyes and says, "But I like Jehovah too! My father says when I marry, I can choose. My father says that Jehovah is everywhere and at the same, nowhere! When he explained how Jehovah is with me when I sleep, when I leave the house, when I miss my mom, when I cry, when I'm happy, he's everywhere, that makes sense! But nowhere? No matter how he tried to explain it, his words didn't make sense, so he suggested I ask you."

Young Ofra touched the core of Gershon's reality. This is the exact dilemma he faces with the people of the tribes, helping them understand the idea of this invisible God.

"I think your father meant to convey that Jehovah sees everything and yet we cannot see him."

Ofra suddenly realized it was getting so late. On her toes and looking across the grove she panics, "Gershon, oh my. It's late and Ezra is looking for me. I must go!" Before Gershon had a chance to respond, she darted away, only to turn and wave her goodbyes.

The sun was setting in the sky and the celebration and festivities would be forthcoming. Ofra would be long gone by the time the fire pits would be roaring.

The farmers with their inflamed egos were boastfully carrying their leather wine skins, big and small, each one based on their earnings. The girls were scheming as they paid attention to the size of the wine skins, knowing who earned the most and who earned the least. Trailing behind the farmers, the landowners were each carrying a lamb around their neck with the limbs of the freshly slaughtered animal in their hands. Once they reached the cooking pit each animal was placed above the fire. The aroma of the sizzling meat with the newly made sweet wine aroused their senses, along with the freshly baked hot bread coming out of the oven.

There were colorful displays of dried fruit, an abundance of bread and honey, more than could be consumed. It was bountiful.

There were five musicians each tuning their wooden instruments, some with strings and others with flutes and two musicians joining with their ram horns each varying in pitch by the musician's embouchure.

Ofra and Ezer still in earshot of the grove, heard the music as they headed for home.

The dancing, drinking, and eating continued throughout the night.

In the early morning hours as the fires were smoldering the men dropped to the ground passing out from the food, wine, music, and dancing.

The remaining women who chose to spend the night, sneaked beside the intoxicated men and under the influence let the man have his way with her knowing that if she got pregnant, by the law of the land, that man must marry her.

Ezer made sure to bring Ofra home before dusk because her father always insisted on eating meals timely. As she rushed into the house, Ofra placed the small basket filled with grapes which she earned for her efforts at the grove. In the corner of the room, under the stairs leading to the roof, she walked toward the sizable clay jar and scooped water into a wooden cup. For the past eleven years ever since Ofra's mother passed, Safta, took very good care of Ofra, her father and their house. She came down holding the laundered clothes that had been drying on the roof. She looked at Ofra, who was still wearing that enchanted look from the grove and emanating a strong flowery cinnamon perfume scent. The old lady wiggled her nose and sniffed the lingering fragrance in the air. She was around long enough to characterize this kind of conduct and recognized what was happening to the young lady who had just stormed into the house. "The table is set, and the food is ready Ofra. Your father is going to arrive very soon."

The old lady smiled and acknowledged Ofra's idyllic mood.

"Thank you, Safta," Ofra said as she rushed to her room.

Chapter 10
"Matchmaker"

A week passed since Ofra attended the harvest and the warm sunny weather was hinting they were entering summer. Ofra widened her steps heading for home as she did not want to make the old lady worry. She walked from her neighbor Malka's house, after spending all of midday playing square and pyramid. This was her favorite game because she was good at collecting and placing the tiny stones in the squares and hopping over them. Home was a few cobble stones away and she entered the main yard through the sole entrance which was shared by three other families. It was surrounded by a stone wall that acted as a security buffer. Some of her friends and neighbors were looking at her and giggling having recognized the matchmaker by her enormous, long white scarf singing *'I wish all the wars were like Jericho, where no blood was ever spilled'* as she entered the house before Ofra's arrival. Unaware, Ofra laughed back without realizing why. People knew this matchmaker and if she was in the house a deal was in the making, or at least an offer was coming. The matchmaker dressed in a black dress with a white embroidered trim, and her hair covered with the recognizable white trademark, sat on a low straw four-legged chair. She was talking to Ofra's father who appeared to be revealing his usual positive disposition.

"Good day." Ofra joined with a smile as she entered and sensed the friendly atmosphere.

"Ofra, I made sure the donkey has enough feed, don't worry about that." "Thank you, Safta," Ofra picked up her small red clay pitcher which was still half full. The continuous breeze from the roof kept the water jar a bit cooler. Ofra poured a little water on her right palm so she could cool her face and neck. Water was scarce in all the land, so she always tried to use it sparingly. She then walked over and stood across from her father who was talking with the matchmaker.

"… and I hope that Koshan the ruler, the wicked, will one day be choked on the honey and the salt he is accumulating, and leave us alone." The matchmaker stated as she concluded their political conversation.

Ofra stood in the corner with her arms folded, staring at the old lady unsure why she came to visit Abba.

The Matchmaker beckons Ofra "Come here, my daughter, sit next to me. More and more you resemble your beautiful mother. May she rest in peace in heaven."

Ofra wanted to hear more about her mother but was annoyed that the matchmaker might be stalling with small talk before conveying some bad news, so she didn't inquire how she knew her mother. Ofra refrained from asking her any questions and certainly didn't want the matchmaker to interfere in her life now that she had met Gershon. She emphatically would be uninterested in anyone the Matchmaker had in mind.

Knowing what the matchmaker is known for and fearing the worst, Ofra abruptly injects "What tribe is he from?"

"Is it important my daughter? As long as he treats you right?" the Matchmaker shrugged her shoulder. "You will never have to go to bed hungry" she continued. "You still didn't tell me which tribe he is from!" Ofra smiled in order to soften her stance.

"He is a 'well to do' Levite, a man of our Almighty." The Matchmaker answers, starting to feel that this young Ofra does not appreciate her services and is quite resistant to her expertise.

"In my youth, we were lucky just to have a man. Oh heaven, the more there is freedom in the land, the choosier they get" as she wiped her nose with a handkerchief. She drags the chair to sit in front of Ofra's father.

"They call him the noble one" continued the matchmaker "He lives close to the holy tent of our creator, as is appropriate for a Priest from the Levite tribe. He lives between the tribes of Benjamin and Ephraim, where the sons of Aaron, the high priests, rest in peace, are buried. But this Priest comes down here, to Bethlehem very often. And now this Priest commissioned me for this mission to find him a wife." She took a deep breath and although intentionally said 'wife' restated her words correctly and said, "A concubine."

She looked at Ofra's father to detect a reaction to the word 'concubine', but none was noticed so she continued in an assertive tone. "… to be a helper to him, especially when he attends the orphans, widows and the work of our creator in the holy tent, in Beth El and Shiloh."

Ofra pacing back and forth is unable to speak afraid she might erupt after the Matchmaker discloses the name. She hopes that her father who has been sitting quietly breaks his silence.

"Maybe you have heard of him?" says the Matchmaker "His name is Gershon."

Ofra, shocked and in disbelief, stopped pacing, eyes wide open, slowly exhaled with relief as she had been unintentionally holding her breath. She was in a state of panic thinking they had someone else in mind. Her father noticed a complete change in his daughter's face and body as he saw the relief when she heard the name Gershon.

"Oh, how clever that Gershon is" Ofra thought while she was not able to hide her initial excitement after the Matchmaker left. "First, he shows his interest in me, right there in the grove, and then in the same week, he sends this lady to seal the deal with father." Ofra was entangled in a million thoughts. They were running through her in every direction. For every beautiful romantic thought there was a reversal to panic. She was flip flopping from jubilation to rejecting the offer of marriage. On the one hand she was thrilled that she would not be like others, who

met their future husbands for the first time on their wedding night and conversely, she would unwaveringly decline the offer of marriage. She adored Gershon but knew she wasn't ready to leave her father and Safta. Going to the Triangle would be an adventure but leaving her friends was unfathomable. She couldn't stop the tidal wave of contradictions.

He was able to read his daughter like the palm of his hand. "I know this is a lot. Take your time. Time is on your side. You have my blessing if this is what you want. Remember, this Levite is a servant of God of Moses before he is anything else. He is not a member of the prestigious Baal and the Ashrah priests. He is devoted to his cause daughter. Not all the people are practicing the Ten Commandments of Moses, and many might have resentment. I love you more than my own life Ofra and this will always be your home. Go rest now."

Overexcited but exhausted, Safta gently walked Ofra to her room where she collapsed into a deep sleep.

Chapter 11
"Ada"

In the Goshen Center in Bethlehem Judea, Ada, Gershon's wife did the cooking and cleaning together with another woman. The two women were paid for their work through proceeds from the people of Bethlehem.

Ada was attentively cleaning the center, holding the palm branch in her hand sweeping and clearing the leaves that were ushered in like a windstorm. She welcomed Gershon as he cavalierly walked by to meet with the high priest.

"Good day" Gershon said with a tentative smile and his intention quickly became serious.

"Good day" the two women responded, Ada appearing slightly uncomfortable. "Are any of the high priests here?" "No" she replied quickly lowering her head, nervous and overwhelmed, knowing she must be prepared to discuss the inevitable.

"How is your father doing Ada?" he asked warmly "He is getting thinner. I was told by the healers that this is not a good sign, but my sister is arriving from Beersheba and she is going to stay with us for a short time. Her growing family needs her, but she wants to spend time with our Abba."

Ada stopped cleaning and looked at Gershon.

"I'm not going back with you to the triangle" she slowly articulated each word.

"Well, I figured that out by now. You have not been with me for a while" Gershon replied in a resigned tone. "Your family's needs always came before mine. It was always this way."

After a moment of silence, she said "Bethlehem has been good for my family … and me"

"And besides, you devote your life to your new God in heaven and you forgot about *your* family. You forgot about your Ada, and you have a son." Turning away from Gershon's eyes she continued. "Now I have a home and a roof over my head. There is bread to eat when I'm hungry and when I'm home, I'm never alone." "I'm happy to hear you are never alone" his voice became gentle when he saw the tears she tried to hide.

"And who is going to help me, Ada?" Gershon's voice sounded a decibel louder while regaining control. "Your God will provide." She subconsciously stabbed using Gershon's words she heard so often.

"Aren't you the one who decided to leave?"

"Did I have a choice?" Before she continued, her voice softened while still avoiding his eyes "Am I too old? Is my body not strong enough?"

Before speaking and careful not to hurt her any more than she was, Gershon decelerated his breathing and continued. "In the future, are you going to be searching for me? Will you be looking to share bread? You are welcomed to share it with us?"

"Us?" Ada laughed feeling bad for this nameless woman and unable to imagine she would be going through what she went through. "You mean the matchmakers offer, Gershon?"

He lowered his head. "I cannot be alone. You know that. I need help. It is not good for a man to be alone Ada." "I don't wish for you to be alone. You cannot be alone, Gershon." He was relieved to hear her sympathy, but she persisted callously "You claimed my virginity and we have a son."

"You know I'm a Levite. You know I have a mission. You knew about all my duties and obligations. I'm sorry, Ada. I'm dedicated to the triangle serving the three tribes."

"Ah, and this new concubine, is she a woman of mission? Take a slave girl Gershon, she will become accustomed to being alone, and lonely." "I'm surprised to hear that from you Ada. I do not wish to spoil my seed on the ground. Besides, you know that the priesthood shy's away from the use of slaves for procreating."

"So now you think you're going to make use of this concubine, the same way you made use of me?"

"I think she will be willing to join me in the triangle. Come with us, bring our son, and when I'm doing the work of our God, carrying the holy ark on my bruised shoulders between Bethel, Shiloh, and Kiriat Yarim, the three of you will not be alone at home. And if you decide not to join us, I will still share my bread with you always."

"Gershon you are a Levite. You live on donations. I'm sure you cannot feed the four of us." Ada said in a candid voice, then paused, forced a smile, and continued. "When Yareike has completed its cycle, I will by then have the advice of the Elders."

Remembering the days she was left alone and hungry with little to eat for a week and many times longer, Ada was certain she couldn't live with Gershon and his concubine in the Triangle. She was uncomfortable thinking about Gershon and a new young maiden. She couldn't express these feelings to him at the moment but knew the Elders would help with their guidance.

"May God of Moses give a fast healing to your father, Ada" Gershon spoke before he walked to his room in the Goshen center, in the Levites quarter. He knew a good rest would be necessary because in the morning he was planning to ask for Ofra's hand in marriage.

Chapter 12
"Proposal"

The next day, before father opened the door, he peeked through the small security window and the voice outside the door announced, "Peace be on you, dear Amorite, father of Ofra."

Both knew the reason Gershon was standing at the door.

"Peace be on you Levite" replied her father as he motioned the old lady "Safta, set for us the table for this great occasion." Having been accustomed to the many quests he hosted, the old lady quickly set the table with bread and wine.

Ofra's father offered Gershon a chair.

"As I'm sure the matchmaker told you" Gershon spoke as he was seating himself on the wooden chair, "I'm asking to marry your daughter."

"Safta!" The father addressed the old lady, knowing his daughter in the next room could hear them but would wait until she was asked to come out. "Did you hear that? The Levite wants to take my last daughter away from home. My young Ofra."

Ofra's father knowing that Gershon, the Levite sitting in front of him, a member of the emerging young Priesthood, a man devoting his life to God could create a challenge for his daughter's future.

"The time has arrived, like it does for everything " the old lady spoke merrily. "I live in the slope of the Ephraim mountains, but you know I come here very often to Bethlehem. We are not far from each other" Gershon said, in a full confident voice.

"My Ofra is young," he made sure to emphasize the word young, while momentarily wearing a somber look.

"*Young*?" commented the old lady stretching out the word young. "This generation into the new land have strong minds. They know what they want, and they do it."

"You are right. You know her and have always been like a mother to her" the father articulated.

The old lady feeling an immediate need to look out for Ofra's best interest, pulled out a small wooden chair and felt comfortable enough to sit down and get into the conversation between these two men who were deciding on young Ofra's future fate. Before sitting down, she looked straight into the Levite's eyes. "… and Ada, your wife, what has become of her?"

"Ada, is good and well, taking care of her ill father, and her brothers…" He took a pause and continued. "… and working at the Goshen center, where I've been staying before going back to my assignment in the Triangle."

"I love Ofra" murmured Gershon to the old lady in her ear. "Here again, what is it about love and this generation." the old lady said while tapping her knees with her palms. "Let us celebrate the wellness for the young priesthood of Jehovah, God of Moses in this new land" declared Ofra's father as he took a sip from the pomegranate wine.

"Safta, bring us the grape wine instead; this day deserves a true celebration!"

He drank the last remaining sip in his cup, and when she handed him the clay bottle, he generously poured the grape wine.

"I will let my daughter's free will decide. For who can slave the matters of the heart but the heart. And before our young Levite departs, Safta, prepare some bread and olives for his departure. ... and one more thing young Levite." The father turned and looked at Gershon "I'm older than you, allow me to ask, what is man's purpose in life?"

The Levite smiled and realized that Ofra's father was either checking his future son-in-law's perspective on life or perhaps his perspective on marriage and was waiting to see if it would be answered honestly or with the answer he wanted to hear.

When Ofra's father asked her daughter's prospective husband the question, he was hoping to reveal the man's main preference to benefit his Ofra. He wanted to know if Gershon is a good man, and that his priority will be love, trust and commitment to his daughter.

"For me, father!" Gershon responded, "a man's purpose in life is to worship the creator, our maker El in heaven. I take it upon myself to teach new values and traditions to our people."

Anticipating a response and cutting into the silence, Gershon smiled pensively, swiveled in his seat, and asked the father "Allow me to ask, what is man's purpose in life to you?"

Without a moment's hesitation his reply came easily "A man's purpose is respect, and always be kind, value friendship, be a good father, feed the hungry, be honest, and if you can, never miss on a good jar of wine when it comes your way, because life is but a breath."

The old lady walked in with a basket of stuffed grape leaves, olives, cheese, and bread and placed it on the table near Gershon.

"We will have an answer for you when Yareke is full in the sky" the father's assuring voice made Gershon the priest feels hopeful.

Gershon, knowing he would still require the father's answer, needed Ofra's assurance. By now he felt he loved her but was not sure about her love for him. The old lady reading his mind and understanding his predicament called out "Ofra! Gershon the Levite is here, come and greet him."

Within seconds, Ofra appeared and so quickly, as she had been listening to every word spoken from behind the cloth that was separating the rooms. Gershon wanted to step outside so he and Ofra could talk privately and looked at her father for consent. Ofra's father nodded and with his approval they both rushed to the yard where the big fig tree stood in the center.

Ofra stepped outside and her giddy feelings of infatuation of days past turned into an uncomfortable anxiousness. Walking nervously toward the fig tree her head hanging low and having overheard all the conversations between her father and the Levite, mountains of thoughts were circling around in her head. She was unexpectantly questioning his plans and intentions. She ran to the fig tree and Gershon followed to catch up to her.

"Ofra, I asked your father for your hand and for his blessing."

"Gershon! Do you really love me?"

Provoked by the conversation that preceded in the house and encompassed with the most unexpected immense momentary excitement, he fell on his knees, his arms wide open, and full of passion proclaimed "I'm bound by my love for God and feel I'm bound to you with the same devotion. Come with me Ofra, I'll take care of you."

Time stood still seeing Gershon on his knees and hearing those affirmations. She was speechless. She wanted to embrace him and at the same time run away from him. She couldn't resolve her conflicting heart.

He reaches into his robe and with the afternoon sun shimmering on the gold, pulls out the most beautiful bracelet.

Her eyes sparkling from this exquisite piece of jewelry, she spoke directly to him, "Why should I? Why should I go with you Gershon?" Her voice was sincere as he reached for her hand to adorn her with the wristlet while he says "Marry me Ofra, I'll be there when you need me. I'll take care of you." Slipping the bracelet over her delicate hand she says, "My life here is just fine Gershon. And your life ..." her head and hands up, she couldn't help but marvel at the stunning gift Gershon just bestowed on to her, continues her thought "...belongs to God."

"So, help me be what I must be, Ofra, daughter of Hebrews!"

She stood under the fig tree, and from its branch, reached up once again admiring the gold bracelet, picked a green unripe fruit, just as she always did. She squeezed it with her hand until the milky juice dripped out, and oozed among her fingers, but this time only three small drops landed on Gershon's face. Ofra giggled as the drops fell and the atmosphere immediately changed. Things lightened up and Ofra was so thrilled with Gershon's gift, and they exchanged pleasantries. But her mood quickly switched back to serious.

"Why should I go with a man who lives like a wanderer chasing a God! A God no one can swear, has ever seen!" she continued in a loud voice while she walked away laughing to herself still thinking about the fig juice on Gershon's face and how he surprised her so unexpectedly. She then extended her open arm to him before she entered the house. "Upon your return, Gershon, and upon my free will, I will have my decision" she said out loud, remembering her father's words.

Leaving him in the yard and walking to the back door of the house, she wondered 'why should I go with him?'

She turned and watched him wiping the milky juice from his face and then he too walked to the back door. He stood there with a puzzled look and deep in thought 'she sure is a feisty girl behind that pretty face.'

Prior to his departure Gershon said goodbye to her father and Safta. While riding his donkey back to the Goshen house, his mind was racing and digesting the events of the day and reflecting her father's words about letting Ofra make her own decision? *'Her free will and matters of the heart will decide'*

What an irony. Ada's father made the decision for his daughter. Now, Ofra is going to make the decision? Times are changing. Is her free will the outcome of freedom? Gershon continued to reflect and stretch the inner dialogue further.

Isn't Ofra too young to choose, even in matters of the heart? Maybe this refreshing air of freedom allows a person to mature sooner. She weaves her web and lures me into her world. How defenseless she makes me feel, as she inadvertently provokes me with her beauty and how she looks at me so innocently but purposely and unintentionally enticingly. Then afterward, while I'm still intoxicated by her haunting looks, and mesmerized by her aura, she reaches out to me and throws me back to reality. Then she hurls daggers into my heart with her words: *'Why should I go with a man who lives like a wanderer chasing God.'* She certainly has a way about her. She occupies the deepest part of my essence. She invades my domain. I can admit sincerely that this beautiful girl who I just asked to marry may know parts of me that I myself have not yet discovered. Contrary to what Ada said and suggested, maybe Ofra will decide to join me in my mission. I admire this young woman and hope she will agree to come with me. '*Gershon, you are falling in love*' he continued his self-dialogue. "*I can clearly understand how a man like Jacob worked fourteen years (and more) for Rachel. Love is surely powerful.*"

The donkey diligently measured each step to the rhythm of his rider. Maybe he sensed his owner was deep in thought. Gershon noticed Ada walking towards her home as he reached the Goshen center. He was glad to arrive in perfect time without having to engage in a conversation with her.

Chapter 13
"Visitor"

Ofra's mother resting in heaven, died when they were just fifteen years into the land. Ofra hoped she would come to her in a dream to coach her, the way the neighbor's daughters were prepared by their mothers prior to their weddings.

It was a half Yareke that night. While Gershon slept soundly at the Goshen center, Ofra was overly exhilarated and sprung off her rectangular wood bed before dawn. She felt particularly pretty in the new golden and beige tunic linen gown her father bought from his last trip. Next to the stairs leading to the roof was the water jug and a lit candle encased in its clay vessel. A soft breeze kept the water chilled and using the wooden spoon to scoop the water, she splashed her face and neck with her fingers, cooling down her light sweat. She peeked at the retreating night above the stairs and followed the soft pale moonlight up to the roof. Pieces of night were scattered upon the face of dawn. She tiptoed to the four corners of the roof, looked up at Yareke the moon God and slowly spun her body into a dance. Her feet and hands followed her hips, and her head was rolling in full circles. She knew she was imitating the dancing of the Canaanite girls who embraced the pagan's goddess Ashrah. She and her friends loved to see them dancing at the festival of fertility, sneaking to the forbidden side of town which she knew her father never would have approved. She was always shocked how the girls stretched and twisted their bodies in the utmost extreme way.

Ofra couldn't imagine how their bodies didn't snap in two. In these early hours, the pigeons were her audience, and their love humming was her rhythm and melody. Aroused by the previous day's events, when Gershon declared his love, and proposed, she started to sing.

"Fate knocks down on my door, oh heaven smiles at me, I am just a young soul. Fate knocks down on my door oh heaven smile and brighten my destiny. Make me fruitful, make me whole, shade your blessing on me. Lighten up my heart, make me laugh, bring all that is joy to my life. Fate knocks down on my door, heaven smile at me, I am just a young soul."

At the far corner of the roof, she sat down on the wooden bed. Feeling so enchanted she continued singing "But then again your eyes love me, and then again, it is true, I bow down to your wish, and I will make our dream come true, I want to smile and be married rather than be without you."

She buried her face in her palms and lowered her head fatigued. She heard footsteps, snapped out of her trance, and pretended she was collecting the dry clothes hanging on the wooden sticks. "Is it that time of the month, my daughter?" said Safta who always made sure to have an early start. She would wake up early to take care of the house and show her gratitude. "It's ok" she continued, sensing Ofra's ambivalence to her unknown future.

"Before I left my father's house, I could not sleep either, but that was a long time ago." She smiled while shaking the dew and the sheep fur from laundered linens. She then walked downstairs with a handful of clothes but returned minutes later. "Ofra, will you take advice from this old lady?" "Say it Safta." The old lady took a deep breath. "I'm listening" continued Ofra with a bit of impatience. She felt like a grown woman and was ready to take advice for what is to come next in her life. "When you are longing deeply for your father's house, be strong, and put your trust in his name, our creator, and stay by your husband."

Descending the stairs and feeling parched, Ofra stopped to drink a cup of water. She was trying to make sense of Safta's words as she went to rest in her room.

Not too much later that morning, Ofra heard someone at the door. She opened the tiny window; a young woman was standing there. She was tightly veiled holding a basket and wearing a black dress with a pattern of white circles around the border. She held the child with her left hand. "My name is Ada." Ofra quickly lifted the wood latch which secured the door. The two women examined each other, neither recognizing the other. "It's Gershon's child" Ada spoke before Ofra had a chance to inquire. Ofra rushed and brought two cups of water. Ada sat on the green olive stump and grabbed her son and possessively placed him on her lap while recognizing Ofra's youth and beauty.

"He is a busy man, and he will treat you fine, as long as he is around."

"You mean Gershon?" Ofra vocalized. "Yes! The Levite. The priest. And be ready to launder the priesthood clothing. And to spend time alone." Ada tried to smile to overshadow being blunt and direct. Or maybe she was just being candid. "That's why he needs a second wife."

"So, is that why you've come here today? To prepare me? To alert me? To frighten me? To warn me?" Ofra's voice although low, was reacting like a grown woman ready to take on life and its challenges. Now, at this unexpected moment, Ofra is confronting Gershon's other wife. Her first challenge.

"I was told you are young and beautiful. I see it's true" Ada reasoning Gershon's decision to choose this beautiful young girl.

Ofra smiled as a form of thank you. "You're no less beautiful. I was told your father is ill, and you care about him very much, the way a daughter should be." Ada forced a smile back "I will not interfere with matters of the heart between you and Gershon" she looked up, away from Ofra's eyes. and paused. "And I cannot stay in the triangle. Maybe you can sister. I have four brothers here in Bethlehem and a sick father. They all need me." Ada continued after a short pause "Since the day my mother died, I had to make a decision between taking care of my family or follow a man who is following an imaginary God in heaven."

Ada took Ofra's hand between her own and gently said "You have my blessing Ofra, maybe you can give him happiness. More than I was able to." She paused again, lowered her head, sighed, and continued. "There is one more thing. The elders made a request. The Levite must have a meeting before you and he can go to the triangle."

"And now you know everything, so I will leave you with that, for now" Ada said as she was lifting the child from her lap to give Ofra a warm goodbye. Ada wiped a few tears from her face.

Ofra brought grapes. "To sweeten your throat and the child" Ofra said while looking at Gershon's child. The small boy, examining Ofra, looked into her eyes, in a grown-up manner. He reached for a grape.

"I should be getting back. My father is very ill, and he needs my attention." "Wait" said Ofra, "you walked all this way with the boy from the city gate?"

"It's ok I am accustomed to walking a lot. I do the food

shopping for the Goshen center." "Come," Ofra's heart was full of understanding.

Ofra went to the back of the house and walked out her donkey. The three of them climbed the poor donkey. Luckily, Ada was petite and skinny, she embraced the child.

The old lady stormed outside "Ofra" she yelled "where are you going?" "The city gate Safta." "Wait, Ezer will accompany you."

The elderly man chiseling the stones in the back of the house, rushed out and followed them on his mule. Ofra turned her head while riding the donkey, and quickly looked at Ada sitting behind.

"I heard what you said to me, but tell me, what is the meaning of your tears? Is there more your heart wants to express? You love him huh? You can come back and join us anytime you wish, Ada. I will make room for you and your boy."

"Thank you, Ofra." They reached the city gate.

Ada's words rang again in her head, 'I had to make a decision between staying with my husband or attending to my sick father and family.' Ofra couldn't imagine being in that situation.

By now it was all known in the Judean enclave that Gershon the Levite proposed and asked the Amorite for his daughter's hand. He was a member of the fast- growing Jehovah priesthood. Gershon was a father to his young son, a husband to Ada and a man devoted to the God of Moses. He carries the Ark on his shoulders and serves three tribes in the triangle. And besides all that, he has many duties to his masters, the Cohens. And now Young Ofra was to become a concubine to this man's enormous commitments and responsibilities. She had no idea what she was about to embark on.

Chapter 14
"Accepted"

After the proposal, Ofra made her decision to marry Gershon and follow him to the Triangle. The Levite, waiting in great anticipation for the year to pass, was concerned that his young Ofra could have a change of heart and be claimed by another. Contrarily, Gershon knew that respecting the customary year after asking for her hand, as promised to her father, had many advantages. Gershon accepted it wholeheartedly, also knowing that her father wanted to wait until Ofra turned fifteen.

Ofra's father reminded Gershon that Ofra was a virgin and surely not pregnant. He told Gershon not to be concerned and that no other man has a hold on her. Her father knew that waiting for the traditional year to pass would resolve all those matters.

A significant matter still revolved around the customary money that Gershon will have to pay. Her father, with all his persuasiveness, could not convince the Levite to retain the expected dowry.

"It will serve as a little token to the young priesthood" the father insisted.

"No. Keep it. Save it for her." Gershon knowing it was unethical and illegal to accept that kind gesture continued "It's the law of the land, my Judean father." In the end, the strict one, Gershon the priest, prevailed.

Her father accepted the money but was more preoccupied about the preparations for this very big wedding and all the pending arrangements. Gershon knew that this upcoming extravaganza would take time.

"I must make it back to the triangle. The work of the Almighty is enormous, and time is short" the Levite said gently asserting his time restraints. "I understand, the father smiled, but my dear son, we cannot rush a wedding. It is not a good omen for things to come." "The olive grove will be great for this occasion," Safta inserted joyfully.

"Good idea" he prematurely responded. "But we would need to carry all the cooking there. I think our yard will be just fine. We will have to remove the remnants of the chiseled stones which were not sold yet and the acacia wood. Then we will lay sheep furs on the ground for our guests and open our house and our hearts."

"My dear son" he turned and addressed the Levite. "You don't have any objection that our friends, my partners, the Jebusites, mingle with us on my daughter's joyful day? They will be offended if they are not invited."

"Not at all. As long as they share our slaughtered meat." "My friends will not object to eating meat that was inspected more than once."

Chapter 15
"Wedding"

Many people showed up for Ofra's wedding because her father held a preferred status. He owned his own home and was admired in the community for his success as an honest wealthy merchant. He was respected by the Judeans and the natives of Bethlehem because he traveled for a year crossing the Sinai back to Egypt and then traveled back to bring the papyrus and clay tablets to the Goshen center. As a trader, he had the ability to sustain this rigid trip and cross borders but personally he promised Ofra's mother, a Hebrew Egyptian, that one day he would fulfill her wishes to bring back those significant inscriptions. He knew that those treasures from 400 years of the Hebrews living in the diaspora were left there after the exodus and could be lost forever.

The Levite, a member of the new emerging priesthood also shared a preferred status. Gershon was known and revered for his complete devotion to the work of the almighty Jehovah the God of Moses. This religion in Bethlehem was the fastest growing divinity. Sheep and goats were deftly selected not to have blue marks which could indicate injury or illness. Only those healthy enough were slaughtered. This was all according to the new code "deity of reason" as it was called by some in this pagan society. The Levites wishes were taken into consideration during the food preparation for the wedding, as was his strict observances serving his God. Members from the Priesthood, and from the

Goshen center were among the guests. The whole town and all the people from the enclave heard about Gershon the priest. He just turned thirty, and now is taking a second wife, a concubine who just celebrated her fifteenth birthday. Ofra invited all her friends from the Goshen learning school. Rachel, the princess, arrived side saddle style in her pretty dress and slid from the donkey gracefully. Just like a lady is supposed to. One young Judean guest commented "She descends the donkey like Akasha the wife of Ataniel and the daughter of wealthy Caleb."

"Well, didn't Akasha receive two large parcels of land as a result of her poised and elegant ways as the beloved princess of Caleb?" said a young man humorously while he stared at Rachel. They all laughed. The young man was eyeing Rachel all night long.

In the decorated yard of the house, the Jebusites, the father's invitees, formed a circle under the wide shadow of the fig and olive trees. It was customary to devote the shaded areas to those special guests. All the others formed two groups seated in a smaller circle in the semi-shaded area.

In front of the house the children were marveling at an Egyptian chariot with two black horses. It was brought here by a rich Canaanite guest, a very well-known horse-groomer. It is said that this chariot participated in the battle of Kadesh when Ramses the II led the war against the Hittites. Under the watchful eye of the driver, children ran their tiny fingers on its wood, bronze, and iron wheels. Camels with their knees folded, a dozen donkeys and equal numbers of horses were all stationed in front of the Amorite's house.

At the Levite's request, the meat was to be consumed only after it produced its aroma. This was a sign that it spent enough time under fire. Eight brilliant torches lit the corners of the roof where a young boy played the flute beautifully. The old ladies in charge of the cooking all agreed that the neighbor at the far end of the four-family dwelling prepares the best savory bread in all Judean Bethlehem.

They all waited to see a glimpse of Ofra's face when she would be unveiled, her passage from a child to a woman. She looked beautiful on her wedding day. Her mother's southern Nubian Judean beauty shined through her olive skin. Her long towering neck and big brown eyes glowed and sparkled. Her poise and charm was inherited from her Amorite father. Ofra the bride was ushered outside to the yard. She was surrounded by Rachel, Zilpa and a dozen other friends.

A big roar sounded from the attendees at the very moment her father removed the veil uncovering her beautiful face. Gershon was standing no more than an arm's length to the two of them and Ofra's father placed his right arm around Gershon's shoulder and guided him towards Ofra. Some words were exchanged between the two men and Ofra's father moved over to make way for Gershon to get closer to his bride. Ofra was radiant in the soft white flowing dress. Her youthful flushed pink cheeks complimented her exquisite shiny black hair that was flowing freely around her arms and down to her thighs. A stunning hair weave was adorned with strands of gold and silver braided down the middle of her back. She was the envy of all the girls many that helped her prepare for this day. Ofra felt like she was suspended like a feather floating through a soft wind. Gershon noticed her delicate innocence and her magnificent glow. He was mesmerized by her beauty. Gershon and Ofra exchanged occasional gazes while the ceremony was being conducted. At the conclusion, while the crowd made loud congratulatory noises with their tongues flapping, Gershon reached for Ofra's hand noticing she was wearing the gold bracelet he gave her a year ago. They had a momentary amorous glance with one another before the guests approached with well wishes.

"More grape wine over here." Voices were heard from the back "More sweet pomegranate wine over here." Voices were heard from the other side.

As the guests wished the newlyweds many sweet days to come, they placed small gifts on the low table in front of them and the larger gifts; the lambs, rams, birds and larger offerings were set beside them near the tree. The woman brought kohl, scented candles and jasmine perfume for Ofra.

"It looks like this Levite can afford a concubine." "We shall see." said another standing by. "Does it really matter if she is a concubine or a first wife? Only a woman knows her self-worth in the eyes of her man" said another woman with a big smile.

Although it was not his first wedding, the Levite was certainly not expecting this extravagant wedding.

Big round clay trays and larger wooden ones were filled with sizzling goat and sheep. They all shared the same platter as they dipped and mopped up the juice with their bread. The fragrant cooking was ushered out by the Judean twilight breeze and was mingled with the soft sounds of the flute. The gentle wind carried the aroma of the roasted meat that was seasoned with apple, thyme, bay leaves and oregano. The scent was sweet and inviting. The people in the surrounding hills recognized that another Judean girl was claimed tonight. The dishes of cooked meat, savory bread, grapes and olives were displayed on the colorful fur covering the ground in the middle of each group.

They all praised Ofra for the delicious fig cake she prepared, of course under the watchful eye of Safta. Gifts of honey were brought in clay dishes just as they were accustomed to sharing during the new moon. It was always a significant gesture for sweet years to come.

Like all weddings, the music drew the listeners, the meat aroma drew the poor, the loud laughs drew the neighbors, but this was far from typical.

By the side of the house, the blind, the poor and the sick were given generous but limited portions of the feast. They each gave their blessing in turn. "May El protect this house." 'May the Baal bring the wind and the rain." "May the Ashrah come quickly to bring fertility to the wedding couple." So, the poor blessed the newlyweds, the rich brought their gifts, and the music played. Three women dancers circled around lit torches which made their brown skin gleam in the light of the fire. An exceptional dancer traveled from the city of Shiloh and her movements were hypnotic. They danced for hours just short of collapsing to the ground motionless. The guests too moved to the music of the harpist and the rhythm of the tambourines.

"One can tell by the amount of money the father spent on this wedding" one woman commented "… that Ofra was untouched." "The bigger the wedding, the more assurance it is, that the bride is a virgin." "With this generation of freedom, I don't know anymore" said another woman in laughter.

"The veil looked beautiful on you Ofra." Gershon's voice was loving. "And Ada, is she here?" whispered Ofra, "she promised to come and help." "No, she did not. Her father is ill, and she could not come." Gershon answered softly.

Although Ofra's father appeared to be delighted for his beloved daughter marrying into the young and premature priesthood, he still had trepidations. *Was this Levite like all other Priests he thought?* His daughter did not marry into the Baal and the Ashrah Canaanites priesthood, which was prevalent in the land. In the eyes of Ofra's father, this man who just married his daughter, genuinely commits his life to Jehovah, God of Moses. But more than anything else, his son in law Gershon devotes and dedicates his life to his God and those portions of engraved stones that dwell in a wooden acacia box. Gershon and the people who believe that Moses came down from mount Sinai and threw the stone tablets from his hands into fragments, also believe that Jehovah, this invisible God himself, came down and assembled those pieces back together which were named the Ten Commandments. The Ten Commandments, the holy of holiest, was carried in this acacia box which came to be known as the Ark of the Covenant. Gershon the Levite, the decedent of Moses, and Aaron the Cohen, along with the other Levites, carried the ark from Beth El to Shiloh and to Kiriat Yarim. Only a small fraction of insightful men and women began to practice the new code of the Ten Commandments, which distinguished Jehovah as the obscure and only God, one God, over all other Gods and Kings. The Commandments meant that all the people are to be judged equally under this code; rich and poor, strong and weak. No one shall be above the new rules of the land.

But not all the tribes accepted the new God of Moses. And justly so! Canaan was a dry land and seriously lacked the resources to sustain the influx of the former slaves. They rightly worshiped the Baal and the Ashrah, the Gods of rain and fertility to maintain their existence.

Ofra's father agreed to give his daughter to this man who worshiped a new God with stringent demands and a new set of rules. The image of this imperceptible God was not engraved into a stone like the statues of the Baal and the Ashrah. It could not be placed in the entrance of their house. He doesn't even know if she will sustain the marriage knowing that this abstract deity is replacing the pluralistic pagan society that has been such a big part of her life. Despite feeling the contradictions and foreseeing the relentless task ahead for her and her husband, Ofra's father was still pleased for his daughter's happiness. And he was especially encouraged by the news he heard just the other day that the tribe of Dan chose to follow the God of Moses deity and needed a Levite. He was reassured that the Priesthood was gaining popularity.

Gershon was unmistakably happy, and it was obvious to everyone that it was all about his sweet Ofra today. And beautiful Ofra was deliriously giddy and excited about the best day of her young life.

Chapter 16
"To the Triangle"

They had a long journey ahead and the Levite had no time to waste. Ofra was hardly able to eat the morning meal and knew she would begin to feel hungry on their journey. She was thinking about how nice it was going to be to enjoy the food Safta prepared for the two of them for the midday stop. Safta hugged Ofra extendedly, missing her already. Her father tried to convince them to stay longer "Gershon, stay at least seven days, as it is customary for a wedding." Although his daughter was married as a concubine, to Ofra's Amorite father, a wedding is a wedding. But Gershon thanked her father, the two men embraced and then he grabbed his daughter tightly and blessed them for a safe journey. "Come back and visit soon" were her father's last words. Although it was still very early this first light of the fourth morning of the week, Gershon and his newlywed rode into the new dawn.

While riding, Gershon was jubilant thinking how happy he would be with Ofra beside him and in his arms. He would sleep peacefully, like he did last night up on the roof. He would inhale her youthful scent once they arrived home. So much joy is awaiting him with her help and vivacity.

She, on the other hand, still possessed the exhilaration from all of the planning prior to the wedding and the excitement she felt throughout her special day. She knew it was every girl's dream. How much love she felt from her father and Safta who were so supportive, and her friends who helped her so much and of course her Gershon who was smiling every time she looked his way, and it was often. She was enthusiastic thinking about their arrival at her new home.

Loaded with gifts, and knowing they had enough time, they stopped at the Goshen center upon Ada's insistence. Two blind elders were sitting in the center of the room on the ground in their usual back-to-back style, serving as the conveyors of communal affairs. They commanded a strong and outstanding capacity to memorize instructions and messages. The people of the community relied on them for many communications. "Yes, Ada was here" responded the blind man to Gershon's question. "And congratulations, long live the newlyweds, good luck." Rocking, the blind men were recalling Ada's message. "Ada regrets that she cannot join you in the triangle. She must attend to her sick father and her young brothers. But she said that in the future she might join you. Those are her exact words."

"One more thing," said the other blind man. "She also asked if the situation permits to send some provisions for the child. If you agree, she will arrange with the senior priest of the Goshen center to give her a small portion from your earnings to buy food and clothing for the boy."

The blind man pulled out a beautiful cloth from a small box. "Here" he said. "She asked to give you this parochet. Ada made this tablecloth. Give it to the Cohen, the high priest. If he likes it, they can use it in the holy tent in Shiloh."

"It's so beautiful" Ofra's surprised voice echoed all over the Goshen center.

She gently folded the exquisite cloth and walking out with Gershon to their donkeys, placed it carefully with her special wedding gifts in the leather pouch that Ezer made for her. They made a hurried exit through the gate to reach the caravan.

They arrived at the intersection outside the walls of Bethlehem, where the caravan was gathered at their usual meeting point. Sheep, goats and cattle were queued aside the salt blocks and grain sacks that were carried and transported by donkey's, mules and camels. This particular caravan was aiming for the port cities of Sidon and Jaffa on the Mediterranean coast via Gezer, the Egyptian fort. Gezer now looked more like a Canaanite town because of the exchange of goods between the Egyptian soldier's and the locals. There was much trading conducted to sustain the soldiers in their fort. Other caravans targeted the southern route heading to the town of Beersheba. The crossroads started to fill up quickly, with travelers from all tribes. This gathering point of Bethlehem was the largest in a young and new vibrant nation. Four hundred years earlier, this Bethlehem crossroad was not far from Jacob's wife Rachel's burial site. She died here while giving birth to Benjamin.

Today, the security riders were from the Benjamin tribe. One can tell by their well-kept bows and arrows, and by their arrogance. Everyone knew that the Benjamin's were the best archers. Members of all the tribes recognized their archery skills and their air of aristocracy. A proficient archer is a life saver against lions and the many thieves and bandits roaming the land.

Noisy bells on the necks of the sheep and the goats were not sufficient to scare away the lions and the wolves but to the shepherd's ear the bells were the way they recognized their flock. Now all can hear the bells everywhere mingled with the braying donkeys bellowing for their food.

The travelers who knew the Levite were glad to see him. They greeted him with "good day," "congratulations to the newlyweds" and wished each other a safe trip. The guards finished collecting the fee for the security riders who protected the caravans against bandits and mountain lions roaming the Judean hills & mountains. As did everyone in the caravan, the Levite and his newlywed paid the guarding fee with honey and grain precisely measured.

Travelers knew how to stay close to each other. When the sign was given, and all at once, the well-orchestrated caravan was on its way. Fewer camels were seen on this route because heading east, the road is mountainous. They rode past the small town of Evos, leaving the town of Bethlehem fading behind them. Ofra trailed behind Gershon sitting sideways on her donkey on the sturdy blanket made by Safta. She also made Ofra a fully covered hooded long brown linen dress decorated with a white border. Gershon was gently pulling her behind him with a hemp rope while softly striking his donkey's lower belly with his leather sandals. The donkeys showed no signs of stubbornness because maneuvering the rocky surface kept them diligently busy. The newlyweds, with the caravan, rode to the end of the long valley. The shadow finally gave way to the rising sun. With a welcoming light breeze they reached the foot of the mountain. This is where the Judah territory ends, and the boundary of the Benjamin territory begins. They continued on.

They finally arrived at the crowded resting area at midday. The Levite nodded each time he was greeted. Ofra raised her covering just enough to shade her eyes from the glare of the sun and was experimenting and learning how to manage a veil. Instantly she started attending to her responsibilities and began demonstrating her newfound capabilities as a wife. Fervently she spread the fresh grape leaves Safta packed and arranged and rearranged them on a cloth on the ground with the bread and olives. She did it with so much care and pride. The Levite stood next to her, amused at the extent of her devotion coordinating this meal. She raised her head and handed him the pouch containing the pomegranate wine. He brought a round flat rock for her and one for himself and then sat next to her.

Voices from a group of men sharing a meal were close enough to be able to hear their conversation. They appeared to be quarrelling about current events. "Let's see what the Levite says."

"Yes, let's see what the Priest's opinion is?"

Gershon turned his head.

He wanted to steer away from any kind of political argument, but he had an obligation to take a stand and express his views. Ofra looked up at him with her big sparkling eyes in anticipation of how Gershon would resolve this disagreement.

Gershon responded "There is a danger in a one-man rule, but, if that is what the people want, let the people have what they want, let them have a king." One of the men says, "There is too much freedom in the land, many people take the law into to their own hands."

"Is it not, blessed be he, what our creator promised his people. From slavery to freedom?" Gershon voiced his belief. "I agree, but I'm worried most about the Benjamins. There is no unity among the tribes. They feel betrayed and sequestered by Judah and the priesthood."

"They forced self-isolation on themselves! They feel they are more qualified to lead the people! Better than Judah! Judah always embraces the priesthood. They feel threatened." Another man spewed. "The people are talking about a king. We just left one in Egypt." another man injected.

"So, that's what I was saying, let a king unite us" replied another and continued. "Each tribe with their families must discover how to live amongst themselves before coming together as one nation." The Levite whispered to himself "Oh yes, kings can divide, and kings can unite, but like the king among the animals he always demands his lion's share."

Ofra packed the leftovers and covered it with clean grape leaves. She folded the wrapped food into a fabric, which she brought from home. The caravan was on its way again. She thought about the controversial conversation she heard and agreed with Gershon's perspective. She enjoyed what she heard from her husband, the Levite and began to sing her favorite song. When she reached the last part "heaven smile to me, I am just a young soul," Gershon began to sing his favored part. "I heard your voice. It goes straight to my heart. Fate smiles on her, making her dreams come true. Day by day, Yareke by Yareke, a shining Shemesh to rise on us two." The words were beautiful, and she was emotionally heartened. She was hoping that a man with music in his heart will be sensitive, adoring, and kind, but she knew this Levite is different. Back at home she met other Levites visiting her father's house who were less strict interpreting the new laws. Her father had his door open to everyone. Ofra often joked with her father when he mentioned about so and so not coming for some time saying, "Well father maybe because you feed them to death." Ofra like to tease her father from time to time. She loved her father, and above all, respected him. Deep inside, she knew he understood and trusted her. She smiled and thought to herself "*Ofra, you are hardly half a day away and already thinking about your father and life at home.*" A conversation between two travelers passing by on their donkey's heading north in the same direction as the Levite and Ofra, interrupted her thoughts like a lightning bolt. One traveler said, "On our way back, we must stay overnight in the city of Evos in order not to run into the night." Their loud words broke her attention. "The Jebusites are not as friendly to the Hebrews as past days, they do not fear our God anymore as in the times of Joshua" said the other.

"On our way back, if we run into the dark, we can stop on the Hill of the Benjamin territory rather than in Evos. I'm sure we will be treated better among our brothers" the traveler said. Nodding their heads farewell to Gershon and his newlywed they sped past.

The Levite lived in the Triangle territory. At the border between the tribes of Benjamin and Ephraim from one side, and the Judeans on the other. This triangle was the hub of the young federation, which consisted of the twelve tribes. It is mostly hills and mountains where the Hebrews settled. The valleys and the flat land started to fill up by the Philistines, the newcomers to the land. They entered the land via the sea up north, from as far as Macedonia and some believed even further. They were known as the sea people. The wedding couple were riding into this hub. From this location the Levite was able to serve three different tribes. He hoped that after serving his brothers, he'd receive a larger take from the harvest. He settled here because of its proximity to Shiloh but mostly for its closeness to the holy tent in Bet El. During the major pilgrimage, the Holy Ark traveled between these settlements.

The early evening breeze cooled the donkeys which allowed them to run faster. Their big ears perked up each time the Levite raised his voice singing, "kings unite and kings divide.' Gershon turned his head continuously checking on his beloved Ofra.

At sunset, another group of travelers exited the caravan. The sign of the Ephraim tribe was painted on white stones lining the road demarcating their boundary. Ofra and Gershon's donkeys increased their speed, recognizing the scent that home is near and feeding time was eminent.

Chapter 17
"Gershon's Home"

They arrived at the Ephraim territory, just short of dark. Ofra stretching her upper body while still on the donkey tried to take a better look at the small stone house, her future home. It was precisely on the slope of the mountain along with two other small houses, one to the left and the other on the right. She measured the close proximity of the three houses, pleased that her neighbors were not too far away. Getting closer, she noticed two wooden poles holding dried animal skins in the front yard. She presumed it was for the Levite's use, for his writings. Near the entrance there were pieces of clay scattered around, she supposed was used for writing as well. A young man on wooden crutches, crippled in his left leg, hobbled toward them. He was tall, olive-skinned, long faced with high cheekbones, the Egyptian type, and medium length black hair. Gershon spoke highly of Boaz during their midday stop, which reminded her that she was already missing her Ezer.

"Welcome back Levite, I'm happy to see you." "Peace be on you, Son of Benjamin." Gershon's voice was calm but tired. "Did you keep an eye on the house?" "Yes, I did" the man said in a proud voice. "Nechushtan bandits might have wounded my leg but don't worry, I can still protect us. My guard is not down."

"I know Boaz. Please meet my new wife Ofra and give us a hand. Help her with her beast." Boaz knew the Levite meant the donkey. The Benjamin looked up at Ofra still on the donkey, examined the Levite's choice in selecting a concubine, and nodded his head as an introduction as well as a silent approval. After she slid off, Boaz walked both donkeys to the back of the house.

"Boaz. I got some new candles in that pouch. Put some light and lock the doors." The young man tried hard to accommodate the Levite because he was grateful for the roof over his head. As crippled as he was, he still managed to perform many duties. He placed the thick piece of wood across the door, latching it closed and securing it for the night. By the time Boaz went to retrieve water to clean Gershon's feet from the big water jar in the corner of this tiny house, Ofra had already located the water, the bowl, and the jug. Remembering how Safta washed her father's feet, Ofra carefully carried the bowl with the small pitcher inside the center of the basin and approached Gershon. She leaned down to wash his feet. She was not experienced in the art of feet washing like Safta back home. She looked at Gershon sitting on the edge of the bed awaiting his approval and he instantly smiled. She poured the water and as she tried to remember, gently started rubbing his feet, imitating the old lady. She made sure not to leave any dirt on Gershon's feet as she knew it attracts flies and bugs and this could disturb one's tranquility at night. However, in no time, Gershon fell asleep in this sitting position.

She looked full circle at this one room house with stairs leading to the roof. She untied her veil and took a deep breath looking at Gershon motionless. His chin was hiding behind his black beard. He looked funny to her in that position. She smiled to herself, lifted his legs, balanced them in a better position and covered him.

"Call me Boaz." He spoke softly. "Here, I got you this covering. Use it with the other bedding over there" pointing to the stone rectangle bed in the far corner of the room. "I put your belongings there. I will be sleeping next to the stairs. Wake me up if you need anything." "Thank you, Boaz."

She arranged her belongings in the back corner of the room. She pulled out a figurine of Anat the healer, Ashrah the fertility Goddess, and even El who was boring to look at. She placed them at the head of her bed. She pulled out an extremely large piece of the pink silk fabric she brought with her to act as a curtain. She tied it around the wood ceiling beam on the right side of her bed and slightly stretched it across to the other side and tied it. That was her private domain for now. She brought water in a jar and poured it into the big clay dish, sat down on the floor and took off her brown dress. With the palm of her hands, she bathed her upper body, neck and face and washed herself in the faint candlelight. She washed her entire body down to her toes. When she completed bathing, she felt refreshed in her magnificent new tunic night dress. A draft entering from a small hole in the middle of the ceiling, that usually collects the rainwater, sent a chill to her body. She stepped out from behind her domain, all clean in her new clothes and combed her hair. She felt good and started to sing as softly as she could, careful not to wake Gershon nor disturb Boaz. "I found love, and love has found me, what a lucky girl I am. I know he loves me; they say he only needs me, but in his eyes, it's only love I see. Mother, you always say, for true love only time will tell. I'm too young, too young to know, but what I feel I love him so." She was admiring the beautiful new garment and the hair adornments her father gave her. Approaching Gershon, she covered him well, with sheep fur as the cool crisp mountain air seeped inside the house. She went behind the fabric curtain. Laying down on her bed, under a warm fur covering, it was still hard to fall asleep. She stared at the night sky through the opening. Her mind was racing in all directions. The wedding, her new home, the journey, the new surroundings, the cold air, the strange noises of the jackals in the distance, and now sleeping or trying to sleep in a new bed. She knew that, until such time when Yareke had completed a full cycle, the Levite would not look for her signal that it was time to come to his bed. She will let him know she is ready, but only after the full Yareke cycle has completed. Only by then, both will know each other. She gazed at the stars while drawing imaginary lines forming a pyramid, she then formed another one and placed it in the opposite direction and created a star with six corners. It reminded her of the way she played squares and pyramids back home, jumping over small marbles.

"My creator" she whispered with her tired mind. "Let me be welcomed among the tribes, the sons of Joseph. I promise to be a good wife. Ashrah, make my body fertile so that I shall bear a child and that we both shall live."

She continued to reflect on the past few days and the future ones too. As she did not like darkness, she was able to fall asleep the moment the candle was extinguished. The timing was perfect.

Chapter 18
"Welcome"

At dawn Boaz was ready to open the door. "Wait a bit longer. Let the warm rays of Shemesh cleanse the night's misdoings." Wolves, foxes, and lions inhabited the highlands, especially on the slopes where the Israelites settled. Bandits and armed gangs would prey on newcomers traveling on the roads and people living in the mountains. Each tribe was responsible to manage their own security. The Levite was a strict man especially when it came to the protection of his home. He made sure to safeguard the animals and his belongings, and to close and lock the door at dusk. He was conscientious to his rigorous interpretation of the laws of the land. On this particular morning Gershon did not rush to open the door as he was preparing himself for the flood of people who were anxiously awaiting his services and advice. He had been gone for two months and word spread quickly last night when neighbors saw the Priest arriving back to the Triangle with the Amorite girl.

As soon as the doors opened, the first group of tribe members showed up to greet the Levite.

"We were waiting your return Levite" an old man was getting down from his donkey with a basket of grapes. "Hope you gave my regards to the High Priest in Bethlehem." "Yes, I did brother." "The vines are ready" continued the old man. "They are ripe and ready for harvest. The men on the third slope are waiting for your inspiration and the inspection. And your blessing of course."

"I know, I know brother, just hold on to your belt son of Joseph" the Levite said calmly. "My daughter is getting married" said another local Ephraimite emerging from behind the house. "The groom is from the tribe of Menashe." He was making a point about the Ephraim and Menashe tribes and their preference to marry among themselves and how they are both sons of Joseph from Osnat, the Egyptian wife. "And if she marries a man from the tribe of Simon, will that not be in line with you brother?" The Levite commented with a smirk. "Not at all, but it is better to marry your own. As my wife says, they know this piece of land better." "A tribe boundary has no meaning brother. Love crosses all boundaries. Love has no boundaries," another man remarked.

"We fought together for the land, but we live apart." interrupted another local man changing the subject.

"Brother, we are united by the Ten Commandments. We must learn how to live apart in peace, before being able to live together."

The Levite nodded his head and agreed to the response of a woman who was collecting wood for her cooking fire.

"And what's your name brother, I have never seen you here before?" Gershon asked the young man who stood there quietly, apart from the others. "Elipaz." He paused. "The shepherd. I live uphill, Levite." "What is your father's name?" Gershon continued.

"I'm the Son of Yoel Ben Ephraim. I never knew my father nor my mother." He took another pause and continued. "I was with my mother only nine months. That's what my grandmother wants me to answer when people ask. Nechushtan the wicked! May El erase his name!" The young man angrily responded in hopes of clarifying the horrible events of his parent's death. Elipaz, having been in his mother's womb for nine months and having no mother or father because of this horrible ruler, was justifiably cynical.

"The Philistines captured and robbed some cows the other day" another man bitterly injected. "Gone are the days when they fear our almighty and respect us. Today they steal our cattle, tomorrow they will demand our blood. Times have changed! Oh, how times have changed." The man lamented.

That morning many more people came to visit the Levite and meet his concubine. Ofra was up and walking in the direction of the small muddy oven in front of the house, carrying a large amount of wood in one hand, and a water jar in the other. Boaz, the cripple, rushed to help her. At this time of the morning, the cattle were out grazing. The scent of the burnt wood and leaves lingered in the air like incense. Morning seized the land and the people in the settlement were up working.

"The young girl is only a day around, and you are working her like an ox" the short thick lady said in a serious voice greeting the Levite. And glancing at Ofra said "Move aside my daughter." She leaned down with feet apart to balance her shorter leg and helped revive the half-moon oven which had not been used since Ada left. "They don't know how to construct ovens these days. Look, you cannot even shelter the fire from the wind. Anyway, spill the water here daughter, and a bit there." Ofra poured the water gently from the clay jar, while the woman's large hands stroked the muddy surface trying to repair the wall of the oven. "Daughter, let the fire burn for a while before you put the dough inside. And remember when you cook the food it's easy to burn a lentil. My house is just a skip away if you need me."

"Thank you, mother," Ofra lowered her eyes feeling a bit shy. "My name is Rachel; I know your name is Ofra. The Ephraim mountains are the tribe's ears." she looked at the Levite. And raising her voice a bit. "Men always prefer a young woman, as if they work harder, or stronger! I was not good enough for him" she chortled, then burst into laughter. Ofra smiled, looked at Rachel with an understanding gesture and they both entered the house.

The stream of visitors continued throughout the day. Ofra felt tired but more relaxed. She really didn't know what to expect the first day in her husband's house and what outcome would prevail. Now, she felt comfortable about everything. She realized from comments she heard that she was Ofra the concubine. To others the Levite's wife. Some called her the Amorite girl, and many referred to her as the girl from Bethlehem. But all she wanted was to be liked and accepted.

Chapter 19
"Consummate"

In this first week, Ofra observed the Levite's daily routine. She was surprised, how at the end of the day when the doors were closed, her Gershon would retire to his corner and start writing on the new leather pieces Boaz prepared. If, of course, Boaz wasn't busy taking care of his majestic mare. He made sure the horse always had fresh water, and continually brushed the sleek dark mane of this beautiful stallion until the last hair was shining like a star. One time she even heard him talking to his horse in a quiet manner. But for now, in her second week, she was adjusting to the new routine, the local people and her different surroundings. *"After all,"* she thought *"I'm a city girl from Bethlehem but now I'm living in the Ephraim mountains and forest."*

It was too early to think about the holiday season when the Levite would leave the house to attend his duties as a caretaker of the Holy Tent. He was a guardian in the house of God in Bet-El and Shiloh depending on the orders he received from the Cohen's.

She used Yareke as her calendar and observed it diligently especially when it got bigger and brighter, and when it was nearing the beginning or the end. It indicated the start of a new monthly cycle. She knew Gershon would not come to her until a full Yareke appeared. She heard stories about wives who wanted to become pregnant who conveniently stretched the truth shortening their monthly cycle and others who lied to their husbands to give and receive pleasure.

Gershon didn't put any demands on Ofra and was content knowing she was adapting and resting behind the curtain in her own domain. He waited patiently for her to reach the correct time of the month, and at her signal they would consummate the marriage. Thanks to Rachel, the room was prepared wonderfully and Ofra was surprised to discover her gentle caring benevolent ways.

Rachel wrapped two stone pillows with a goatskin which she brought from her house and positioned a sheep pelt on the top to give it a softer touch. She did the same thing with the rectangular stone bed preferring to put double goat and sheep fur as bedding. People here in the mountains believed that a stone bed with good cushions, helped a woman become pregnant, sooner than on a wooden bed.

Rachel made sure to put two pomegranates, one whole, and the other split oozing red juice, along with a small clay plate of honey and grapes next to two half-filled wine cups. As a decor, on the far corner of the room, Rachel placed colorful cloths made out of straw and assorted tree leaves on a high stone table.

She addressed Ofra. "Daughter" she said, "Gershon is a Levite, a member of the new priesthood. He is strict in the ways of Moses and modesty."

"Which means?" Ofra turned her head and looked at Rachel skeptically anticipating her response.

"Love him NOT like the Egyptian way." "And how is the Egyptian way?" "Mm, it's the back way." She paused while she searched for the right words. "The dog's way. Insist on looking into his eyes" Rachel whispered to Ofra.

"I'm nervous Rachel" Ofra said while exhaling deeply.

"Because you are a virgin Ofra." said Rachel smiling as she was leaving.

Ofra and Rachel prepared the marital bed. Ofra waited for Gershon while she sat in the middle of the rectangular stone bed with her feet folded. She wore a white linen embroidered dress held by a bright leather cord. When he arrived home, he came straight to her room. His black beard looked longer to her. He reached for the clay cup filled with wine and extended it to her lips. She did the same in return while they looked at each other tenderly. He climbed on the bed right knee first, supported by the palm of his right-hand, fingers flat open on the bed. Gershon's coat of colors held by a leather belt opened and she finally saw his wide musclebound chest. She was staring at the bruises on his right shoulder. "It's the ark lifting" he whispered. She brushed her fingers gently over the marks. His leather sandals fell to the floor. His black curly hair was hanging loosely resting on his wide shoulders. When his beard brushed her leg, she shivered. She felt a strange and new sensation. He climbed closer, being careful not to put his entire weight on her fragile young body. They stared at each other, and as he approached her, she leaned back resting her head on the pillow. He continued to gaze

longingly at her and when she closed her eyes momentarily, she felt his beard brushing her soft supple body. She trembled. As she opened her eyes, his face caressed her small breasts. She leaned back further and the cloth covering the bottom part of her body slid down. He began kissing her entire body. She enjoyed his tenderness. While he inhaled her sweet-smelling skin on her neck, he entered her gently. "Go slow" she murmured.

Chapter 20
"Boaz"

Days quickly passed, memories of home and Bethlehem continued to surface. It had been only five weeks since she arrived at the mountains, and already she missed home, her town, and its daily heartbeat. She remembered the sounds of clicking sandals on the newly fixed cobble stones. She longed for the curved streets leading to the busy market and more than anything else, her eyes begged and desired to see the colorful noisy city in contrast to the stillness of the isolated mountains. She looked at her long fingers. The ones that had playfully stroked the stone walls. The same fingers which caressed the multi-colored fabrics that arrived from Egypt and Damascus, that are now pounding dough, and sorting out bad grapes and peas daily. She looked again, this time at her palms, the lines, and marks where the sugary juice of the pomegranate left its dark stain. She placed her palms over her small bosoms, her fingers pushing deep into the center of her chest, squeezing and releasing the blocked breath stuck inside of her. Heaving, she started to cry. "*I miss my father's house. My Safta. My Abba. My room. My friends. Or maybe, it's just this place.*" She continued to ruminate. "*Or is it me? True, I am relentlessly inquisitive, as my Safta knows too well. I love the shades of kohl and the sweet smell of jasmine. I adore the gifts of colorful scarves from my Abba. I miss walking with my friends and stroking the stone walls. My people here are so different. They are reticent. The women are most concerned about the color of the milk! They're devoted to their vegetable gardens and their flocks. Everything here has the fragrance of pine, sheep and earth."* Her thoughts were interrupted, and she forced a smile when she saw Boaz bringing freshwater to fill the jar. He rushed outside and quickly brought her a branch overflowing with ripe dates. "Somebody from a neighboring tribe, dropped off these dates." he said politely avoiding her watery eyes. "Something to sweeten your heart" he added to lift her apparent melancholic mood.

"You're always shy" She blurted spontaneously. "Or is it only towards me?" She said too quickly.

"I am not shy of you!" he chuckled with confidence. "It's just that …" "… the Levite asked me to look after you."

Boaz words rescued Ofra's nostalgic tears, and she broke out in a loud laugh. "Oh, yessss?" They both shared a conciliatory moment and Boaz with ease of tongue and in his usual arrogant ways engaged in a conversation with Gershon's concubine.

"I am from the tribe of Benjamin" he said in a proud voice.

"I know that by now. One can easily distinguish a Benjamin" she said softly knowing the discussions Abba and his guests spoke about the Benjamins and how overconfident they are.

He rushed outside again and this time he brought in firewood. "I do not like to leave anything outside for the night because come the morning, everything is gone!" Amazed, she looked at him and how he was able to walk on one foot supported by a wooden stick under his arm. Boaz caught Ofra staring at his impairment.

"I am from the town of Parah in the Benjamin territory. Nehoshtan, the wicked murdered my father. My mother tried hard to take care of my brothers and sisters with the help of the tribe's elders. She was a great woman. She always made sure to feed us before herself. She consumed whatever was left if there was anything left. Sometimes at night I would stay up late and watch her mix grinded pieces of Cherub, pomegranate seeds and grapes. And then she added water to the mixture. On the nights when there was no food left over, she drank the mixture which she felt gave her strength. We seldom ate meat." Ofra held back her tears and Boaz continued. "She died shortly after my father passed. My uncles did not rush to take us in, because my father always sided with the Judean tribe in every conflict. My uncles, the Benjamin's, disliked him for that. They took each one of my siblings to live with them. But not before the tribe's elders got involved and made them accountable to do that, as it was the law of the land. My father's words echoed in my ears. *If you become an orphan*, he said to me, *do not build your future with the Benjamin tribe*." Ofra was thoroughly absorbed by the words from Boaz and did not interrupt him at all. He continued "Their hearts hardened by the Egyptians way back in Egypt. Gradually the Benjamins put distance between themselves and the Judeans and the rest of the tribes. I remember my father's last words. He told me … *run to Judean Bethlehem, my son, a big city always provides food and shelter*. And so, I did, but before I got to Bethlehem, I earned some money guarding and feeding the horses and catching runaway bulls in the outskirts where the grazing is good. It was an unsafe place since it is close to the valley in the Philistine territory. It was especially dangerous because the soldiers of the wicked Nachostan who controlled all of that land, climbed up from the valley. And as you probably heard, they did this in order to rob and steal. They demanded money from the owners, stole the horses and cattle and foolish me, I tried to stop five experienced soldiers and paid dearly for that reckless decision. It is one day I will never forget because I lost half my left leg." While staring at his missing limb Ofra was distressed at the horror Boaz encountered.

Boaz continued "Weeks later, in Bethlehem, the Levite saw me at the gate wounded and hungry. He took me in and saved my life."

"Thanks to the almighty, you are now alive, Boaz. Please do not try to take on five soldier's next time." She smiled while she looked intently at him in high esteem. "Boaz, do you regret following your father's advice to leave your Benjamin tribe?" Ofra asked genuinely.

Boaz continued speaking in a deeply somber tone "No! Besides my father's words, which of course I took earnestly, I did not want to make my living by the sword, as a Benjamin soldier, like many of my friends did, and are still doing." A moment of silence filled the room. Ofra could not hold back her tears. Her emotions about missing home as well as the tragic story of the life of Boaz reached their tipping point. Boaz motioned to her knowing it was the right time to get some fresh air and hoping to see Gershon arriving home. They both walked up to the roof and stepped outside. From there they could see if the Levite was returning from the neighboring town as he went to pick up ropes which were needed for his work in the holy tent in Beth El. The Pilgrimage season was about to begin. Before complete darkness descended, Ofra began collecting the laundry that was drying and Boaz gave one last look scanning the road leading into the settlement. Finally, they saw Gershon, fatigued and sweaty, emerging from the side road on foot pulling his donkey behind. Ofra abandoned the clothes, dropping them in the basket, and took off rapidly, while Boaz limped as quickly as possible.

"I took the side road to beat the falling day." He was speaking as Ofra was running to him. "The almighty helped me, and I made it in time." Ofra rushed to him, and he hugged her with his free arm. As Boaz approached, he handed him the donkey and said, "we need to lock the doors Boaz." Now with both arms around her they warmly embraced. Having a rough day herself and with Gershon gone all day and knowing traveling on the roads is dangerous, Ofra was enormously grateful he arrived home safely. Boaz attended to the donkey and once inside locked the doors for the night. When Gershon finally had a chance to sit down, Ofra rushed over to him, and on her knees, washed and rubbed his feet with so much tenderness. It only took a few minutes to help him feel revived after his long day. He discarded his dirty clothes and washed up for the evening meal. Ofra brought the wine, bread, and food she prepared and arranged everything perfectly on the table. They all sat down at the small table.

"More Philistines are coming from the big sea, and now they're pushing deeper into the land." Gershon commented while eating their simple dinner.

"Tell us more Levite, and the tribe of Dan?" asked Boaz. "There are a growing number the Philistines crossing through their territory. The tribe of Dan is no match against those 'iron' people" Gershon continued "I also heard that more families from the tribe of Dan escaped from Egypt and are arriving here looking to join their brothers."

"Ofra the bread is exceptional tonight" Gershon said giving Ofra a reassuring smile while continuing his conversation "But thank the almighty, the tribes of Zebulon and Naphtali are safe on Mount Tabor." The discussion continued throughout dinner.

But having been walking since sunrise and after eating a warm meal, Gershon succumbed to a compelling fatigue and was moving slowly to his bed.

"The people must unite. They must unite" Gershon whispered his last words before falling asleep. Ofra looked at him, his head tilted to the side.

"It looks like the whole burden of the twelve tribes are resting on his shoulders." she thought while crawling next to him. "Does this man have time for me? Does this man have love for me?" She was too depleted from her own emotional exhaustion to answer these overwhelming questions and fell into a deep sleep.

Chapter 21
"Alipaz"

Boaz walked to the rear of the house to check on the animals. "Brother Alipaz, what are you doing here in the middle of the day?" The young man was hunched with knees bent in the corner behind the donkey. "Oh, Brother Boaz, something terrible has happened. Is the Levite here?" Alipaz asked with a trembling voice and bloodshot eyes.

"Yes, tell me, brother what happened?"

"Her brothers are after me, I ran all the way from the hill to find shelter here." "Whose brothers?" "Debora, you know, the girl who always helps Ofra fetch water."

"Ofra!" Boaz shouted. "Bring some water to drink, and my left-over food." "The brothers are after you? Why? Did you force her in the field?" "No brother Boaz! I would never do that. I aimed my stone slinger at the herd to bring back a goat to the fold. Seldom do I miss. But I think I might have hit her on the face. I don't know why she was there among the sheep to begin with. I think she died. And I did not mean to do it brother, it was an accident." Elipaz, the young man was shaking and sweating.

Gershon the Levite, hearing the commotion of the shepherd and Boaz, came dashing out the house. It became clear the situation was dire. People came to the Levite for help, for many situations. This incident could have a most disastrous outcome without immediate intervention. The Levite spoke clearly and quickly. "I heard you, my young brother, there is no time to lose."

"Please believe me, Levite, I didn't mean to harm her, it was not intentional." "Head for the refuge city of Shechem, my brother. Your journey will be long and dangerous."

"Do you own a horse?" asked Boaz "No! You know I'm a poor shepherded." "An orphan" whispered Gershon while looking out, expecting at any moment for the arrival of Debora's father. "Her father and brothers will be here shortly looking for him. We must avoid the spilling of blood, if of course he's speaking the truth. The elders in the refuge city in Shechem will decide. We must get him there before Debora's brothers put their hands on him."

"I will make sure he will make it to Shechem" Boaz stepped forward.

"Are you sure you want to take him? You're risking your life. Debora's brothers, and especially her father will not like you helping a murderer escape" continued Gershon with a worrisome voice as he stepped inside the house.

"Not if the elders are convinced that this young man speaks the truth. And I do believe Alipaz speaks the truth" Boaz said assuredly still in earshot of Gershon.

With these words, he extended his left hand, and helped Alipaz climb the horse. "Wait" yelled Gershon rushing out. "When you get to the city gate in Shechem, with Gods help, give this tablet to the elders." Gershon handed Alipaz a clay tablet.

"Yes Levite. I will." Ofra rushed and handed Boaz his left-over food, some bread and grape wine. They rode in the direction of the designated refuge city of Shechem in the Ephraim tribe territory. It was less than a day's ride on their horse.

An hour later Debora's father and his two sons stormed into the Levite's house rightfully thinking that a man might find temporary safety and advice at a Levite's house before attaining protection in a refuge city.

"Is Alipaz here?" the outraged father demanded.

"Father let us pursue and kill this man Alipaz who killed our sister!" shouted the oldest brother.

"I would not dare do that if I were you" Gershon spoke a bit louder with a convincing tone in his voice. "He is in the hands of Boaz, a courageous Benjamin hero and a strong and abled fighter."

"Then we'll kill them both" said the youngest, furious brother.

"He'll kill you, young son of Ephraim. Boaz and Alipaz are on their way to the refuge city of Shechem where *justice* shall be served. The elders will decide if Alipaz killed Debora intentionally or if it was an accident" the Levite spoke slowly trying to calm an understandably enraged father.

"Ride fast my sons!" And before Gershon could utter another sound, the father shouted "Wait! Don't confront Boaz. The Levite is talking sense. One death in the family is enough. We will all go to the elders and speak our truth." The father and his sons stormed away from the Levite's house.

Boaz and Alipaz descended the hill, riding in a north-west direction to Shechem, the refuge city. After a short silence Boaz said, "Do you know Debora's brothers?"

"I do, brother Boaz, they are very protective of their sister." "They sound like good brothers."

"Did you ever see them riding a horse?" continued Boaz.

"Only once. I saw the youngest brother ride a horse when he came to take a jar of fresh milk."

"How many brothers did you come in contact with?" "As I know, there are three brothers." "We shall stay in Shiloh for the night."

"Why Shiloh brother Boaz?" "They know we are aiming for the town gate to speak with the elders. They will ride through the night, and we will rest through the night. If they don't know we stopped, they cannot find us. They will be waiting for us when we get closer to Shechem, but they won't know when." Boaz paused and continued. "Who nails the target? The tip of the arrow nails the target. And the tip of the arrow is Shechem." "You are a true Benjamin, my brother Boaz" said Alipaz while still shaking.

"Oh no. If I were a true Benjamin, I would be by now in the Benjamin territory among my brothers." Boaz said in a softer voice recognizing that Alipaz doesn't know anything about his history. Changing the subject Boaz says "Now my young brother Alipaz, calm your mind and stop shaking your body like the Baal priests. And stop your heavy breathing on my neck. Tell me, how old are you?" "My uncle said I'm 13 years old, but my other uncle said I'm 15 years old, so I think I'm 14 years old." "That's good enough."

"I think I need to empty my stomach" said the young Alipaz

"Go empty your body behind that pine tree over there. And by the way, what will you use to wipe your butt?"

"I always carry leaves wrapped in a cloth. My uncle insisted, I do that." "Good, you don't have to show me. I believe you. Then go wash your hands very well in that pond over there. I will be watching over you, so hurry up, time is short." "Yes, brother Boaz." Alipaz followed Boaz instructions very well.

In the late afternoon hours, they approached the city of Shiloh. "Don't be afraid young man." said Boaz, still feeling the heavy breath on his neck.

"Why are you helping me, brother Boaz? You're risking your life for me." Alipaz probed.

"Alipaz, if you insist, I will tell you." Boaz paused for a moment, gathered his thoughts, and continued. "Some people like to collect coins. I like to collect deeds. I know how it feels growing up without a father and mother. This is one of those deeds. I'm a deed collector" he said with a smile.

They entered Shiloh, an upcoming city in the Ephraim tribe territory. Shiloh was known for its dancers, singers, and poets. Alipaz pointing in the opposite direction of the painted stones on the ground questioned Boaz. "Brother Boaz isn't Shiloh that way?"

"My young brother Alipaz. We are going to the old section of Shiloh. The signs direct us to the new part where the Hebrews dwell. That is where Debora's brothers could be waiting for you. They could think you might be hiding in the holy tent, under the watchful eyes of the Levite's." "I understand, brother Boaz." "And besides that," continued Boaz "the fine wine of Shiloh and the women and dancing is this way." Boaz pointed to the left with a smile.

"No one is going to look for us there, unless the hearts of Debora's brothers are set on a Shiloh woman. And I don't think so." "I hear you Brother Boaz."

They crossed through the old market, and many looked and marveled at the beautiful horse and the two riders as they stopped at the tavern. A young disabled man approached Boaz and took the reins in his teeth and walked the horse to the back of the inn.

"Peace be on you my crazy friend Boaz, son of Benjamin. Welcome back to El Varuni."

"Peace on you, my dear friend Naim. This is Alipaz." The two friends hugged and kissed cheek to cheek.

"I heard you prefer doing business here in Shiloh, rather than in Gezer, my friend Naim." "My friend Boaz, the Egyptian soldiers don't spend much money over there. Besides, Shiloh's Mountain air is cooler and full of inspiration. And we have the grape wine you like Boazzzz." He said stressing the letter "z" giving a strong indication by his pronunciation that he was not a Hebrew from Egypt but was like everyone else in this tavern. They were Canaanites.

By the time Boaz had a few drinks, the young disabled man bounced into the room. Boaz threw a coin in the air and the young man caught it easily. "That's including the feed, for the horse, brother Mo."

"Thank you, Brother Boazzzz." He also stressed the "z" like his master. Boaz whispered words in Naim's ear, and he signaled to an old lady. Her face powdered and painted and a strong whiff of perfume, she walked the two men through a corridor and into a room. Then two young girls brought a big jar of water.

"We are safe here, my young brother Alipaz. We will satisfy our hunger and tomorrow morning we will be on our way." "I'm very hungry, brother Boaz?" Laughing Boaz says "Yes, we will satisfy all of our hungers."

"All of our hungers?"

"One is for food, and the other for a woman's love."

"I never experienced hunger for a woman, but when I saw the pretty girls walking to draw water something happened and when I would sleep and dream, the next morning my bed was wet when I woke."

Smiling widely Boaz says, "Tonight, you will lose your virginity."

"Well, brother Boaz, I better not start with that."

"I wish it was that easy." Boaz chuckled. "Many men, including me, would have chosen not to start with it. Now look around you, in this humble tavern. There's no telling when a woman will come your way after you enter the refuge city. Hunger of the body my young Alipaz, can drive a man senseless."

For the first time in his young life, Alipaz feels like he's being treated as an equal. "Have you ever tasted wine before Brother."

"Pomegranate wine, yes, once or twice," said Alipaz

"That's good. Put your belongings in that corner and ask Naim the owner, where you can wash yourself. He will show you the way.

Before Alipaz leaves to bathe Boaz speaks. "Tell me, son, close your eyes, count five stars, and tell me if you prefer a black girl, a white girl or a Nubian?"

Alipaz blushed red, turned his face sideways and said the first thing that came to his mind, "It doesn't matter, just a pretty girl."

"Well, tonight you will have a good meal, a good bath and a pretty girl."

Chapter 22
"Hathor"

Boaz was enjoying drinks before he was escorted to his preferred room with his favorite woman.

"You owe me a visit from last time, son of Benjamin" she teased pointing her finger in his face. "I've been wondering why you never came back to pay me a visit. You know I can heal that foot with my magic hands" she spoke seductively. Then talking as if he wasn't in the room, she joked tongue in cheek "It's easier to conquer a land, then conquer this Benjamin man with one foot."

She stood up facing Boaz, spread her legs and held each breast with the palm of her hands and moved them gently forward.

"I don't like what you are wearing around your neck, daughter of Canaan." Boaz said in a drunken voice.

"Oh, you mean this Hathor golden Egyptian triangle necklace. I will take it off, just for you!" Boaz was enchanted by this beautiful Canaanite girl, and in a singsong drunken stupor chants "Oh, that triangle which men desire, a lion's might, cannot devour. A mouth, is it a sea of pearls sparkling in beauty? Or is it a dark cave that rots and lurks in a man's plea for a woman's pity? A pair of rosy breasts each stamped with a ring and a nipple, soft in a baby's lips. Was it all created to tremble men's senses and desires?"

"Oh" she said tauntingly "Is Shiloh`s air sponged in magic tonight inspiring this Benjamin poet?"

She unfastened the colorful chain holding the Hathor plate and threw it around his neck. "You are no longer an Egyptian slave, you handsome Hebrew man! You are now my slave!" she said, while laughing and circling Boaz with a dance. She pulled him down to the floor.

"Come, behind me with your love" she said with her captivating voice.

"Ah, a Canaanite woman with an Egyptian touch" Boaz said in a drunken voice.

Their lovemaking was prolonged as the night slipped away.

This passionate Shiloh girl along with the excessive amount of robust house wine and combined with the permeating coriander and tamarisk perfume finally exhausted Boaz but he still managed to stand up and walk to the adjoining room.

He glanced at Alipaz deep asleep in the far corner of the small room. Naim appeared briefly. Boaz thanked him with a look, nodding his head as a thank you for taking care of young Alipaz. Boaz closed the wooden door behind him and crashed to the floor making sure to block the entryway to the room where Alipaz was sleeping. He was guarding Alipaz and making sure he was well protected. They slept well, but at dawn, Alipaz woke up and when he attempted to leave the room was unable to open the door. Thinking he might have been abandoned, Alipaz started knocking and screaming hysterically.

"Boaz, Boaz." Alipaz shrieked in his high-pitched voice.

Boaz, now sober but his head pounding, was annoyed at the noise. He opened the door and with a stern but reassuring look, calmed Alipaz with his nonverbal gestures.

The girl who brought their bedding last night came with a wrapped breakfast. "Take it with you Boaz, you never have time.

You're always on the run, or a chase." She handed Boaz cheese, honey, and a piece of bread all bundled in a cloth. "I will say a prayer for you, for a safe trip" she said.

As they were departing, Boaz compensated Naim with a small bag of grain which he always carried for trade and payments.

They rode all morning with not a word spoken. Suddenly Alipaz said "What's going to happen to me, when I get to Shechem, Boaz."

"Oh, you found your tongue young man."

Alipaz smiled. Boaz always knew how to diffuse tension with his good humor.

"Now we are equal. You are a man now. Say it out loud Alipaz. Make those mountain lions hear you! Like a lion's roar! In fact, I think, I hear one roaring right now."

Alipaz gripping tightly began worrying that there really was a lion nearby.

"Calm down Alipaz. There's no lion interested in us right now."

Boaz paused for a moment and continued. "Did you roar like a lion last night?"

"I did not roar, but she sure was nice to me." "What language did you converse Alipaz?" "We did not speak." "Well, that's a good sign" he laughed inwardly.

"She bathed me, sponged me, and sprayed scented water with flowers. Thank you, Boaz."

"Welcome to manhood Alipaz. Remember you can level with a man without knowing him the way a man knows a woman." He continued, knowing that Alipaz will be surrounded by experienced men knowing men in the sanctuary city. "The mark of brotherhood is in the spoken words, not in the acts of the body."

Alipaz wasn't experienced with these acts between men or women. After a moment Boaz continued "These words which I just spoke are things a father tells his son. Allow me to play that part. But take this seriously, my young Alipaz."

"Yes, I will."

Boaz was silent for a moment then he continued "You asked me what will happen, when we get there. Well, first they are going to give you a bath and then they will feed you. They are going to ask you many questions. Before you answer, you must connect with your mind, and then, only then, reply. Remember to speak only the truth Alipaz." after a moment Boaz added "Do you know how to do that Alipaz, to speak only the truth?"

"Before my father died, he used to say, Son to tell the truth, you must connect your heart and soul with your mind."

"Do you know how to connect those three, Alipaz?" "Yes.

- My breath is my heart and soul. Above my brow is my mind.
- My heart dwells on the left across from my upper arm.
- My words are true when I connect all three.

Those are the words of my father. My uncle conveyed his words to me. And the Levite taught me how to wrap the small box and leather cords. He says they symbolize our Ark with the words of the Ten Commandments."

"Well, your father was a man of truth and you explained that better than I could. You asked me what will happen when we get to the refuge city. If you tell the elders the truth about what happened when you aimed your sling, they will allow you to stay as a free man in the sanctuary city. You will be protected, and Debora's father and brothers will not dare come after you. It's the law." Boaz stated with assurance. "And then I will have to spend ALL MY LIFE in the refuge city Boaz?" Alipaz spoke in a crying heart wrenching voice.

"All your life? No. When the High Priest dies and goes to heaven he connects with the almighty. Then, the almighty in heaven will extend you the truth. And you will be allowed to leave the refuge city. Debora's father and brothers will have no hold on you. They will not dare to touch you. Remember, it's the law of the land, Alipaz." "What is the name of the High Priest, and how old is he Boaz?"

"Pinhas Ben Eliezer" Boaz replied.

"I heard an old man in our village mentioning that name, which was around… from the time of Joshua. He must be old, right?" "Well, that's your luck Alipaz." Boaz responded in a low voice. "They will explain all of that to you. But don't wish for anyone to die. We don't immortalize anyone." "I see Boaz."

"Remember Alipaz, always be humble before El our creator. And among people, be humble, but be alert and awake. The heart of a shepherd is guided by nature. But not all are shepherds like you. Where you are heading now, there are no goats and no sheep to obey a shepherd's command and there are some men who act like wolves and dogs."

"Oh Boaz, don't be hard on my heart" said Alipaz sadly. "I see you are preparing me for what's to come."

"Do not fatigue your heart. Put your trust in the hands of the God of Moses. We are almost there. Don't be afraid when you see Debora's brothers. They might be waiting for us in the company of the elders, but they will not touch you. Pass me another grape leaf with cheese and bread. Do we still have water, Alipaz.?" "Yes Boaz."

Early evening, they entered the sanctuary city of Shechem.

"Look at the stone markers Alipaz. We arrived to the Ephraim camp. You see those tents on the right, with the big tent in the center?"

"Yes, I do." "Here is the tablet."

"Yes?"

"Now, make a run for it. The moment you enter the tent, say your name, say you are from the Ephraim tribe and hand them the tablet. Then say in a loud and clear voice. I think I killed a girl accidentally."

"They will take care of you. I will be watching. Go and El of Moses be with you."

Alipaz looked at Boaz, with tears in his eyes, and said "Thank you El, for putting Boaz on my path. Boaz, you saved my life and you have been like a father to me in the moments I needed it most. Thank you." Alipaz started running. Boaz waited until young Alipaz entered the tent. He then set his sight for Shechem's Hebrew enclave before the doors close for the night.

Chapter 23
"Rachel"

Ofra rushed to the door when she heard someone calling her name. Rachel, with her usual limp due to anisomelia emerged from the trail behind the hill. She supported her weight on her right foot using her hand to push down on her knee with each step.

"How are you, my daughter? I'm sorry I couldn't make it to see you yesterday. Here, I brought some bread and lentil soup. Please don't refuse me. I used to say to the Levite, *there is nothing to eat in this house.* He would say *don't worry; His name will provide.* So dear daughter, until such time, you and Boaz need to eat."

"Thank you, Rachel, but Boaz is still away in Shechem, the refuge city."

"I don't know how he managed to ride his horse, with his wounded leg. And poor Alipaz, the orphan. Do you think he meant to kill Debora?

Rachel was excessively talkative today.

"I don't think so. That young man can't kill a butterfly" Ofra remarked

"As petit as she was, she carried water jars almost her height." Rachel recalled "Imagine, to spend his life in a refuge city. So sad. Well, time will tell." Rachel put the food aside on the table knowing that Ofra and Boaz would eat well tonight.

"How can I take food from a widow?" Ofra said looking straight at Rachel.

"I am a widow, Ofra, but I am not sick or dead yet. Besides, the sons of Joseph were very generous to the widows and the orphans this harvest. I also brought some salt and greens. It is good for the stomach." Rachel noticing the unkempt floor, took the palm branch and began to sweep the room.

"I know you are not happy Ofra. I remember the look on your face the first day you arrived. And now you look sad."

" I am sorry to admit but I have been spoiled in my father's house. My husband needs a slave, more than he needs a wife. I know that Gershon loves me, but he is not around much to show it." Ofra frowned forlornly. "Now, I understand Ada more than ever" Ofra continued.

"Oh my! You say he loves you but he's not here to show it? What is it about love and the fascination with the Canaanite pleasures." "Do you fault them for their ways?" Ofra questioned.

Rachel stopped her cleaning frenzy, stood up and looked straight at Ofra "... and what do you mean by that Hebrew daughter?" "You know you are like a mother to me Rachel. I would like to open my heart to you, if you let me, of course." Ofra said hoping to engage in a heart-to-heart woman to woman conversation.

"Go ahead, my daughter."

"I will never question our ways. But I am trying to tell you something. It's just that I am shy about it." "Go ahead, Ofra, open up my dear. Women's secrets are endless, and we can have shared secrets. You can trust me."

"Rachel, what I am trying to say is that the other day, when Gershon came to me, it was hurting so much that I had to push him away from me. He was so angry, and you know what he said? That I am causing him to sin because all his seeds were on the floor. And for three days he did not talk to me. Now you tell me, Rachel, how did I make him sin?" Ofra spoke innocently. "He is a Levite, Ofra. He is a man that is strict in the ways of our almighty. Many men imitate the Canaanites ways and do not care if their vigor is wasted rather than procreating a child." Rachel continues trying not to hurt Ofra's feelings about her inexperience in lovemaking and says, "It is possible that our creator made you too narrow but with time my daughter the pain will go away. Calm your breathing and be patient."

"Thank you for your wise and kind words but I'm afraid that it will never be fine."

At that very moment they heard a horse snort and the two women jumped up and were so happy to see Boaz at the door. "Alipaz is in God's hands. Let's hope for the best" Boaz said in a promising voice." He continued talking "I figured the Levite might still be away and I was worried Ofra would be alone. I tried to make it back, as fast as I could."

"God will reciprocate for your good endeavors for Alipaz and the Levite." Rachel said, praising Boaz.

"Good to see you Rachel" he nodded his head.

"I am glad to see you too, Brother Boaz. How are you doing with that leg?" "It is in the hand of the almighty" Boaz replied while pointing his finger and eyes up to heaven. He continued. "Thanks to the almighty, I did not have to use my sword to protect the young Alipaz."

"Alipaz is a young man, Boaz, I see you're still extending your neck for others."

Boaz smiled. "I see you put more layers of leather on your leg to protect it" Rachel continued. "Yes, I did." "Bathe it in myrrh more often Boaz. It helps to kill the poison." "Thank you " he said preoccupied wanting to attend to his horse.

"The animals are fed, and we have enough candles" Ofra said.

"The Levite is lucky to have you doing more on one leg, than some do on two. May the almighty help you Boaz."

"Thank you for those sweet words, Rachel, you make me blush." "You can take it, son of Benjamin." Rachel continued

"I wish I could spend the night here with you Ofra, but I'm afraid they are counting on me back home. Let's hope the Levite will be home soon."

Rachel left late afternoon but not before she brought in the half-burned wood she scooped from the outdoor oven. She was pleased Boaz was back, which meant Ofra would not be alone. Boaz, now on the roof looked down the road in hopes of seeing the Levite. He wished Gershon would show up in the last moments of the day before Shemesh disappeared into the night. But as night fell, he had no choice but to close the door. He felt sad for Ofra knowing she would be alone again. He always felt saddened in those instances when Gershon was away.

It was noontime the next day when Gershon made it back, tired, but content having accomplished his tasks.

"I knew I had to share you with the priesthood Gershon, with the poor and the sick, but I did not think it was going to be to this extent" she said in a nonconciliatory tone. Gershon said nothing.

Chapter 24
"Loneliness"

It has been three months since Ofra, the young newlywed from Bethlehem arrived at the Ephraim mountains, full of optimism and expectations as any married girl would hope for when arriving in a new place.

The last gasp of spring was blooming, decorating every brown piece of earth which stuck out from beneath the rocky soil. The flaming red soft short lived anemone flowers dominated the surface. Yet, looking at all of that beauty from the rooftop only made Ofra melancholier. She missed her friends, her father, her room, the old lady, the games and craved for the table always filled with food and fun. Sweet spring air fever provoked her yearning vigorously inflaming her longing like a drowning person desperate to get their head above water.

Ofra was alone too often because Gershon was obsessively consumed serving his God and attending to his holy duties. She especially hated the nights. She was so desperately lonely. In the short time she was with Gershon she realized just how much time he spent away and was particularly worried she would never see him with the approaching holidays.

Gershon's main responsibility was Guardian of the Tent and the Ark. The Holy Ark made out of acacia wood contained the Ten Commandments engraved in stone. It was circulated among the three holy sites, Shiloh, Kiriat Yarim, and the old historical Bethel, where Jacob, 470 years earlier fell asleep in the presence of the Shekinah, the presence of the divine. It is the same spot where the holy Ark now dwelled. Presently it was less traveled until the approaching harvest and the upcoming celebrations. The Cohens were the high priests who made the decisions where the holy ark is housed. It's currently stationed in its home base in Bet-El in the Benjamin territory where the Shekinah dwells.

Gershon, the Levite was occupied with practicing new techniques in the art of ropes which helped in dismantling and putting together the holy tent. He spent most of his free time writing, delivering bread for the poor, comforting, blessing and bringing remedies for the sick.

Ofra grew to despise the nights when she had to be alone. Rachel was kind enough to visit often, recognizing Ofra was sliding deeper into that narrow path of isolation. Rachel fetched water, baked bread, and made every effort to cheer this young maiden but still was unable to be a comfort to Ofra at night.

"Go easy on your heart, Ofra," she said to her, days later. "How can I? My husband is entangled with his cause, and I am all alone."

"Yes, I understand you, Ofra, but is bitterness serving you better?" "What am I to do then? Go back home, to my father's house?" "Ofra, I will pretend I did not hear that. I know your husband loves you. Anyway, why would you run away from love which you always talk about?" "Maybe he loves me Rachel, but his silence confuses me and blinds me like darkness. Why then, did he need to take me away from my father's house, when he knew that he was going to spend all his time between Shiloh and Bet-EL? Is he expecting me to be dependent for food on the mercy of you and our brethren? And Boaz too? Some of our brothers and sisters don't understand the duties of the priesthood and I don't want their pity or their donations. Believe me, Rachel,

I understand my Gershon, but forgive my lips. I know it is not good for a man to be alone, as people say, but how about a woman? What about us?"

Before heading home Rachel murmurs, "Oh daughter, now I understand why they call this generation, the children of freedom. I have been hearing that remark more and more often lately." She gives Ofra a warm embrace and waves goodbye as she leaves.

Ofra tried very hard to keep herself busy, but persistent memories of home surfaced like recurring doses of glittering stars in the evening sky. Her friend's foolish laughter, playing the stone games, the old lady hanging the laundry on the roof, images of Ezer tending to the donkeys and all the imagery of home flashed in front of her frequently. It was just a matter of time before it was unbearable to sustain the pain and longing for her father's house.

Gershon realized Ofra was not happy as she spent most of her time alone in the house in her secluded area behind the curtain. Gershon came home just before dark. He spent the afternoon preparing the list and finishing the plans for the sacrifices the Efraim tribe would be taking to the holy tent in Beth El. He saw her lying down, her head supported by a scarf covering the small olive figurine box. He noticed her shedding a tear running down her cheek. He sat on the ground next to her bed, facing her.

"As time passes by, you will be more accustomed to living here. I know my task is heavy. I am a servant of the almighty and I know it is not easy. I'm a Priest, a Levite, and I know how much the people need me. Every tear you shed feels like you are ploughing into me and it's breaking my heart." Gershon's words did little to comfort Ofra because she knew their reality was unchangeable. She closed her wetted eyes and escaped into sleep.

Chapter 25
"Reality"

The laughter of the girls fetching water grew stronger, brisker, and inviting. Although Rachel was twice their age, she was still strong enough to carry water for herself, and proud to bring water to the Levite's house. "How is the Levite's wife doing Rachel?" "She will be fine daughters." " I heard that life with the Priesthood is not that easy" one of the girls commented and shrugged her shoulders.

"The other day someone said that when the Levite is away, poor Ofra is left with no food in the house" another girl said with a smirk on her face. "Oh, daughters, your tongues are faster and slicker than the priests babbling at the feet of Ashrah and Baal. Or maybe, do I hear some voices of jealousy?" Rachel said while turning her head staring at each one intentionally. "He's not a provider!" Another girl jumped into the conversation with confidence.

"I'm sure about that" commented the skinny girl who just joined the group.

"I think she is going to leave him the way Ada left him. Girls, you remember Ada?" another girl said louder. "Girls, you make me sick with this kind of talk. Hurry up. Finish filling up your water. Go home and find a man." Rachel's protective tone was convincing as she hobbled away carrying a jar of water on her head and another small one in her left hand.

Ofra occupied most of the time in her bed behind the curtain.

She was homesick. From her rooftop, she spent some of her time gazing southeast in the direction of Bethlehem. Her mind was signaling conflicting messages about what to do. "*Stay strong, Ofra. Don't do anything foolish. Put your trust in the almighty.*" Safta's words kept echoing in her head.

On the first week of summer, Ofra woke up early Monday morning with renewed strength. She put on her favorite red dress with the flowery border. "Gershon" calling him by his name in an artificially sweet way. "Yes Ofra" he looked at her with anticipation, never having heard this tone since her school days.

"Forgive me for not helping you, as I should." "But you are."

"… by sleeping most of the day? I'm sorry, but I cannot be like Rachel." "I do not want you to be like Rachel" he replied. She sat next to him. "Freedom and the celebrations will begin soon." "Yes, I know Ofra." "You will be going to the Holy Tent of our..." he put his fingers on her lips to stop her from saying God's name in vain. "The other day" she continued, "Rachel said, that she heard that the tribe of Benjamin is very annoyed because the Priesthood doesn't side up with having the Holy Tent in the Benjamin territory. And they're also annoyed with Judah because he aligns himself with the Priesthood." "My Ofra is very much informed in the tribe's matters. The Benjamin tribe …" continued Gershon "… disagrees with the Priesthood and with Judah, especially during harvest time and during the holiday season. Their dispute goes back well into the past, in the years in Egypt. But, can we talk more about that another day?" he said gently.

"Gershon, please talk to me now." She raised her head and looked up in a dreaming mode drifting back to those sweet school days. "The way you used to, back in Bethlehem. Now, you come and go so fast, like the graceful Prinia bird which I saw the other day on my windowsill." She turned back her head, and looked at him, with glossy eyes. "Do you remember how you ignited me with your dreams and your inspirational words about anything and everything. What happened to those days?" Gershon lifted his head up with a sigh, and then sweetened it with a smile and sat next to her. "The tribe of Benjamin" he said "want to live by their own rules. They feel that Judah wants to have the last word. The tribe's affairs are the concern of all tribes in the alliance. The Benjamin's feel they are being left out from the decision making, especially when they see Judah and the priesthood agreeing and seeing eye to eye. The Philistines are entering the land from the great waters in the north and the tribe of Dan is not a match for those sea people. It is important that all tribes be united. The question is, who will lead this young nation? Benjamin or Judah?"

"So what side are you my dear husband?" Ofra said calmly Gershon turned his head, astonished at her interest in this matter.

"You look surprised, my dear Gershon." Ofra articulated in a mature manner. "I heard a lot about the Benjamin's and the Judeans from you, from my father and the many guests who would visit our house." "It is a brotherly feud, you might say, a disagreement among brothers in the family." Then Gershon became serious and said with an assertive voice. "I am a Levite. I don't take sides. I look after all the people. I receive my orders from the priesthood."

Ofra pressed on and continued. "What is the difference between the Nanna priesthood, and the priesthood of Jehovah?"

In a proud voice Gershon proclaims "Oh, the priesthood of Nanna goes hand in hand with the king. The Priesthood of Israel speaks to and serves the people." "My father said that the priesthood, the Cohens, go hand in hand with Judah. So, what is the difference Gershon?" "Judah is not a king. That's the difference my Ofra. The people, nor the priesthood, are in a rush to appoint a king. We are free. Brotherhood will continue to keep us united" he proclaimed.

She walked back to her room behind the curtain, sat for a few moments before fleeing upstairs to the roof bursting out in tears. "Oh Abba" she mumbled, "since I came to this land in the forest, I fetched water, baked bread, fed the donkeys, gathered the wood for the fire, and cleaned the clothes including the extra linens the Levite brought from Beth El. But it is not the hard work that distresses me. Forgive me Abba, I am tired, and my heart is heavy. The fear of loneliness grows deep in me. I don't know if I can bear another night alone while Gershon leaves for Bet-El. It is not easy to be married to a man of God, a member of the priesthood as I once thought." She lingered on the roof with her tiring thoughts and fatigued heart.

Chapter 26
"The Departure"

The maturing fig season was coming to an end and Ofra remembered how she marveled at the natural milky beauty of the fig tree in her yard at home not too long ago. Ofra was enervated from the mental and physical fatigue, longing to be back at her father's house. Now she hears the recognizable vibration of the drums and the cymbals growing louder as a sign of happiness. She can tell by the familiar sounds that the grain harvest was good. The widow, the orphan, and the poor kept their allowed ten percent of the harvest, as this slowly had become the law of the new land.

This year Rachel finally added her name to the list for one of the groups formed and would be traveling a two-day pilgrimage to Shiloh. She was especially happy to see her name written on the clay tablet because it was this harvest that the Ark would be brought to Shiloh. and she would be able to fulfill the deed of the offering of thanks to the creator. She was also going to meet her daughter's family coming from Chavat Yair settlement, which was located in the eastern half of the land of the Menasha tribe which was beyond the Jordan Passage. She hoped they all might group together and buy a sheep to sacrifice. Her contribution would be olive oil.

A few weeks later, summer heat filled the air of the Efraim mountains. Donkeys demanded more water, and the lines at the well grew longer. Ofra became increasingly concerned, saddened, and was dreading Gershon's upcoming departure.

"Gershon" she whined the night before his departure. "I know that there is enough food and wood for cooking, but you know I cannot be alone at night. My sleepless eyes are already too tired anticipating the morning light. The other day Boaz killed a snake right in the back of the house. And you know how much I am afraid of snakes. And the Jackals with their howling calls." "Ofra, then come with me to Shiloh, and you can stay in the big tent with the rest of the women." "I wouldn't like to do that. I heard that the people treat the women like the Baal and the Ashrah servant girls. I wouldn't be safe with those men who sneak into the tent. I would feel like a prisoner. I like this house, but only with you in it." "Well then, I will be back in two weeks, and by then, maybe you can think about joining me back to Bet-El for the rest of the big season. Until then, Dina and her family and Boaz will be here. It's a full house. You will not be alone." "Yes, I know Gershon. it is still hard on me. Come summertime, the pilgrimage season, it's family time. I long for my home, my father's house."

"I know Ofra. Please extend patience in your heart. Find strength in his name the almighty. I know the elderly can use some help in the settlement. One day, you will call *this* place home."

"I miss Bethlehem Gershon." "I can understand that Ofra. This is a settlement in the forest which the sons of Joseph inherited. I know this small village is not Bethlehem, but it will do for now." "I desire a permanent house, Gershon, as you promised me." "Yes, I know Ofra. I know I gave my allegiance to his name, and to my masters, the house of Aaron the Cohens, the priesthood. And while I'm in the holy tent walking and guarding the house of the almighty, I know his name will walk with you, and will take care of you."

Trying to believe his words, she went to bed early after the discussion knowing they would need to wake up early for Gershon's departure. She planned to help him load the donkey. It was the Levite's first of three journeys this year. This one to Shilot, then to Bet-El and lastly Kiriat Yarim. The night before the departure was a restless one, mostly because of the anticipation. It was more difficult for Ofra. The thought of being solitary and depending on the neighbors for anything annoyed and humiliated her. However, she was there early in order to help the Levite. Boaz, with his wounded leg got worse with each passing day, yet he insisted on carrying the heavier loads, wincing with each step. The two donkeys were finally loaded. One would be carrying the small sacrifices and the paraphernalia. There was oil, salt, wine, incense, grain, and cages of small pigeons. The sheep and other cattle, which were customary sacrifices, were to be brought by the pilgrims.

The donkey carrying Gershon and his personal items, included ropes, pegs, extra wooden stakes for the tent, food, wine, bread, cheese, and water. Before he left, Ofra ran to the house to bring him extra honey and figs that she had prepared.

They had a proper goodbye with a tender hug and Gershon knew he was leaving Ofra in good hands.

She ran to the rooftop and saw his silhouette starting to disappear down the gravely road. She burst into a cry. "Come back soon" she yelled from the rooftop and saw him waving before he faded away.

At the gathering point, help was waiting to accompany Gershon all the way to the Holy Tent in Shiloh.

Chapter 27
"The Well"

Later in the afternoon on that day, two local guards from the tribe pulled into the yard and knocked on the wooden door. Boaz, not able to move his infected half leg, stretched his head out of the roof's small protective wall. At that very moment, Ofra recognized the guards through the small window, and opened the door. "Did anyone show up here today?" "Not that I know of" Ofra responded with a surprised look on her face. "Well then, be on guard for yet another runaway who might be looking for the Levite for guidance before they make their way to the refuge city of Shechem. Knowing that the Levite is away, the elders asked us to keep an eye on the place."

"Thank you," Ofra's voice was clear and respectful. The Guard continued "Oh, the well down the road has dried up, but the one down the mountain slope near the sycamore tree, that well is still active. You know, where the Canaanite girls fill up their jars." Ofra thanked them again. Boaz managed to make it downstairs, all sweaty and breathing heavily, but the guards had already left. His leg, not completely healed, had actually worsened. Just when he reached the last step, he collapsed. Ofra rushed and helped to get him back on his one good foot. She saw tears in his eyes when she supported him with her arm but felt so helpless, unable to ease his pain. "I am afraid I have no choice but to cut whatever is left from this sick leg" he mumbled while licking the tears dripping from his upper lip. "I am sorry to hear that Boaz, maybe when you get to the almighty house in Bet-El, the healers will cure you." "I don't know if I will make it Ofra but thank you for always caring about me. I'm so ashamed and feeling so powerless." "Don't be! It's not your fault that you tried to stand up to that wicked Nechushtan, and his bunch of thieves. May the almighty erase his name." "Well, the almighty did! But now Ofra, please help me climb back up to the roof, the evening breeze will help cool my burning body." Once Ofra helped Boaz, she rushed back down to open the door for Rachel. Her loud knock echoed throughout the Ephraim Mountains. Ofra was glad Rachel, before leaving for the pilgrimage, arrived as planned. Upon entering Rachel and Ofra exchanged pleasantries and inquiries about the health of Boaz. Rachel placed one of her large bundles on the table and they both quickly rushed to see him on the roof.

"This is the Egyptian stuff I told you about." She pulled out a wrapped cloth, asked Ofra to hold one side while they tautly spread the material. It smelled like garlic mixed with a variety of other medicinal elements. She then bound it tightly around his leg. His painful scream stretched as far as the Judean Mountains. "You are going to feel better!" she said when she finished dressing the wound. She gave him a strong fermented drink she had brought with her. He swallowed a sizable gulp and began to cough. His face turned red, and with a scratchy voice said "Thank you Creator, for sending me these two angels. I don't know what I would do without them."

The two women went downstairs, unpacked the rations Rachel brought, then carried the food back upstairs, and they all ate.

Before Rachel left for home, Ofra explained she was planning to wake up at dawn to have an early start to get to the distant well by the sycamore tree. She described how the Guards came by to warn about a runaway and also mentioned that their well dried up. Rachel did not want Ofra to walk the long distance by herself, so they planned to go together in the morning.

*****

The next morning, on their way to the well, they ran into the settlement Guards who were keeping a close eye on the Levites house knowing that Gershon was away. Rachel and Ofra felt good that the house was being protected.

Everyone had an early start that morning to go to the water well.

The Hebrew girls muttered to each other "The Canaanites girls will be there."

And the Canaanites girls whispered to one another "The Hebrew girls are coming." Some of the Canaanite girls were servants. The string of beads they wore had a strong erotic implication. Despite the existing suspicions between the locals and the newcomers, the girls were able to be respectful and maintained a nice exchange, taking turns filling up their jars under the watchful eyes of the Hebrew guardsman and the Canaanite farmers. This helped keep peace and order. The Canaanite's chose to grow their crops closer to the well for ease of irrigation and to make sure their girls had men watching over them. The Canaanites having been living peacefully in the land for generations strove to coexist with the Hebrews who were new to the land.

Water was sacred. They all needed to survive in some kind of harmony. The girls, realizing the gravity of their situation and trying not to exacerbate the tension, were courteous to each other.

The Hebrew girls did more of the gossiping today. "Look up there at the girl I told you about. That's the Canaanite girl the Hebrew man ran away with" said one of the Hebrew girls while nodding her head in the direction of the beautiful girl who just arrived. "He married her, and I heard they ran away to the town of Gezer. But they're back!'""

Another Hebrew girl joined the chatter "As if there are no beautiful Hebrew girls here?" she added while rolling her eyes. "Look who is coming down now" whispered another Hebrew girl.

"The Egyptian girl. They say that back in Egypt she was priestess to the Golden One." "You mean to Hathor, the mistress of love and beauty?" "Yes!"

"She still wears the hair style like the priestess" another girl said noticing the bouffant tresses with the big curl at the end. "We praise the golden one! We extol the lady of heaven Hathor the golden one!" One of the Hebrew girls said playfully and theatrically, imitating the Egyptian women hailing Hathor passing in a procession.

"The Levite's wife is here! Watch your tongue Hebrew girls. We do not wish to be cursed by Jehovah the God of the Levites" another girl scolded softly.

"You mean the concubine?" replied another girl. She paused and said, "We heard she is the daughter of an Amorite, a wealthy man from Judea Bethlehem." "No" another girl insisted. "The concubine is from the family of Shalmon Ben Nachshon from Judea Bethlehem. That's what my father says."

"And my father told me, she is the daughter of the Amorite. But listen to this. I heard Alipaz, you know, the shepherded that killed Debora, will be set free. But he will need to spend his life in the refuge city until the High Priest dies. Then he can leave."

"How sad, I really liked him" another girl made a comment. "Well then, wait for him." the other girl said teasingly. "I will be old by then" she answered. "Unless the High Priest dies soon."

"They say that he is very old" another girl commented encouragingly. The girls knew she was insinuating that there was hope for Alipaz and for their friend. "That is if you wait of course" she giggled.

Another group arrived from the Hebrew side. "Good morning" Dina's voice greeted them sadly.

"I thought you were in Bet-El by now" Rachel countered quickly. "My father wants more family members to join the trip because he thinks the roads are too dangerous." "With three girls, I would think the same," Rachel responded. "Boaz asked about you?" Ofra said softly while looking at Dina. "How is he doing?" "I think he will be doing much better, if you will be next to him" Rachel said suggestively.

"Well, that is not what my father thinks. I feel bad enough about it without you having to make such a comment." "I'm sorry Dina. It's just that it hurts me to know that Boaz has no one by his side to be with him." "I know Rachel" Dina said with a cry in her voice. "Your eyes sparkle when you see him. It is easy to see," Rachel added. "My father thinks that one cannot live on love and that it will be hard for a crippled man to put food on my table." "Well Dina, if your father had to decide between a good man on one leg, or a bad man on two, he should go for Boaz and his magnificent horse." Rachel and Dina hugged.

"When are you leaving Rachel?" "With the almighty's help, next week. By then the Levite will be back." Rachel said while looking at Ofra, who appeared to be daydreaming and was oblivious to their conversation.

"You know Boaz is going to join the caravan to Bet-El, on his horse of course. You know how much he loves that horse. He told me that one time his horse saved his life. Well anyway, he is going to see the healers. I promise you Dina, I will help him as much as I can. I will bring him back healthy." "Thank you, Rachel. You are a good friend" said Dina beaming with gratitude.

Ofra and Rachel waited until Dina completed filling her long-neck clay jar. Israeli farmers used this type of jar while the Canaanite girls were filling their short clay jars.

The three girls left together and walked back home. Dina went to her father's house and Rachel went with Ofra to the Levite's house to spend the night.

Chapter 28
"Lonesomeness"

A week passed since the Levite left on the pilgrimage to Shiloh. Dina too, finally, also left. Rachel spent her days going back and forth between her house and the Levite's house making sure Ofra and Boaz were sustaining themselves, but everything was not going well. Ofra was spending way too much time thinking about home and how wonderful it would be to spend those sweet days of summer with her family and friends. She wanted to go to Bethlehem and did not want to stay here in the mountains. Her disposition continued sliding downward, longing for her father's house. She had a heaviness in her heart, the kind that makes it difficult to breathe. Festering inside, Gershon's departure made her emotions even stronger. As her mood declined, she spoke less and less to Rachel and Boaz. But she made sure to help Boaz whenever he interrupted her thoughts. He would call her name from the rooftop especially when he heard her sobbing these words:

"Night is falling, night is fading, a glimpse of hope, is he coming. A chance he may or may not. Another night of yes or not. Another Yareke had passed, and I keep on falling. To hope, I cling with all my might, but it looks like I lost the fight. Loneliness is here, I'm young, too young to bear. Must I go or must I stay, oh, loneliness, please go away."

Ofra became increasingly distressed. She cried constantly. She spent her time lamenting and couldn't sleep. She was lonely and hungry. The little food Rachel brought disappeared rapidly, except for a few sweet, ripened dates, carobs and two pieces of bread. She walked up the stairs.

"Is that you Ofra?" Boaz called. "Yes" she answered in a weak crying voice.

He jumped up, off the wooden bed, while approaching her, supporting himself with a wooden tree branch as a crutch. "I'm sorry Boaz, I'm afraid to be alone, please share these sweets with me." She sat down on the corner of the bed and opened the cloth holding the dates and the carob, but when she saw his leg discharging yellow and oozing with a horrible infection she yelled "Safta in heaven! Mother in heaven! BOAZ! You must now go to see the healers. You cannot wait any longer."

Changing the direction of her thoughts, and sitting down next to her, Boaz says "Ofra, yes, I know. I will go. Ofra, are you ok? I hear you down there. I'm worried about you."

"I left my father's table of milk and honey, just to be with a man who lives on dates and bread, and he is not even here with me to share it."

Exhausted and depleted, she mumbled a few more words while resting her head on Boaz "how funny love is" and she collapsed into a sleep.

Chapter 29
"Dina"

E arly morning, Boaz hobbled quietly down the stairs on one leg. His badly infected limb was tied to a wooden stick using extra pieces of fabric and held together with a leather belt. Ofra appeared at the door of the backyard of the house where Boaz was preparing his horse. "Boaz, where are you going?" "You were right. I must go to the healers at once if I want to see the light of a new day. Gershon will be back in a day or two and Dina is back, and we heard she got married to a man from the Benjamin tribe. So don't worry, Rachel and Dina will take care of you."

"Why did you wait and suffer? Was it because of me? Was it because you wanted to make sure I was fine before you decided to leave for the healers?" He didn't answer, his painful look said it all. While slowly exiting the yard on his horse he turned to Ofra and said, "Tell Dina I hope she has a happy marriage."

"I know you love her Boaz." He took off before she was able to bring him any food for the journey, and anyway there was little food in the house.

Coming down the road, Rachel saw Boaz in the distance traveling down the hill. She was spitting words, "How can he get to Bet-El with his leg like that? Please Jehovah watch over him, he is a good man."

"Ofra. What is happening?" she said as soon as she entered the house. "I could not stop him from leaving, he was in so much pain." "He can hardly ride that horse, with his leg hanging like a palm branch. And on top of it, I'm worried because you are all by yourself."

"Thank you, Rachel, for caring so much. Is that true that Dina got married?" "Yes, she did, but they're back now."

"What tribe is he from?" "They're Benjamins!" "Funny, her father never liked the Benjamin's and he's a Benjamin!" "Will they be moving to the Benjamin territory?" "You can ask her. I am sure she will be here soon. Come Ofra, you look tired, I have sweet figs, they will give you strength. Your face looks swollen. Aren't you sleeping these days?"

"I am so tired Rachel. I am not sleeping. I know much you care about me and the work of the Levite."

"Let's just hope that your husband will be back soon, just as planned because I must be on my way to Bet-El soon. You know, my young daughter Hanah is giving birth with his help, our creator. You can come and stay with me until the Levite comes home." Ofra nodded at the invitation.

They walked the mile downhill to Rachel's house. Before long Rachel saw something unusual when two horses appeared in her front yard. It was her son-in-law and his friend from Chavat Yair.

"Mother, Hanah needs you. Somethings wrong. She's having pains too early. She's so worried. You must come now."

"Do not say it my son, don't evoke the evil eye." "Jonathan!" Rachel called the old man who stays in her house. "Go to Dina s father's house and tell him that the Levite's wife is by herself and please, let the elders and the guards be alerted." Ofra, distracted from her own dismay, watched Jonathan rush out. She placed her hand on Rachel's shoulders affectionately with sympathy and understanding.

Rachel quickly packed her belongings and before too long, they all departed, and dropped Ofra at her house.

Knowing that Dina's family members would be coming soon, Ofra decided to sweep the floor and tidy the house.

Dina's father arrived at the Levite's house. Having been blessed with three daughters, he knew how to resolve problems as over the years he had his cup filled with emergencies. He was a Benjamin who chose to live in the Ephraim mountains and although he hoped his daughters would marry a good man from the triangle, Dina was betrothed to a Benjamin.

The newlyweds, Dina's father, Dina's sister and her husband all relocated to Levite's small house awaiting Gershon's return. Dina's brothers stayed behind.

This Benjamin family had a lot of respect for the new priesthood, and an appreciation for the Levite's work in the community. They were happy to keep Ofra company, so she didn't have to be alone in the house. There was never a dull moment in the settlement. Ofra didn't know how she stepped into the middle of this commotion. With all the people in her house, she still felt very lonely. The noisier the house became, the lonelier she felt. As the longing for home intensified, the heavier the burden became. That night Dina opened her heart to Ofra and told her that if it was up to her, she would have married Boaz. Ofra felt sorry for Dina for the choice that was made for her and sorry for Boaz who had no choice. Ofra escaped early into the night tranquility but could not find peace. The jackal's hollering in the mountain sounded closer than usual and kept her awake all night. Her thoughts were racing in all directions.

Chapter 30
"Run-Away"

At dawn on the fifth day of the week, Ofra left her bed and walked to the roof. It was Thursday, the designated market day, occurring close to Shabbat, the holy day, the day of rest. Significant numbers of people started to observe this day. Its biological importance to the human body and spirit gained its sacred acceptance in the logical magnitude of the seeds of the Ten Commandments. The Cohen's who gathered the fragments of the tablets Moses shattered were now resting in the acacia box in the holy tent guarded by Gershon and a group of his fellow Levites. The young couples in Ofra's house left earlier than usual heading to the souk before dawn. From the rooftop Ofra could see the trail of a few scattered people heading towards the market to set up shop. She decided this was going to be her last sleepless night in the house and went downstairs with unrelenting determination. She carefully arranged her figurines and some small perfume clay vessels and rolled them into her wedding dress. She placed her precious gold bracelet and some coins into the small olive jewelry box making sure to leave a few coins in her pocket. She gathered her tunics and then placed everything into the center of her largest scarf. She tied up the scarf from the four corners and knotted and bundled it together. She went to the back of the house to make sure there was enough feed left for the donkey which Dina and her husband were now using to carry their vegetables to sell at the market. Ofra veiled her face thoroughly and slung her belongings over her right shoulder and secured the house as best as she could. She hurried her steps with conviction so to be able to join the small Thursday morning caravan heading for Bethlehem Judea.

Dina riding on Ofra's donkey heading back to get a fresh load of vegetables to sell at the market noticed a young girl who resembled Ofra. "Ofra, Ofra," Dina calling her twice, was sure it was her friend, but Ofra s face was fully covered, and the girl was walking quickly with her head down. Dina did not get an answer. She thought maybe it was not her after all. And at that very moment Ofra, not wanting to be talked out of her plan, disregarded looking in Dina's direction and continued walking towards the exit of the settlement. When she passed Rachel's house beyond the high stony wall, Ofra gasped and caught her breath thinking that Rachel would not approve of this daring departure. When she arrived at the caravan gathering point there were a small group of riders with their horses rubbing their hands together trying to ease the morning chill. A young man stepped forward and inquired about her destination.

"We can go as far as Bet-El, from there you can switch and take another caravan to Bethlehem," said the young man. She took out a few coins from her pocket and as she was getting ready to pay, another rider arrived on his horse. and said, "Is that Ofra, the Levite's wife?" She recognized him. He was the guardsman who policed the settlement and always kept an eye on the Levite's house. "She is heading as far as Bethlehem, but we can only go as far as Bet-El" the young rider shouted. "Well, it will be my honor to escort you to Bethlehem. That is exactly where I'm heading right now. My mother is ill, and I need to hurry and bring her some provisions."

Ofra immediately handed the guardsman the coins. His face lit up and he looked up to heaven and spoke, "Thank you El, you always provide." "My father needs me, and he is all alone in the house. I heard that the old lady who takes care of the house and my father is ill ..." Ofra's fibbing was gaining momentum the more she started speaking and thankfully the guardsman and the young man were involved in exchanging something and not paying attention to her excited nonsense. He handed the guardsman a cloth saddle with a divider which they use for women riders. "Use it for the young lady, just make sure to return it when you're back. By the way, thank you for helping us with that runaway bull the other day." "I'm glad everything turned out fine with that animal. I will make sure to return the divider and return it back to you, brother, Thank you." "Did you ride on a horse before?" The guardsman was addressing Ofra while helping her climb up.

"One time only, but I ride my donkey a lot" Ofra grinned. "That helps" he remarked. There were thieves and threats from animals so very seldom would you see a rider solo in the Ephraim mountains or on mount Gerizim next door. They waited until other passengers arrived and then departed. By the time the word was out about the Concubine's departure, they were already making headway in their long ride to Judea Bethlehem. She traveled with a strong conviction about her decision to go back home. She assured herself about her determination to pack and leave and felt justified with her actions. They stopped at the rest area after the long morning ride. The donkeys and horses were all huddled under a fig tree sharing the shade from the Shemesh sun. They were constantly shuddering flies from their skin. Ofra looked around and even with her face covered, she was still recognized. "Isn't that Ofra, the Levite's wife, riding alone in these dangerous mountains?"

"The Concubine on the Hill" observed another man. She ignored the cynical comment and turned her head away. "Come my daughter don't listen to these men." A well-dressed woman accompanied by a slave said to Ofra in a comforting voice, "Men always have something to say when judging a beautiful young woman." She then turned to her slave and said, "Help feed and water their horse."

"Come daughter, have some wine and bread with me, unless you are with child? In which case, the wine is not good for you." The woman shared bread with Ofra, but Ofra was unable to eat because she was so preoccupied with thoughts of her father's reaction to her arrival.

"Thank you so much" Ofra's voice was full of sincerity.

Her mind was flying, *"What should I say to my father? I hope he will understand."* In the early evening hours, the first houses of Bethlehem appeared on the horizon and her heart started racing. A nervous excitement overcame her.

They entered the main street. It was quiet with a few children playing near her father's house. The guardsmen helped her descend from the horse and gave her the satchel with her belongings. She hesitated for a moment her heart physically visible beating out of her chest. With her head sinking lower, and her steps dragging, she made it to the door. Her father, hearing a noise outside and thinking someone was approaching by horse, opened the door and was shocked to see his Ofra.

Her first words were "Oh Abba, forgive me. My pain overcomes my mind."

She collapsed to the floor.

Chapter 31
"Home"

On the third day, emotionally exhausted and physically sluggish, Ofra finally found the strength to come back to herself. No questions had been asked yet. Not by her father, nor by her friends nor any family members. Her father motioning with his chin was directing Safta to go to Ofra. He knew the two women could have a more successful conversation without his interference.

Ofra's weight loss and fatigue were noticeable. The old lady, made sure to encourage her to step out of her trance, but it was only on that day that Ofra finally emerged from her oblivion. Ofra fell into Safta's arms, and her warm embrace felt so loving and familiar. They walked outside to the yard and the desperately needed fresh air.

"I'm sorry for letting you and my Abba down. Yes, I know your words were always in my mind, but I failed everyone."

"Daughter, I am sure you tried hard, but you know what? Come Ofra, sit down right here."

Ofra sat down on the trunk of the olive tree. "Listen Ofra, daughter of freedom, listen to me, this daughter of slaves, look at these hands" the old lady showing her palms. "From the time of Joshua, these hands baked bread, fetched water, washed clothes, and soothed wounds of our children dying for this land." She continued "So tell me Ofra, what happened to you? Did he work you so hard like a daughter of a slave?"

"Nothing happened Safta! I missed you. I missed father, and I missed home. And I missed my room, and I missed my friends."

"Your father is getting old, your brothers and sisters are all gone to their families, one day you will not have a home to come back to."

"Oh mother, you are too hard on me. That is too painful to think about."

"So Ofra, please, tell me what happened?"

"I don't want to be left alone at home, Mother."

"I understand Ofra. But daughter, sometimes it is not always how you expect things to be. It is how you make the best of the situation. Extend your patience and take things lightly."

"I don't want to live on donations. When he leaves for Shiloh and Bet El he doesn't leave enough food. Rachel and the neighbors must bring me food."

"You wanted to marry Gershon. You married a Priest. You married a Levite. You say you live by the donations of others? Accept your husband's mission and make the best of it."

"Oh mother, you are too hard on me."

The old lady paused for a moment. "I hear you, my daughter. Now look in my eyes and tell me. Do you accept your husband's mission?"

"I love Gershon … if only he would find the time to be more at home, and not let me battle the nights alone."

"Do you accept your husband's mission?"

"I don't know mother." Ofra took a very deep breath.

"Ofra, you know the law. He has the right to come and reclaim you. You will have enough time to rest and reflect. I think that your husband will show up after the counting of the Omer, when the harvest is concluded."

The old lady lowered her look at Ofra's belly. "I'm not with child Safta!" "I'm not saying you are!" "I never agreed to go with Gershon when he attended to his duties, so I never spent time in the woman's tent. I was never forced upon." "Well then, here, chew on this carob fruit for some strength." "Thank you, Safta."

"The almighty will be with you Ofra. Your father always warned me about your stubborn ways." she said lightheartedly. "Safta, you look tired. Let me help you more, in the house." Ofra voiced her sincere intentions to be more helpful. She was feeling guilty for resting so much in the last three days. "Maybe I'm just getting too old" She smiled. "That's nice that you want to help me. You can start by ..." Ofra completed the sentence before Safta could finish "I know! I can start by making lentil soup for dinner!"

"But remember" the old lady started to say and again Ofra interrupted "I know, it's easy to burn a lentil!" They both laughed.

Ofra was home most of the time helping the old lady. She learned the art of sewing, and sometimes fetched water instead of paying for the neighborhood services. As the days passed, she managed to find things to do around the house and learned how to bake unleavened bread. This became the symbol of remembrance celebrating thirty years of freedom in the new land.

There was a sense of satisfaction in the land, even the tribes of the sons of Joseph, Menasha, and Ephraim, who settled in the harshest of terrains, realized it was possible to cultivate farming even in the rockiest of mountains.

Safta kept Ofra's father informed about everything that was transpiring with his daughter and knowing how fragile she was, he tried not to stir up any additional tensions. Naturally he was very concerned about his daughter's health and happiness. He was aware that her husband was devoted to God and helping people, and knew it isn't easy to marry a Levite who must wait for the third year to claim his take for the harvest. This had become a new regulation for the Priesthood as the scope of their duties had increased in popularity with the rapid growth of this young tribal nation. On the other hand, he also knew about the dissent with the tribes and the enemies of the Priesthood, specifically with the Benjamins who were not satisfied with the way the Priesthood was managing affairs.

There was a conflict about where to place the ark and the Benjamins and the people in their 24 villages were angry. In the blessing from Moses to the Benjamins it was said that the ark shall reside in Bet-El in the Benjamin territory where the Shekhina dwells. Ofra's father knew the difficulties his daughter, by virtue of her marriage to the Levite and the Priesthood, was experiencing. He wanted only the best for his daughter and was grateful she was safe and pleased to see her back to her natural state of wellness and equanimity.

Chapter 32
"Heartbreak"

While still in Bet-El, Gershon felt heartbroken with the news of his beloved Ofra going back to her father's house. His disparaging feelings compelled him to channel his momentum into his work in the Holly Tent. He tried to chase away his feelings of guilt mingled with feeling deserted but could not. Missing Ofra was unbearable.

The Pilgrimage ended, unity triumphed and Gershon's duties finally came to an end in Shiloh. He was back home. When he stepped into his domain, the emptiness and loneliness hit him like a stone wall from his chest to his groin. It ached like mysterious fingers ripping into his heart. He realized he loved her more than he was willing to admit. He felt her presence, she was in every part of the house, her perfume penetrated the stony walls. In the back room where she created her privacy, he was unable to go beyond the silky curtain. He was hoping she left the silky curtain intact intentionally and while he was engulfed with a flash of hope he was thinking that perhaps she was planning to come back. His pain was too hard of a burden to carry so he started to vent. It was the best way he knew how to ease his pain.

"I wish you were here, to lighten up my heart. I wish you were here, to brighten up my night. Why did you have to leave? You left me here to dream alone. Like a blind man in the dark which has seen a glimpse of light before. You left me longing, anticipating, and waiting."

He felt like a stranger in his own home. The next morning Rachel showed up earlier than usual realizing the shock Gershon must be experiencing without Boaz and Ofra in the house. His devastated and annoyed look said it all. "Don't tell me you're blaming her because she packed and left?" Rachel said while flitting around straightening and arranging the place. "I thought she was fine. I asked her to join me at Bet-El. I told her she could stay with the other women in the big tent." he mumbled. "She was not fine! And I'm not sure she would have stayed, even if I was still here."

"I think you're right Rachel. I heard about your daughter." He lifted his head "Congratulations on your grandson's birth. I'm glad everything turned out ok. We all prayed for a healthy outcome. It was all in God's hands." "Thank the almighty, I got there on time." Rachel, still cleaning, had mixed emotions about her quick departure and having to leave Ofra at this fragile time. She hoped Gershon would not harbor any resentment. "Look at this mess. They didn't even have the courtesy to clean the house. It was Dina's father, Dina and her husband and the rest of them. I made sure they knew how to watch over Ofra. Even the guards were told." "I hear you sister. Thank you for being there for Ofra."

Chapter 33
"Tell Her ..."

One hundred and thirteen days passed without his Ofra. According to their customs, the separated couple would need to wait accordingly as a reconciliation period. If no other man claimed her and she was not pregnant, Gershon could finally reunite with her. He hoped that she would be happy to see him, would be interested in speaking with him and would ultimately agree to go back to the hill with him.

By this time, Boaz was back. The healers cleared the infection, and he was stronger than ever. He was an enormous help for Gershon, tending to all of the house chores but could never find the precise words to comfort Gershon's longing for Ofra. He was inconsolable.

Gershon came to the realization that he can no longer live without his Ofra, not even for one more day. Sitting on the wooden bed, he supported his chin with the palm of one hand. Deep in thought he was contemplating how he could persuade her to come back home. He promised himself that if she was willing to return, he would take charge as a husband and would ameliorate their lives, especially now that his earnings from the three tribes were starting to materialize.

A knock on the door interfered with his lamenting and yearning. It was Rachel carrying her usual basket.

"Well, time has passed so quickly, Gershon."

"Not for me. My work for the almighty is not as gratifying as before. It's tiresome. I'm too distracted. Time is like a slowly moving ox plowing rocky soil." Gershon said sorrowfully.

"Love will do that to you. Maybe after all, youth can teach us a thing or two about matters of the heart. Admit it Gershon, you miss your Ofra, and you find it hard to live without her."

He avoided her look and then he said, "How do I get her back, Rachel?"

"Go to her! Tell her everything will be different from now on. Tell her she will never have to go to bed hungry. Hire a helper. Tell her from now on, she will be treated as an adoring wife. When she attends to the cooking, the helper will collect the wood for the fire. He will feed the donkey and fetch the water. First, load your donkey with supplies. She must feel that her father is not the only one that can master the art of how to host. Try to be home more often, Gershon. She is too young to spend time alone."

"Rachel, you are talking to me like a young boy."

"Maybe I do. In the face of love, your foolishness encumbers your age." she continued. "I left some bread and cheese. It turned out tastier now. Go get your wife Gershon. She is a good young woman; I miss her here."

Rachel was heading to the door to continue her day when Gershon spoke "Rachel I'm sorry, I forgot to give you this small olive bag. I intended to give you this from my last trip." Gershon handed Rachel a small leather bag full of olives. "Thank you Gershon" she continued to leave then turned back and added "Go get your wife back and if you truly love her …" Rachel hesitated "… tell her."

After Rachel left, he realized how wonderful this woman is. Full of grace and wisdom, and always there when he needs her.

Early the next morning, on his way out, Gershon made a stop at the home of a neighboring family in the settlement. He knew they had taken in a boy from Moab to help ease the burden of the boy's struggling mother. He knocked on the door.

A young voice from the roof yelled "It's Gershon the Levite!"

"Good morning!" Gershon addressed the lady of the house. "Good morning to you, servant of the Almighty." "Do you still have the boy? The one from the Moabian mother?" "Yes. He is a good boy and great helper," said the wife.

"Can you spare the boy?" asked Gershon.

She looked at her husband with a reassuring look. The husband gives an enthusiastic approving nod. The boy looked healthy, around twelve years old, with sparkling eyes, which insinuated he possessed a sense of alertness and good health. The family was grateful to have one less mouth to feed. "Thank you, Levite for taking our "sacrifices of thanks" to the Holy tent. We heard that this year's celebration was a big success. We just could not go this year, but with the almighty's help, hopefully next year!" The husband was heartfelt. "Yes, with the almighty's help next year" repeated Gershon. "Hurry up, boy, collect your things." said the husband.

His wife whispered in his ear "… do you think the Levite is leaving to get his Ofra back?"

Once they were out of the house, Gershon says "We have a caravan to catch up with, the day is pressing on."

After a moment of silence, the boy asked, "Where are we going?"

"Judea Bethlehem, son."

Chapter 34
"Bethlehem"

Gershon and the boy caught up quickly with the departed caravan heading to Bethlehem. Neither donkey had provisions loaded because the Levite decided to shop in Bethlehem. He planned to get a fresh load of goods to show Ofra that he was changing his ways and thinking about her needs. He hoped she would see how much he was trying and how much he was willing to do, to make her happy. And of course, he was most concerned whether she would agree to go back with him. Gershon knew that he had the legal right to claim her even against her will if he chose to do so. This thought crossed his mind should she refuse to go, but he quickly abandoned the idea because he wanted to reignite her love. Gershon and his new helper entered Bethlehem in the evening when the merchants were beginning to close their shops. It was customary that Levites were invited to be a guest as it was deeply believed to be a blessing to the house. "Gershon, Levite" one of the merchants called "Where are you heading?" "The Goshen Center" said Gershon.

"Please, be my guest in our newly built house, it will be a great honor to host a Levite."

"No, let him stay with me. My daughter is ill. His presence and advice will serve as healing. Although our home isn't quite finished, we will make space" said another merchant, with determination.

"Ok. Let the Levite go with you. Prayers for your daughter" the man easily consented.

Gershon and the boy followed the man to his house. It was in the last stages of completion. It was almost dark and a few workers from the neighboring city of Evos chiseled stones in his yard before they headed home. "With the almighty's help, I hope to celebrate the blessing of this house soon. It's getting hard to find good stone workers among our people to do this job," said the host. "It takes a while to learn a skill, especially for this young generation in our new land. Or maybe ..." continued Gershon "... they don't want to continue to do the stonework their parents slaved in Egypt."

"Yes, it's going to take some time to heal. Time will tell" agreed the host.

The Levite's feet were soaked in water as the man made sure to be a traditional host and follow the rituals. The donkeys were fed, and they all sat down for dinner. After the meal, the Levite recited a blessing for fast healing for the young girl. Gershon looked at her eyes and tongue and then suggested boiling an herb in the water.

Gershon advised the owner to follow the new rules for the upcoming dedication so the house will be blessed. "Salt the meat with Jericho salt, let the meat aroma get stronger on the fire and if the sacrifice is a calf, it must be at least two years old."

"Why Jericho salt?" the host asked curiously. "Oh," said the Levite, "they wash the salt better, they have sufficient water."

As soon as the sun rose, the host insisted that the Levite and the boy accept a bagful of dried green peas and figs before departing. Word was circling around town about the Levite and that he was possibly reuniting with his beloved young concubine. His host was aware of the chatter but chose not to engage in any such conversation as they made their way to the square. They all headed for the main street.

Gershon and the boy went into the market and stocked up on provisions. Wine, cheese, salt, honey, anything he could put his hands on. He saved enough money and maybe subconsciously knew this day would come. He knew the figs he bought from the Jebusite lady were the ones Ofra especially liked the most. She gave him extra figs and asked him to say a prayer for her ill son even though she was a Canaanite. She heard about his God's greatness, and the miracles with the great Moses and Joshua. Some people in the market wanted to give him donations but he insisted on paying for every item. He preferred not to accept gifts for the young Priesthood during this binge shopping. Bethlehem was always good to him. He liked the hospitality of the Judeans and their close brothers of the tribe of Simon. Gershon heard the talk in the street about this newly emerging Judean figure by the name of Ben Kanaz who continued to stand up against the wicked "Nehoshtan" for eight years. Gershon liked what he heard.

Gershon was pleased with his decision to hire the boy. He was smart, attentive and could be helpful to Ofra. The closer they got to her house, the more unbearable it became. Gershon was formulating his persuading words, which he was anticipating using the moment they were alone face to face but all the words he was preparing in his mind sounded useless. At the end, he realized a simple I love you or come back to me, would do. Be direct and sincere, he kept telling himself. Submit to love Gershon. There comes a time when love is bigger than any man. Admit it! Look her in the eyes, and say to your Ofra, the concubine, I love you, I cannot go through another day without you. His mind was racing, and he was arguing with himself. Don't even think about dragging her out of the house against her will, like other men. He remembered telling Ofra that freedom roams in the heart and the mind like the rainbow with many colors' roams in the sky. Well, Gershon he thought to himself, let your beloved Ofra's free will guide her heart. That's what love is all about. He surrendered and knew time is changing and yet he was so preoccupied with his thoughts that it actually seemed like time was standing still.

Chapter 35
"Parting Paganism"

In the morning hours, Gershon realized they greeted into the neighborhood by the sweet smell of burning wood and freshly baked bread. The children ran towards Gershon and the boy because they recognized the Levite and knew he would be bringing candies.

Gershon was unsure what kind of welcome he was about to encounter. When the old lady opened the door, her weary, tired, old age, mixed with the multitude of emotions were noticeable on her face and demeanor.

"It is good to see you, servant of his name. The master of the house stepped out and will be coming soon. Make yourself comfortable." "Thank you, mother," he replied, always addressing the old lady with those words. He looked over her shoulder, hoping for a welcome from Ofra. The old lady read his mind "Yes, Ofra is here. She locked herself in her room. We heard you are in Bethlehem." She spoke pragmatically. "How is she?" "Good and healthy."

"Thank you, Hashem" the Levite whispered. They sat down. The old lady brought him a bowl to wash, water to drink and a piece of bread. She then looked at the boy, and concluded Gershon finally hired a helper, so she hurriedly brought him a piece of bread and a cup of water. "I see you have a nice boy with you, Gershon. A helper?" she spoke intentionally loud making sure Ofra could hear. Then lowering her voice, she continued talking. "Why is it the tribes have to quarrel after every pilgrimage? It's the same old argument! The Holy Ark should be in Shiloh! No! The Holy Ark should be in Bet El! And the tribe of Dan, in the far north, who are so distant from Bet-El, and travel the furthest for the pilgrimage, complain the least."

"Yes, wise woman, but I'm sure ..." Gershon continued, "... the tribes will come to an agreement." What he didn't tell her was that he sided with the opinion of the majority of the tribes who believed that the holy ark should be shared communally in Shiloh and not exclusively in Bet-El. The Benjamins strongly believed that Shiloh could not, should not and will not be crowned as the home of the ark. Gershon was not in agreement with the Benjamin's because there was a strong need to allow all the people access to enhance their newly acquired conceptual spiritual needs of a God in Heaven. The Ten Commandments in the Ark embodied this abstract belief and the departure from paganism was building momentum.

"Talking about agreements," Gershon continued while nodding his head at Ofra's door.

"Well, if the question is between to beat on the rock or talk to it, I suggest, start by talking." said the old lady while she laughed, and made use of what had become a metaphor. She was referring to the confrontation between God and Moses when they crossed the desert. Moses said to God that the people needed water and God told him to talk to the stone but instead Moses beat on the stone.

Then the old lady continued, "With this freedom generation, I don't know anymore."

Gershon thought he saw Ofra's straw door sway a bit and hoped she might be stealing a glance at him.

Father arrived not surprised to see Gershon in his home and greeted him. His first words were "Did you eat anything?" Ofra heard her father's voice, and her door suddenly opened, but she was not out yet. "Ofra," her father's voice was formidable. Persuading her with a softer tone, he spoke, "Come! Come and greet your husband."

Ofra walked out slowly with her head down. Gershon thought he never saw her so beautiful, just like when they first met. His eyes examined her faster than a bolt of lightning. A lot can have happened in a year and four months. He continued and waited patiently to connect with her, but she still avoided his eyes. The old lady and Ofra set up the table and then Ofra sat next to him and said nothing. Her father insisted the old lady fill the table abundantly and made sure it was a most festive midday meal. The hospitality of the Judean master of the house didn't escape Gershon's comprehension of his own incompetence. Ofra's father knew that Gershon, his son-in-law, was not conducting his life in a balance between the body and the soul. He strongly believed that food for the body is no less important than food for the soul, conveying to Gershon how he raised his daughter. "This is not only about the book of life and the great causes. This is the land of milk and honey! Let us enjoy it! Pass the wine dear." he said in a joyful mood. Ofra helped the old lady. She rushed in and out of the outdoor oven checking on the freshly baking bread and when done brought it in for everyone. Although meat was not consumed on that day, there was still plenty of olives, cheese, honey, wine, and bread. Gershon tried so hard to trap Ofra's eyes, but his attempts were in vain. She kept herself busy and the only words she said were "Yes Safta, yes Abba" all day long.

That night Gershon went upstairs to the roof and waited. He thought he heard her footsteps following him, but that turned out to be his desire which probably ignited his imagination. This would be a perfect time to speak with her and to open his heart, just when everyone is asleep. She might even agree to go back home with him. He filled his lungs with fresh Judean Mountain air spiced with the strong aroma of burning wood. He waited and waited, paced back and forth on the roof, and marveled at the beauty of the starry night. But she never showed up. Maybe she was waiting for him in her room, he reasoned. But no. She knew he would not go there due to the respect of her father, the master of the house and of course to respect her domain. He finally went to his bed. He tried very hard to balance his breathing as he was so tired and fatigued. Earlier, in a single moment, he saw her so beautiful and calm. Now with this intense body heat and the sweat covering his body, he realized how much he loved her even more. He felt helpless. He knew he had the right to claim her back, but still chose not to. It was her heart he wanted to reclaim. The heart he conquered when she was taken by him, when her eyes were inflamed with every word he would say. When they were full of passion when they first met. The heart he lost. *"Proceed slowly with caution, and remember, it is one thing to conquer a woman, but nurturing love to blossom is another."* These words he once heard from a friend about love were relentlessly haunting him like the unending creation of honey in its hive. And it never stops.

This time I will not let her go, he promised himself before falling asleep.

Chapter 36
"Reunion"

Gershon's strategy paid off because late the next day, although she was still silent, he was glad to see a smile on her face. She walked toward the water jar and looked directly in his eyes. It was the perfect timing he had been waiting for.

"Boy, go and ask Ofra, if there is anything she needs." It was odd and somehow transparent, but she felt it was thoughtful.

The Levite presumed there was now hope. He would like to be on his merry way with Ofra next to him. But not so fast. Father sensed his son-in-law's dilemma and jumped to the rescue. "Levite!" His conciliatory tone sounded like a peacemaker. "I know that the work of the creator is pressing on you, and you must go, but one must find time to take a break, especially after such a busy harvest season."

"Safta!" He turned to the old lady. "Set for us the table, let us eat and enjoy our evening meal." He then looked at Gershon. "Another day, you shall leave!" he said in a compelling voice. "If my staying here another day will make you happy, then let it be" Gershon responded an octave higher than usual with his arms elevated. So, another table was set, and Gershon recognized the role Ofra's father was portraying. He was accentuating the importance of always having the time for your family and having ample food on the table. Gershon went along with it, and felt he was taking a crash course on how to run home or become the head of a household. But Gershon neither had the experience nor the means to run a home like her father. The wine finally exhausted Abba, but not before he voiced his opinions about the state of the young tribal federation.

"Freedom can unite and can divide. We need a king to fight our battles and unite us," He proclaimed, "And one more thing!" he added with a drunken voice before he crashed into bed. "A word of advice for a healthy marriage. As they say, my young son, servant of God, keep a woman's belly full, don't forget to clothe her back, and for eternal happiness, bring her ointments to soothe her aches. And one more thing Levite! A lonely woman at home is an invitation for the snakes of all colors. Be with her and hope and pray that love will grow." Gershon did not have the chance to respond because her father fell asleep, and they all had to carry him to his bed. At that exact moment, Gershon gently touched Ofra's arm signaling her to join him, and she didn't indicate any resistance, so he went up to the roof and this time she followed him. Gershon, although in full control, still did not escape the influence of the wine. It was a beautiful Judean night that revealed its magical starry exquisiteness. When she reached the roof, not looking at him, she walked with her head tilted to the side. Gershon was tongue tied and all the beautiful words he prepared the previous night on the roof escaped his head and he burst out in a sincere tone "Ofra the fig tree is no longer milky. It is now ripe like honey. I brought some figs for you." She quickly gave him a glance and even more quickly looked away. Gershon saw her roll her eyes and said "Ofra, come back home to me." She turned and looked at him, "What for? To be home alone again?"

"I need your help, Ofra."

"Oh? You need my help, or you need me?"

"What do you want me to tell you, Ofra?"

"I want you to tell me that you will make me a wife like all other wives, have a home like all other homes, and a husband that will not leave me alone to battle the nights." "My Ofra is always better with words than me." His voice softened. "Ofra, a Levite I am. I know my difficult mission. I will never be able to match your father's provisions. My life is in the hands of our creator; let us put our assurance in him, come back to me and help me be what I am, and what I ought to do, and be."

A moment of silence ensued and to Gershon it signaled a possible truce.

"I love you Ofra, I need you in my life."

Her eyes suddenly sparkled and looked even brighter on that clear and illuminating night. He waited.

She took a long pause and stared at Yareke, the silvery moon and thought, 'I know he loves me, but he's not around much to show it. Should I go, or should I stay, should I go or should I stay. Or should I let love lead the way.' Softly moving her attention from Yareke to Gershon she finally whispered, "When did you hire the boy?"

"Two days ago. He is a good boy and will be a great help. Things will be different from now on" he paused and then continued. "I also spoke to the priesthood about the coming season to schedule less traveling if possible." Focusing her vision on the night sky, her ears and her heart were listening. "I desire a permanent home, Gershon. With a big roof that will always be looking up to heaven."

Standing there for a few moments under the stars and opening their hearts, they gently kissed.

Chapter 37
"Departure"

Gershon thanked his God for fulfilling his wishes. Ofra too, thought how after all, her Gershon is so very special and so much more unique than her friend's husbands. She never heard them saying their husbands possessed the courage to say, "I love you" to their wives. Up on the roof last night, after they renewed their vows, they each retired to bed.

It was now Thursday and Gershon was the first to wake up in the very early pre-morning hours.

"Prepare the donkeys," he said to the boy who hardly had his eyes open. "We are leaving this morning." The boy diligently responded to his master's order.

The old lady emerged from the back side of the house and saw the Levite and the boy bustling about. The glowing look on the Levite's face said it all. She was delighted at the thought that the two lovers re-united and came to a good resolution.

"The roads are getting more dangerous; we must go at once, and early, in order not to run into the dark." said Gershon.

"I know, I know," she said with an understanding voice.

"What's the hurry? Let us put a piece of bread in our stomach and thank our creator, and after, you will be on your way." The awakened father said wanting to seal the happy ending with bread, butter, and milk. Ofra, listening to the conversations, entered the room and looked at Gershon to see if he was going to accommodate her father's breakfast invitation. She was waiting to see an approving look from Gershon as she knew her father would be pleased if he agreed.

The sweet aroma of baked bread and butter determined the outcome. "We Judeans," the father said, "very much respect the people of the hills, and the mountains. Maybe we are not better farmers, but our bread is the best!" He dipped a piece of bread in a honey dish, added butter and washed it down with milk. By the time the father completed yet another story, this one of the heroic battles of Joshua conquering the land, the sun was above the horizon. The neighbors, Ofra's friends and some family members came to give their renewed wishes and say goodbye and of course more food was served. Ofra's father made his point that a man cannot live only by the Book and deeds, especially when he had to feed, take care of a wife, and raise a family.

Gershon, concerned about this unexpected delay, stood up and announced "Thank you for this beautiful farewell but we cannot stay for one more cup of milk. We must leave at once."

They finally began to pack up and leave. The neighbor who came to say goodbye to Ofra, whispered to her husband, "God picks and choses, but in the end, we succumb to destiny." Then added, "and I hope, she'll stay and not leave him, the way Ada did." Her husband heard those words and in a chastised tone shushed his wife and spoke. "It's hard for a woman to marry a priest. We wish them luck."

Just before Ofra climbed the donkey, she broke down, and burst into tears. Safta rushed to her and wiped away her tears with her fingers, and said, "Judean daughter, do not fatigue your heart. Your husband dwells in the realm of the almighty, and now you do. Trust his name, and you will find tranquility." The soft-spoken words helped Ofra, she lifted her head up, and off they went.

Chapter 38
"Caravan"

Approaching the city gate, Gershon was surprised to see the entire caravan at a standstill at the gathering point. They were greeted as they approached. It looked like there was a delay. The camels were sitting motionless on their folded knees, the donkeys stood sleeping under the shade of the fig trees. A mountain lion making its way through the Jordan passages, was now spotted right on the trail. Two additional riders on horseback were hired to accompany the caravan. Finally, the camels stretched their legs, the donkeys' ears were pointed, and new bells were attached on the neck of the animals, to scare away the bad spirits, and alert the lions. The caravan finally got on its way, later than usual. Gershon was becoming concerned that it might be too late before reaching home. He was uneasy about what would happen and where they would stay for the night. During all this time, the Levite was silent. The boy saw his master's worrisome face knowing traveling at night was dangerous. There were rumors that not only one lion, but two were spotted on the trail. Gershon had to decide; to continue, or to exit the caravan. "Master," the boy said, "how about staying the night in the city of Evos which is close by." Everyone knew about the convenient lodgings and feeding stations for the animals in the Canaanite town of Evos.

" Boy," replied the Levite. "I prefer to stay the night among our brethren, the Hebrews. Let us push ahead."

Just as night fell, they made it to the outskirts of the Benjamin territory, known as the "Hill". "Thank you El for helping us to reach our brother's domain" whispered the Levite, more relaxed. They rode into the small city. Last minute merchants were closing shops. It was as quiet as if someone intently spread a sheet of silence over the town. It is customary in the Hebrew towns to offer a guest a room for the night, especially when they recognize a Levite approaching. Gershon looked in all directions, but no one came towards them to offer any accommodation. How strange the Levite thought, this was not expected nor typical for his brothers the Israelites. Suddenly an old man emerged from behind a tree tightening the rope around his waist after having relieved himself and walked toward them. "Where are you heading?" The old man inquired.

"The house of the almighty. Night has caught us here, my concubine, the boy, and I." Gershon responded.

"Oh, servant of the almighty, I am from the Ephraim tribe, but I live here in the Benjamin territory with my daughter. Come to my home and be my guest. Your presence in my house will be a blessing for us."

"Thank you, son of Ephraim." They were thankful after having such a long and tiring day. He escorted them to his small simple humble abode.

The man customarily washed the Levite's feet. He respected and followed the old customs; the way Abraham washed the feet of the three angels seven hundred years earlier. This ritual continued to be practiced by this Ephraim man/ He had seen and heard about it from his father and his father before him. He perceived life in the same ways he learned of Abraham and made an immense effort and was exceedingly privileged to host this

Levite. They all sat down at the modest table and were grateful for the small meal prepared by their host and his daughter. As soon as the old man finished reciting the blessing over the bread, a thundering knock on the door jolted them from their seats and the forceful commands pursued.

"Old man! Bring the man out of your house, that we shall know him! And what are his intentions in OUR Benjamin territory?" The old man's daughter peeped through the tiny window, and she saw the town's people gathered in the yard. Men, women, and children. She had never experienced anything like this before and she didn't understand what was happening. Ofra too hadn't witnessed such a fright.

The old man stepped outside, "Brothers! The Levite, his wife and their helper, are only passing through, and they are guests in my house for the night." "Oh? Old man. They are only passing through?" one of the Benjamins shouted cynically with the cheering of the townspeople.

"… and when they decide to stay, they end up telling us how to conduct our lives!" a man angrily shouted from the crowd.

"Sons of Benjamin" the old man added "the Levite and his wife have no intention of staying in this territory. You know that the Levite tribe is given our almighty right to be wherever he wishes among his brothers. Those are the laws of the land."

"Old man! Don't preach to us the new laws of the land. Bring the man out, that we shall know him, according to our laws and our ways." "Sons of Benjamin, the man is a Levite, a priest. You cannot discard the priesthood by treating him like a Canaanite. Why do you want to know him the way the Canaanites do? Since when do we, the Israelite Priesthood, act like the Canaanite Priesthood? Gone are the days of Sodom and Gomorrah."

The old man remembered his grandfather telling him the story about the people of Sodom when Abrahams nephew had to run away after they knocked on the door and demanded to bring out his guests so they could know them. He articulated this parallel calmly but the more he said the worse it got.

An old Benjamin elder pointing his finger at the house shouts "We know that you, a Levite, and your concubine are siding up with Judah and the priesthood to position the holy ark in Shiloh. Did you forget? You, a man of God, forgot the blessing Moses bestowed on the tribes? To keep the ark in Bet El where the shekhinah dwells, in the Benjamin territory? Where Moses promised it would be!"

The old man turned to go back into the house when a voice shouted, "Old man, our patience is running thin. Get the man out that we shall know him." The tension was mounting, and the men were relentless. The old man turns back and cries "So brothers, sons of Benjamin, what do you want me to do? Are you forcing me to send out my virgin daughter and the Levites wife like Lot, the nephew of Abraham did? Just like Lot, who was compelled to offer his two virgin daughters? For his name's sake, the God of Abraham, do not do such a thing to the Levite. The people will say the priesthood in Israel are acting like the days of Sodom." Revolted the old man storms back into the house.

Gershon, looked at the old man in shock, "To bring out the women?" "Levite, those are our brothers from the tribe of Benjamin, they know the laws not to hurt the women. How badly can they treat my daughter and your wife? After knowing the women, they will take them in for the night. Do you prefer they know you and blemish the name of the Priesthood?"

The old man is driven back outside because of the persistent banging, screaming, and yelling. "Old man, you're offering us your dreadful virgin daughter, and the concubine? Are you making fun of us? You know that the moment one of us redeems your ugly daughter's virginity, we must marry her. We as well know the laws of the land. Are you playing tricks on us, old man?" An elderly woman shouted "Are you offering us the concubine? The Judean harlot who abandoned the Levite?"

A woman much younger screamed "No! She left him for another man. We wondered why he would agree to take her back?"

A senile woman rushed to the front of the crowd, leaned forward, lifted her dress, and mooned the old man. Then she shouted, "This is to you, the tribe of Judah and the tribe of Levi."

The old man could not bear another moment of this madness and went back inside. Ofra was sitting on the floor terrified with her back pressed to the wall, listening in shock. Her mouth, her heart, and her eyes in total distress and her face as red as blood.

"What choice do we have?" The old man's broken voice was drained. "Their words are vile." Gershon whispered with his head down.

"We must not let them discard the Priesthood just because they want to level with you." the old man said sorrowfully.

"It is more than level man to man. I'm afraid they are looking to get even with the priesthood, my brother Ephraim. They believe we took sides with the Judeans and that we abandoned the eternal Shekhinah which dwells in their territory in Bet-El."

"Well, then, I say, let's send the women out to calm down their rage" the old man asserted and then addressed Ofra and lifted his eyes to heaven. "Go daughter, lower their rage, they know they will face the consequences if they hurt any of us. And hopefully, we will all be saved by morning." Gershon looked so powerless *"Ofra, what have I put you through."*

The banging on the door became stronger, almost knocking it down.

Ofra stood up and stepped forward and with unwavering conviction spoke. "I as well know the laws of the land. Let it be known and witnessed by the old man, and his daughter, that I, Ofra, the wife of Gershon, the Levite, am going out against my will. And if I will be forced upon and disgraced by my brothers the Benjamin's, the truth will be on my side. And they will face their judgment."

Gershon with tears streaming from his eyes, held her hands tenderly and murmured "Am I going to survive this because of you, Ofra?" Gershon's words left the old man recalling the story of Sarah saving Abraham while passing the border to Egypt and he said "With Gods help, this will get resolved in the same manner as it was for Abraham and Sarah. May God protect you, wife of Gershon."

"Let them see that you are going out there against your free will" Gershon said knowing that it is illegal to force a woman without her consent and would deter the Benjamins from harming his beautiful young Ofra. The old man opened the door, Gershon pushed Ofra forward, against her free will, and for everyone to see, and forced her out. She showed a gentle resistance, as if to say, it is against my will.

"Go" the old man stuttered "and may the almighty be with you." He quickly closed the door behind her afraid those thugs might force themselves into the house. She stood with her back tight to the closed door, frozen, not able to comprehend any rational thought.

Chapter 39
"The Unthinkable"

It was a full Yareke, a starry night. The moon, always the eternal witness of the night's occurrence with heaven shining it added light into the yard.

"Why am I afraid?" she thought. "Isn't Boaz a Benjamin? And Dina's husband, and my friends, and some of their husbands? Aren't they all from the Benjamin tribe? Be strong Ofra, stand by your husband. Put on a strong face with these people and everything will be fine. Bring them back to their senses, save your husband." she continuously mumbled.

"Our Levite likes pretty girls" said the first of three men.

"He likes them young" he continued while distorting his face mockingly.

"Isn't the Levite, the man of God, like all other men? We want to know him. You must know him woman?" said the elder of the bunch. "Is it so hard for a Hebrew priest to come down and level with his people the way other priests of other lands do?" said the third man who looked smarter and younger and then continued "What is your name?"

"Ofra! Why do you want to know him the way dogs know each other?" she said bluntly recalling her school friend Rebekkah describing a story her uncle repeated and how they were making fun of the absurd idea and started making dog noises and giggling.

"And he likes them gutsy."

"Introduce yourself to the young woman." said the first guy who was the stupidest and ugliest of the three guys. They were all laughing and making faces. "They call us the wicked Benjie's," said the smart one.

"But we're not that crazy," the stupid guy interrupted "We are worse!" "And you are from the tribe of Judah, right?" said the elderly man. "You see we are not as stupid as your learned and educated Levite husband might think. Now, you are going to do the talking for him. For the Levite, and for the Judeans? Ha!" "So far, you're doing all the talking." said Ofra.

"Oh, and he likes them feisty" the smarter of the three men said sneeringly.

"Look woman, you are caught in the middle of this. Our disagreement and disputes are with the Levite, the priesthood, and the Judeans. Unless of course you want to represent and speak for the Judeans? We Benjamin's are tired of being told what to do by the Priesthood and by Judah. The Judeans headed by Judah think they can manage all the tribe's affairs."

The Benjamins began listing their gripes and imitating the priesthood, jeeringly at first and then with their rage mounting said:

"Don't eat this, and don't eat that" the ugly one said contemptuously.

"This is not good for the sacrifice, this goat has too many blue spots, this one is too weak to stand on its feet, this one is ill and cannot be slaughtered." "The fruit trees are not ready to be harvested because they are too young. This meat is not cooked enough to be eaten."

"Don't worship the Baal and the Ashrah. And the Ark shall be going to Shiloh this coming Pilgrimage" said the elder impersonating the Priesthood. He was fuming about the ark not staying in Bet-El in their Benjamin territory and his anger was escalating.

"Listen woman, the Levites, and the priesthood do not listen to anyone's opinions." Then the stupid looking one interfered tauntingly "They listen to Judah, and Judah listens to the priesthood."

"No priest is welcome in the Benjamin territory, from Bet-El to Jericho" continued the ugly of the three. He raised his voice. He was incensed and wanted to make sure he was heard by the Levite and the old man. "Sound the shofars! The Benjamin tribe is going to be free! Our arrows will hit hard into the hearts of anyone who dares to change our ways and customs."

"Save your words," the smarter guy suddenly came up with an idea. It was apparent on his twisted face. "You are talking to the woman, not to the Levite or the priesthood. I have a better way. It will be the only way the Levite and the priesthood will get the message. They will stay away from our affairs and respect us in our territory. And we will keep the ark where the Shekhinah dwells, here in Bet-El."

By now the crowd had all gone to their homes because the deep dark night in these mountains was approaching. The ugly one grabs Ofra's arm and pulls her away from the door and yanks her farther from the house. In turn they drag her deeper into the woods among the pine trees. "Now, let the Levite check these marks on his beloved." The man kicked Ofra's thigh so hard, she collapses to the ground with a cry. "Is there a blue mark yet?" he yelled in madness "To you Judah, this daughter of Judea." He kicks her again and this time Ofra screams horrifically as she is rolling over the hard earth.

"Make that cow stand up. is she still healthy?" The ugly one laughs forcefully while he punches her face and sees the blood gushing out of her nose. He pulls up his robe and before violating her says "now brother, tell me, is there a difference between this Judean woman and the Canaanite girl I had the other day?"

Chapter 40
"The Message"

The old man approached Gershon who was sitting on the floor with his head in his lap. "Go Levite, rest your body and mind. Come the morning she will be at the neighbor's house. They will take her in for the night. They will not dare to harm her." The old man reassured Gershon confidently and comfortingly. "I hope that's true" whispered Gershon. He sat there lifeless with his eyes closed trying to convince himself that the old man's words would be realized. He covered his face with the palms of his hands and continued whispering "It's all my fault, I should have been more careful. Had I just left Bethlehem earlier, this would not have happened."

"Levite it is all the almighty's doing." the old man asserted.

"It is all the almighty's doing. Who am I, Gershon the Levite, to change, to see, or to decide the future." Gershon was blaming himself but interchanging his belief in his faith at the same time "I wasn't thinking this could happen, but God always has his own plan."

"Oh, Almighty God, send us a miracle like you did with Abraham" exclaimed the old man.

Far from the house, deep in the forest among the tall pine trees, poor Ofra was futilely trying again and again to stand on her feet. They pushed and threw her from one to the other as they harmed her weakened body.

"This is all for you Levite! Count the number of wounds on your beloved to

mark the number of the tribes. Inspect the marks on your beloved like you inspect the cow."

They jammed a rag in her mouth to muffle her screams. Ofra finally collapsed, breathless and bleeding. "Leave her there" the ugly one suggested. "No, I have a better idea. Let's bring her closer to the old man's house. At dawn, the Levite will get the message" said the smart one. Nearly lifeless, they quietly dragged Ofra to the old man's house on the hill making sure no one heard them. They left her lying there, in the late hours of the night. Ofra's bleeding body remained for hours on the cold hard stones, a short distance from the entry to the house.

Deprived of sleep, fatigued and worried, the Levite and his host waited impatiently for dawn so they may open the door to the house as the laws of the land dictated. When Shemesh rays emerged, they all stepped out into the morning which naturally looked like all other mornings. Blackbirds chirped during their early habits and tried to ease away the early chill. Their donkeys were still half unloaded. The old man, the master of the house walked tentatively toward the door.

"No. Please. Allow me to open the door" said Gershon.

The old man and his daughter stepped back. Gershon opened the door and saw Ofra, on the ground ten steps from the entry.

"Stand up and let's go." She still managed to hear Gershon's words, but her soul was emerging slowly from her body. Sphere by sphere she was ascending to her ultimate destination. She was glad to see him alive, because by now she knew what those despicable men were capable of doing, especially after their contemptable acts. She realized she was the messenger, and her marked body the message. But why? What were their motives behind this cruel ordeal? She succumbed with her belly down in front of the old man's house. Her soul was ignited by her last gasps of breath on earth. People believe that's how souls are propelled into their luminous journey to their resting place. Her consciousness evaporated into heaven's domain the higher her soul continued to climb. She lingered a bit, as if she wanted to take the long way home to heaven, not yet ready to depart. She was about to join other women in heaven like her, who were victims and had died before their time.

Gershon on one donkey laid Ofra's body on the boy's donkey's face down. Gershon pulled Ofra's donkey using a short rope while the boy was running after them. For many hours, Gershon maneuvered both donkeys over the rocky terrain. At one time, Ofra fell off the donkey. The boy caught up with them, catching his breath, and helped Gershon put Ofra back on the donkey, belly down.

"Jehovah! God of Moses! King of miracles! We are in your hands now." Gershon mumbled while he resumed riding. By now, he was in a state of shock and denial. He refused to accept reality and destiny's verdict. What was destiny's verdict? Behind him, he refused to believe he was carrying his beloved Ofra's dead body. How could he accept the idea, or the fact, that the Benjamin's, could brutally harm his beloved wife. It was completely unbelievable. He was not capable of comprehending the brutality, an act so despicable and viciously committed by no other than his brotherly tribe.

When they arrived home, they carried her to the back of the house and Gershon laid her on a fleece blanket on the stone table.

His eyes opened widely in terror at the sight of her assaulted body. Now he saw it all. The broken arms and legs, the excessive bleeding, the horrific blue and purple marks, the horror. He howled to himself and could not control his emotions. He put his ear to her chest but there was no sign of life. He jumped back and landed on the floor, his chest was rising up and down, his lungs refusing to inhale or exhale in any usual way. He sat there for what seemed like eternity in a state of shock looking at her but unable to focus. Recovering his breathing, he stood up, approached her and caressed her first laceration, then the second. He gently stroked her wounds. Twelve in all! It was *him* they meant to hurt. "A message directed to me! Almighty in heaven. These are not acts of my brothers who perceive the world the way I do. Ofra, you died for me!" he screamed. "You sacrificed yourself for me, to save my life and the honor of the priesthood! Only if heaven could have given me more time to prove it to you. Forgive me! Forgive me. God only knows how much I love you."

Chapter 41
Agony

Sitting on the floor facing Ofra's body, in a state of shock, feelings of rage, confusion, grief, and fury were boiling inside Gershon. Dina and Rachel arrived vociferously. He wasn't aware but the house began swelling with people. Word got around fast. Shock turned into anger and a demand for justice mounted. Some were saying that the perpetrators were from the Benjamin tribe. Others believed they had to have been Canaanites. Rumors were flying around the Levite's house from every direction. No one was able to understand why young Ofra was murdered.

It was difficult for Gershon to look at Ofra's marked body. He knew the three thugs from the Benjamin tribe deliberately used Ofra to voice their resentment against Judah and the tribes who were accepting and siding with the Priesthood. *"How will I assemble the leaders of the tribes to see this? They must see this with their own eyes. How do I gather all the tribe leaders from the four corners of the nation to witness what is in front of my eyes?"* His mind was racing. Gershon was sobbing on the floor with his legs folded and Ofra's lifeless body lay before him. He ran his right hand up and down trying to dry his short beard that was drenched from his tears.

"She's not even twenty years old! I'm barely thirty. How did my brothers come to this level of brutality? Our generation never witnessed cruelty like our fathers and mothers in Egypt. I always thought my Benjamin brothers perceived the world like me. To think I preferred to

spend the night among them on the hill just to avoid danger from outsiders! Why didn't I listen to the boy? We were caught up by the approaching night and he suggested to spend the night in Evos. Why didn't I listen to the boy? Why does God want me to go through this? Am I really here to lead our misguided brothers?"

He dropped his head down, in a fleeting moment everything felt futile. So strongly that Gershon not only questioned his own accountability but in a flash doubted God's existence. He was ready to abandon the Priesthood. The immorality was unfathomable.

To Gershon, the Benjamins had to live to the highest standards by virtue of having the Ark in their territory and it was their duty to be the guardians of morality. It behooved them to live with honor and decency. Gershon couldn't reconcile the inscrutable incomprehensible actions of the Benjamins with God's Ten Commandments that dwell in their territory.

With his head still hanging he continued to mumble. "I can put Ofra's body on a horse, and ride to each and every tribe to display the viciousness. They will all see who the Benjamin's really are."

Feeling useless, drained and fatigued, reality plunged his concentration and engulfed his entire essence. He lifted his head with his eyes enflamed.

"The heads of the tribes must see this immediately. It is my duty. They must see with their eyes what words cannot express."

Rachel looked at Gershon and was concerned at his odd behavior. He had a strange look in his eyes. His movements were erratic. She had never seen anyone in pain like this before. Frightened, she quickly turned around to leave. She saw Boaz approaching and with both palms blocking his entrance said "Don't go there! Let him grieve on his own."

"I must make them see this with their own eyes. How else will justice be served?" He muttered again and again. "I must make them see this with their own eyes," he was saying the same words repeatedly.

He continued talking and whispering unintelligibly as he prepared to execute a plan.

Chapter 42
"Horsemen"

He lifted Ofra and placed her on the stone table. He reached for his knife. "Your brutal death will not be in vain Ofra. I will not stop until such time when justice is served. I will not stop until my brothers repent. I will shake the foundation of this young tribal nation. No, you did not die in vain Ofra!"

With trembling hands, he approached Ofra's body with the knife. *Gershon, you must do this for Ofra h*e murmured to himself trying to steady his billowing knees to avoid falling. He burst out in a guttural cry as he brought the knife down quickly. He was unaware that his tears were streaming into Ofra's severed bloody head. "This will be sent to Judah in Bethlehem" he stammered as he tenderly draped it in a cloth.

"And this broken arm full of blue marks will be sent to the tribe of Simon, and a broken foot will be sent to the tribe of Dan." One by one, the remaining limbs of Ofra's body marked by vicious wounds inflicted on her, were severed, and wrapped to be sent to the tribes. With twelve uncontrollable screams of a suffering animal and hyperventilating with each painful chop, Gershon bound the last of Ofra's remains and collapsed to the floor.

Everyone quieted hearing Gershon's low deep painful howling oblivious to what he was doing. Out of respect, Boaz and Rachel asked the throng of people to let Gershon grieve on his own, as heart wrenching as it was.

Gershon emerged from the back of the house holding six cloth-covered limbs in each hand. In a loud raspy tone, Gershon addressed the outraged crowd outside his door. "I need good horsemen who can ride through the night. One to each of the twelve tribes in our nation. You will meet the elders and show them what the Benjamins have done to this young innocent woman. I wrapped their horrific savagery in these cloths."

"Levite, I can leave at once. My horse can carry me to the far north to the tribe of Dan."

"Let me serve the priesthood by fulfilling this privileged commission. I can leave at once as well" another man stepped forward. "Give me the honor to serve you and the courageous woman whom we all loved. My horse and I are healthy, and we can leave immediately."

The Levite handed Ofra's covered remains to eleven volunteers. Only one missing.

Boaz rode up on his beautiful horse and approached Gershon. "You know I am Boaz, the son of a Benjamin. I am obliged to fulfill this deed. I will deliver the cruelly inflicted remains to my brothers. They will see and witness what they did to our Ofra." "Brother Boaz. Is it not enough that we have lost Ofra? We cannot lose you too!

"I am compelled to go to the tribe of my brothers. I must go. It is the least I can do for our Ofra." Boaz looked down at the ground at her remains. His eyes were bursting with tears. He sobbed with his voice full of rage. The Levite lifted his head after a short silence. It was during this pause, at this very moment agreeing to allow Boaz to honor Ofra's life that Gershon began emerging from the abyss. "Go, and El be with you." Boaz mounted his magnificent horse with his sword intentionally pointed toward the territory of his home and declared "Justice must be served where the eternal Shekinah dwells! In the land of the Benjamin's!"

The twelve riders used Gershon's final words as a signal to depart.

"Go! Let your brothers see with their eyes, and judge with their heart. The almighty will be with you."

"Levite, what shall be done after they have been inspected by the elderly?" said one rider. "After they have been examined by the elders, ride to Bethlehem, and there will be the burial. Do not lose time, brothers. May God watch over your safety."

They all rode off to the four corners of the land.

"I think Boaz is going to look for her murderers," said Rachel. "I'm afraid, I hear a voice of revenge?" she whispered to Dina. "Brother Boaz! Don't take the law into your own hands! It's a matter for all the tribes" Rachel shouted.

"I hear your words wise woman" said Boaz sitting erectly on his horse with Ofra in the folded cloth safeguarded under his arm. Rachel imbalanced on her short leg, began running after him, and waving her arm and spitting words "The elders and the leaders from the tribes will make sure justice will prevail Boaz!"

"I hear you, wise woman" Boaz repeated and rode off. "I think you are right Rachel. He is going to look for her murderers" said Dina fearing for her dear Boaz. "Come," said Rachel, "It's almost midday, mourners will be coming. Let's fetch water and prepare food. But first, let's help Gershon."

Chapter 43
"See and Judge"

The twelve riders travelled in four different directions deep into the land carrying Ofra's remains. Rumors about the young woman's murder, the concubine, the Levite's wife, began spreading around the nation. Because the nature of rumors circulates unverified information faster than the truth, there will be no question after the riders arrive. The old man and his daughter who graciously hosted Gershon and Ofra, along with the elders, will now be the eyewitnesses to this horrific criminality.

The riders all agreed on the language they would use to address the leaders; "This is what your brothers did! See and judge!" Their message was to be sent to the elders and judges of all the tribes throughout the land.

The first rider was instructed to move as rapidly as possible, making sure to arrive quickly so Judah and the Priesthood could witness this horror. There was an urgent need to evoke the leadership of the nation, in Bethlehem, and thrust them into action.

After entering the gate, the elders were gathered undertaking their daily routine. "A messenger I am! This is what your brothers did! See and judge!" He then opened the bloody cloth, and exposed Ofra's head. The elders looked at each other shocked; the scene conveyed the message which words solely could not. The eyes validated the cruelty of the Benjamin gang. "How could this have happened?" gasped one of the elders while he nudged his wooden stick on Ofra's purple marks near her eye. The elders spent quite some time trying to grasp what happened, to whom it happened, why it happened, when it happened and who would do such a heinous act. They were firing questions faster than the rider could answer. They soon learned it was the Amorites daughter from their village and immediately sent two elders to his home. Many people started gathering around the square. Most heard rumors but this was more gruesome than anyone could have imagined.

"Go to the Goshen Center and bring the judges! Quickly!" demanded the most senior Cohen. "The Levite puts himself above his brothers" said one of the visiting bystanders who promptly proved to be a Benjamin. His gripe grew louder "The Ark of the Covenant must remain in Bet-El, in the Benjamin territory where the Shekinah dwells, and not in Shiloh, or Kiriat Yarim."

"The *eternal* Shekinah" his friend, another Benjamin bystander corrected, enhancing the man's word. "Every tribe is a master in his land" added the Benjamin with a proud voice.

"Judah is here! Make way! Judah is here!"

"And who appointed Judah as the master of all the tribes?" He continued obdurately as he looked at his friend with a sneer.

All eyes looked in the direction of Judah who was dismounting his horse rapidly. Judah, the head of the fourth tribe was a descendant of the twelve sons of Jacob. He exuded an aura of leadership. He approached the bloody cloth on the ground which was enveloped by the crowd. He looked closely at this gruesome site in disbelief. The injuries were obvious and bore signs of malice, unprecedented cruelty and despicable torture.

"Justice must be served! Convene all the elders and all the judges, of all the tribes in our nation" Judah spoke full of conviction.

A big outcry was heard in every family throughout the land because the riders swiftly reached the elders in each tribe. There were twelve tribes in total including the tribe of Benjamin. The demand for justice mounted. Ofra's name was spoken by everyone. The entire nation spoke about the concubine, the wife of the Levite, the poor woman who was murdered. Her body parts were examined by the tribe's elders, and they all agreed that this level of brutality was incomprehensibly ruthless.

Chapter 44
"Yoav"

Boaz entered Bet-El in the Benjamin territory in the afternoon and rode directly to the city center. It was a crowded area. Ofra's limb was covered in what was now a bloody cloth which he held up high above his head with his right hand. "This is what our brothers did! Come. See and judge what they have done to this young woman." People were trying to get a closer glimpse and saw the blue and purple marks, and the deep cuts on her limb. "Oh Boaz, hero of war. You stand here among your brother's, the Benjamin's, on the ground in your territory, your home. Have you come here to defend the Levite? The Priesthood? The concubine? The Judeans? Side up with your brothers!" The elder stated. "I'm on the side of justice brothers."

"Boaz, look around you at this group of elders. We have been extending justice throughout our territory, in the twenty-four cities from Parra to Givon. We will bring the murderers to justice, but not to the hands of Judah and the priesthood." "Maybe Judean blood runs in his veins and not Benjamin blood," said one of the spectators. His cackling echoed all over the city center. "Side up with your brothers! Side up with your brothers!" The crowd was shouting. Boaz gathered Ofra's limb and decided it would be best to go to the other side of town to spend the night with his friend Yoav. When he arrived at Yoav's military school he was greeted outside by a 'working woman' who had just come back from the center. "For a jug of wine, or a fig cake, I will trade you my honey" she said squeezing her breasts into his face in temptation. "A man who seeks a woman's justice, needs a woman's favor in return." She winked and crinkled her nose.

Yoav emerged when he heard the chatter signaling a visitor. "Peace be on you, Brother Boaz. I heard about your arrival in town." "Peace on you, my brother Yoav." "Itai! Bring some bread, water and whatever is leftover of the grape wine." The young trainee was wearing a facial protective mask made out of goat skin. Itai brought wine, bread, water and put it on the wooden table. "Sorry Master Yoav there is only pomegranate wine." "Oh, ok it will do. Thank you, my young brother Itai." Then Yoav turned around and faced Boaz. "Boaz. You know I don't run the tribal affairs; I stay far away from it."

"I know brother Yoav." "The men you are looking for, are not here, Boaz." "I figured that out, Yoav." "We are awaiting your instruction" the young Itai addressed Yoav.

"Look at this generation, they are short of patience. Look around you, Boaz. They are all born and bred in the new land, children of freedom."

"Isn't he too young for your intense training?" Boaz commented and pointed at Itai.

"Oh no! In this generation they don't count their years. Try him in the bow and arrow. You will see. He is twice his age. I train them to fight the enemy. They are good soldiers." "I know Yoav. But now, I am here because I must find Ofra's murderers. Where are they brother Yoav?" Boaz, on a personal mission, is not interested in the festering conflict between the Benjamins, Judah and the tribes of the Priesthood; not regarding where the holy ark presides, nor the power struggle between them.

"Boaz, the elders don't want to turn the murderers into the

hands of Judah and the Priesthood."

"I want to find the murderers!"

"Do you really think that if you find her killers, it's going to prevent a confrontation between Benjamin and Judah?"

"Yoav, I am on a mission to find those bastards!"

"You know Judah carries the banner of the priesthood."

"Yoav!!! I understand their conflicts. I know the big picture and I don't care! That's not why I'm here!" Boaz, with venom seeping out of the veins on his forehead, stares deep into Yoav's eyes and says in a very slow staccato tone "I just want to put my hands on those low life's."

"Look at those two trainees up there" continued Yoav changing the direction of their conversation hoping to reduce his friend's intensity. "The one on the right, we'll call him the Benjamin. Like us. He's a well-trained warrior. He wants to lead the nation. And on the left, let's just say, he's Judah. He has a different way of gaining respect from the people."

Boaz is annoyed and perplexed by his friend's rhetoric. Boaz is a true Benjamin. He is a warrior like his brothers, and he is obsessed with finding Ofra's killers and has become extremely frustrated and exasperated by Yoav's analogy.

Yoav sensing the frustration of his friend and realizing Boaz is not at all distracted by the Benjamin-Judah paradigm says "Brother Boaz, if the elders agree to surrender the murderers to the hands of the Priesthood and Judah, things might settle down."

"As we both know, the Benjamins will NEVER surrender those men to the hands of the Priesthood, nor to Judah."

"I saw it coming." Yoav whispers and then continues with increased emotion "People don't come to Bet-El anymore. Not like before. People are going to Bethlehem. They're going to Shiloh. The pilgrimage doesn't come here, there's no activity. We're suffering. And the conflict has been building. There's a power struggle, there are new laws that the Priesthood has been injecting and now with these three morons... Three stupid men from our people!"

"Are we facing a confrontation of a brother killing a brother? Is this where we are heading Yoav?"

"What they did to Ofra might very well be what ignites the blaze. And Boaz, you know that I am a soldier. And I will fight with the Benjamins, our tribe. Soldiers are trained to kill; you know that brother Boaz."

"Or be killed" said Boaz and continues

"I know, I know!" pointing to the big hanging clay tablet written in Egyptian with the words:

Put no trust in a brother, acknowledge no one as a friend, nothing is to be gained from them. For a man has no one to defend him on the day of anguish. "You are more Egyptian than a Hebrew, my dear friend Yoav. Are you trying to defend your Egyptian heritage? For that, you could have stayed back in Egypt! And anyway, I don't think you believe in those words up there on the wall." said Boaz with a touch of irony. He enveloped Yoav's shoulder with his right hand. "I believe in those words only in the battlefield Brother Boaz." "And who is proper to lead the people?" Boaz pressed on while he looked at the two wrestlers "The young challenger on the right, or the Judean?" "The one who will win the battle is the one who is proper to lead the people" Yoav paused for a moment and continued. "A challenge between Judah and Benjamin is unavoidable. Listen to the sounds of the shofar getting louder." Yoav sipped the pomegranate wine from the clay cup and said, "And if you ask me Brother Boaz, I prefer to be part of a nation of soldiers, rather than a nation of slaves." "It looks like the Benjamin is winning up there" Boaz pointing his arm to the two young wrestlers. "Don't be sure! The Judean's might outsmart him unless the Judean's commit the number one mistake in a battle." "What is that mistake, brother Yoav?" "Mercy" Yoav replied in a sure and determined voice.

"I was afraid you were going to say that brother Yoav. But I still want to put my hands on the killers, no matter what." "I know" said Yoav. Until then, rest your body, bathe, and satisfy your hunger. Tomorrow is another day" he paused for a moment and continued. "You are welcome to attend the archery and spear throwing competition, Boaz. The long spear, the Romach, is becoming very popular in the art of war, especially after that long war in the north, what they called the Trojan War." "Oh, brother Yoav, my heart is heavy, leave it for another day."

"Atelia." Yoav called out loud. The woman at the entrance, the 'winkler' walked in bouncing. "See to it that my friend Boaz, the Benjamin, feels like he is at home. And prepare some ointment for the boys." "I will master Yoav." She winked again and Boaz followed her across the street to a place where a small group of students, training in the art of wrestling, were housed. She walked Boaz to the back room. A young woman brought water in a jar while she pushed a small wooden chair with her foot. She nodded to Boaz to sit down. She washed one leg and his other half leg. Boaz leaned forward and marveled at her oiled and perfumed bosom. 'I'm a Givonite" she spoke before Boaz mumbled an inaudible question. Then she started to sing an Egyptian song in a soft beautiful voice.

"Seize the day and be unwearied, let not the heart be troubled, enjoy the day as it passes, like a breath on earth." Her soft voice mingled with the loud cheering of the people attending the archery competition. He closed his eyes but managed to see her bouncing away. She could tell this Benjamin warrior's heart was heavy. She turned around to see him collapse to the floor into a deep sleep.

Chapter 45
"Givon"

Boaz was awakened by Yoav's deep voice in the early morning. "Brother Boaz, good morning. The men you are looking for are in the city of Givon."

"How many brother Yoav?" Boaz questioned while rubbing his eyes. "As I heard, three men, brother Boaz. It's futile to go after them. They are protected by the elders."

Boaz disregarding his friends comment and ignoring the warning said, "Thank you Yoav, may El be watching over you and us all." Boaz then splashed water on this face and swiftly gathered his belongings. Atelia followed him out and handed him bread and cheese and was holding something small. He sniffed the aromatic air while getting on his horse.

"It's grinded pines which you are smelling, it will help with the odor" she said with a gesture toward Ofra's remains.

"Thank you" Boaz said in gratitude while mounting his steed. "We are going to Givon my friend" Boaz whispered to his horse. She jolted forward, as if already knowing the direction.

Chapter 46
"To Bet-El"

"To Shiloh! To Shiloh!" shouted people in the Judean Bethlehem city center. "No! To Bet-El! To Bet-El!" bellowed others from the Judean Bethlehem city gate. "Brothers" said Judah to the crowd "We must convene in Bet-El in the Benjamin territory, where the eternal Shekinah dwells from the time of our fathers. We shall gather all the tribes and all the people so we can pursue justice."

"Judah, you want to resolve this conflict in the Benjamin territory?" shouted a man from the crowd. "Yes! We must speak to the Benjamin's in their territory, brother to brother!"

"Judah! We need to wait to hear the voice of the priesthood" came a shout and instantly many others joined in unison.

The three elders standing next to Judah nodded their heads as a sign of agreement. "To Bet-El! To Bet-El, the house of God!" the crowd shouted.

The gathering expanded in numbers rapidly and the amplitude of their voices rose just as quickly. They could be heard expressing their anger about Ofra's death as well as Benjamins accelerating annoyance of the Priesthood. Many were insinuating that the Benjamins might step out of the tribal covenant. Word was spreading fast among the multitude about the opposition. In a chain reaction, the crowd hushed to a dead silence when they saw the messenger's arrival. He declared, "From the High Priest, from the house of Aaron the Cohen's! We shall assemble in Bet-El in the holy house of the Shekinah."

The people began yelling that Judah and the Priesthood were joining forces. "The priesthood is taking sides with Judah," they screamed. "Judah is collaborating with the Priesthood" others suggested. Judah was emerging as the predominate leader and The Priesthood needed Judah's cooperation to unite the tribes.

Chapter 47
"Triumph In Unity"

They all finally convened in Bet-El. People from across the young nation brought their sacrifices to this holy sacred ground where the Shekinah dwells. Each tribe erected tents outside the perimeter of the holy ground accommodating the elders, leaders, judges and guards. Inside the perimeter dwelled the Holy Tent protected from the top by cloth and enclosed by four stone walls covered with leather hides. It looked part house and part tent. Inside was the Ark, made from acacia wood. It was a simple wooden ark guarded by two cherubim angels on its cover protecting its content. It contained stones from the Ten Commandments engraved by El himself. They believed the almighty descended and gathered the pieces Moses shattered. A beautiful parochet, a colorful decorative fabric was laid on the face of the Ark. It served as a separation especially when the sacrificial blood was anointed on the Ark by the priest.

The Cohens were attending to their work of the sacrifices.

The people were streaming in rapidly and the yard leading to the entrance of the holy tent was uncharacteristically crowded. People of the nation were arriving in droves. The Cohen's were assiduously busy because the line of people for sacrifices of mercy went further than the eye can see. It wrapped around and down the mountain, and no one seemed to mind the wait. There was a unified feeling of a sacred mission. The poor brought the little pigeons and birds, and the rich brought their goats and lambs. The Levites were selecting the sacrifices under the watchful eyes of the Cohens.

"Did you make sure this cow is more than one-year-old, no more than three?" "Yes, I did, Levite" responded a young man before he handed the animal to the Cohen to proceed with the sacrifice. "Remember fellow brethren's, those are the new laws of this land," said the Levite.

"I need more salt and water over here," said the Cohen. And so it went, day and night, people arrived from every part of the land to take part in this triumph of unity. The elders arrived in wagons, others on horses, some on donkeys and many on foot. "Peace be on you, brother," they greeted each other, and each tribe took turns policing and keeping order. "How many tribe elders have arrived brother?" Inquired one Judean organizer. "We know the Dan tribe from the north will soon arrive. We haven't received word about the Benjamin tribe, and we haven't seen their flag flying high above any tent yet. Hopefully they are bringing the murderers as was demanded by the council."

48
"The Burial"

Boaz arrived in Givon looking for Ofra's murderers but knew he must make it back to Bethlehem for the burial along with the other eleven riders traveling back with Ofra's remains. He hadn't forgotten Gershon's words *After they have been examined by the elders, ride to Bethlehem, and there will be the burial. Do not lose time, brothers.*

A Benjamin warrior entering the city of Givon is recognizable. He remembered Yoav's advice not to trust a Givonite for help *They kept their distance from the newcomers who came into the land. Look for Nathaniel the Benjamin, when you reach Givon, he will guide you.* And Boaz did just that. "Peace be on you, brother Nathaniel" Boaz lowered his head so he could clear the entryway of the storefront in the city center. "Yoav sends his regards." The man quickly pulled out a chair. "My name is Boaz." "Oh, the warrior? It is my great honor to meet you. I heard only good things about you."

Boaz smiled, "thank you." "Peace be on you, Brother Boaz, what can I do for you?" Boaz looked around and the man understood. They both walked to the back of the store into a room full of bows and arrows. Two men were busy perfecting the art of making this weaponry. "It looks like trade is profitable nowadays," said Boaz. Nathaniel smiled. A child appeared from behind a linen curtain with a beautiful smile and black curly hair. "Abba," the boy said. "

Many others did, at the hands of the Pharaoh and his advisors. May the God of Moses erase their names." "Indeed" said Boaz. "I'm looking for the murderers of ...." And before Boaz could complete his sentence Nathaniel said "... Ofra the Levite's wife, the Judean"

"Yes," answered Boaz. "They call themselves the Doggies. The Benjees! They were picked up yesterday here in Givon by the Benjamin tribe police. Look brother, the shofar has been echoing all over the Benjamin territory, especially after they heard that the tribes are arriving in Bet-El. I'm afraid the Benjamins young militant generation and some elders, made up their mind ..." He paused, "... not to surrender the murderers. The Benjamin's do not accept the union between Judah and the Priesthood, and they don't want to be told what to do! You know that! You're a Benjamin. And they're determined to keep the Ark in Bet-El and not in Shiloh!"

He then asked his worker to bring bread and cheese and to pack it in grape leaves. "I gather you are in a hurry." Nathaniel continued. "A word of advice, brother Boaz. The slinger of the three is the most dangerous. They never separate. They always stay together. And I see revenge in your eyes. Be careful and be smart, don't let it interfere with your judgement. I know those three men brought evil on all of us. Before you go, take these six arrows. They have the bronze tip and they cut into the air faster than all the others." Nathaniel rolled the handcrafted arrows into a linen cloth cured in oil and handed Boaz a distinguished leather pouch. It was outstanding and made from a superior hide. "Peace be on you brother Nathaniel and thank you for your help."

After traveling for hours from Givon, Boaz entered the city center in Bethlehem. Eleven riders had already arrived. They all greeted each other fatigued and exhausted having crossed the country from all four corners of the land. They sat on the stony earth with Ofra's limbs next to each rider. Ofra's father, unable to walk on his own, was supported by two men who would help him get to the burial site. His pale, dazed, distraught appearance resembled a man who hadn't slept or eaten in days. Safta, weak and frail, insisted on coming to Ofra's burial. She too was assisted by a strong man who held her feeble body in his arms. Rachel and Dina met up with Gershon who was unkempt and looked deeply depressed. Ada was there as well. They were joined by the fast-growing somber crowd. The Jevosite old lady, who in days past sold figs to Ofra, walked all the way from the old market to the Goshen center where they were convened. When the people of Bethlehem realized that the Levite was planning Ofra's burial, they delayed their travels to Bet-El. There was a strong feeling of unity amongst them and most wanted to pay their respects for this young daughter of the Amorite and the wife of the Levite. Gershon dropped a blanket on the ground, and each of the riders carefully placed Ofra's remains gently down. There were twelve limbs, which at one time was Ofra's whole body. Gershon tied up the blanket containing her limbs, from each corner and positioned it on the donkey. He walked while pulling the animal behind him. The procession passed the Goshen Center as they all followed Gershon to the burial site. The procession continued and exited through the town gate, outside of the Judean Bethlehem walls. At the 1000-yard mark, on the right side of the dusty road, the procession stopped.

It was believed by all in this large assemblage, that Ofra's soul hovered over her body, before her soul departed to its resting place in heaven.

They stood quietly and powdered their upper bodies and heads with the dry dirt and ashes from the ground.

Gershon addressed the crowd. "Ofra died young." He was choking on his words. He was scarcely able to speak three words. After a long pause, and trying to compose himself, he barely lifted his head. He made several attempts to dislodge the lump in his throat. He looked so tired. He had black circles under his eyes. His beard had grown longer. It's hard to remember the last time he slept but he continued "She died bravely." This wasn't anything he had done before but he mustered the strength to honor his young Ofra and continued, "She saved the priesthood honor. She saved my honor, and my life. Her brutal death will be avenged in the name of justice. I did what I felt was the right thing to do to show the cruelty in which my young Ofra was murdered. Some of you might blame me for sending her limbs throughout the land. But what other way could we seek justice? What choice did I have? Ofra will go to her grave, united, as one body. There is no higher cause, but the search for justice. Rest in peace in heaven, dear Ofra." Before he collapsed, Ofra's father stepped next to Gershon with the help of the other men and the two men consoled each other in tears.

"Rest in peace my beloved daughter, may the years you have lost in this life be rewarded in the next to come." It was heartbreaking and he fell to his knees and broke down sobbing. Through his grief he managed to utter a few more words, "I miss you my sweet beloved daughter." His head fell to the ground and mumbled "Goodbye my precious Ofra. I will carry your smile to my dying day."

Rachel and Dinah held on to one another, but Dinah buckled to the ground and fortunately Rachel was able to prevent her from falling. This was an unbearable loss for all.

There wasn't a dry eye anywhere and everyone was particularly emotional. They lowered Ofra into the ground and a High Priest from the Goshen center addressed the mourners. "Ofra in your painful death you have united us. We suffered as slaves, and we know the meaning of cruelty, but we will not tolerate it among our brothers and sisters."

Boaz standing next to Gershon, knew no truer words could have been said and he thought '*Yes, Ofra, we will not tolerate the cruelty you endured. I will make sure of it.*" Boaz did not hear any of the succeeding speeches nor any of the condolences as he was obsessed with thoughts of avenging the goons.

A young fellow Levite was addressing the dispersing funeral-goers, "It is important to bury the dead right away brothers. Ofra's circumstance was different. Do not let the dead stay in your home, bury them immediately. When you return home today, wash your hands and wash your feet. If you brought water with you, wash your hands now. We must differentiate between life and death, between the clean, and that which is not clean. Make a distinction with your mind, and with your eyes."

They all followed Ofra's grieving father, Safta and Gershon to Ofra's childhood home.

Chapter 49
"Judgment"

They all convened in Bet-El. The young and the elderly leaders of the twelve tribes all looked for answers and guidance from God. People continued arriving from every corner of the emerging tribal nation. The leaders of each tribe, the elders, the judges, and the warriors of the past, all came to demonstrate unity.

"The Benjamin's are here, and they did not bring the murderers" the guard announced outside of the big tent. Word spread faster than contaminated water and before long the entire camp was agitated.

The leaders of each tribe took their seats in the big round tent on the rocky ground in the middle of the camp. Judah sat up front and next sat Simon. Half of Dan, who chose to migrate south to Akron to be in a more secure hub, sat next and beside a small group of Benjamins. Ephraim the descendent of Joseph and Asenath, the Egyptian, sat next. They were from the center of the land. Next, sitting close to each other was Ephraim's brother, from northwest Manasseh, along with Zebulon, Issachar, Asher, Naphtali and a small group from Dan who remained in the north. Completing the circle from the eastern part of the land, beyond the Jordan passages sat Gad, Rueben, and leaders from the northeast part of Manasseh. In the tent, the leaders and their delegates aligned with their respective tribes totaling almost one thousand people. Although the Benjamins sat amongst the other tribes in the circle, a small group of Benjamin hardliners chose to make their presence known by sitting apart grouped together, with their demeanor suggesting that they were ready to fight. Thousands more disconcerted were descending outside the tent.

"Brothers and sisters," the caller addressed the assemblage in a deep loud voice. "We are all gathered here to hear, and to listen to each tribe, on the matter of the murder of the Levite's wife. Secondly, prior to this gathering, runners were sent to the Benjamin's, by the tribe council, to surrender the three men to face justice. Thirdly, to hear and listen to the matter of the Benjamin's treatment of the Levite and their demand to know him in their territory according to the ways of Sodom and Gomorrah. Brothers and sisters, please stand for the anthem *'Don't avoid my eyes, my brother'* by the Levites choir. Brothers let this anthem inspire us into resolution and unity." The disapproving smirks of the hardliners went unnoticed by most. When the hymn concluded, the congregation sat and four men from the priesthood remained standing.

"We want to make it clear that until the three men face judgment, peace will not dwell in our land. The young woman's blood is an outcry, and the covenant with God must be upheld."

The riders who had carried Ofra's limbs successfully reached one hundred fifty elders and leaders from all the tribes: One elder stepped forward. "We saw the woman's limb. We never witnessed such cruelty among us since we left the house of slavery. The wounds engraved on her young body was a message sent to all of us." Ten elders and young leaders from the Benjamin tribe stood up: One elder stepped forward "to that, we the Benjamin's say and respond that we regret the death of the young woman." After that statement, this group of sympathetic

Benjamins nodding their heads, sat back down. "As to the manner and treatment of the Levite" The eldest member of the priesthood stood up and said "A Levite has the utmost right to come and go among his brothers. This includes the Benjamin territory! What has come over you to blemish the servant of his name by demanding to know him like the people of Sodom? Why, Benjamin?"

A Benjamin hardliner stood up and replied, "To the point of 'knowing him' we do agree that it does insinuate a controversial interpretation, but we stick to our practices, customs and traditions from the past."

A member of the priesthood and tribe elder stood up and replied, "The Benjamin's have no right to enforce their sodomizing ways on others, especially those who choose not to engage in that act."

A Benjamin sitting amongst the tribes added, "To the question of the Levite's right to come and go freely we answer it is the not the right of the Levite to come into our territory and tell us how to live. It is not the right of the Levite or the Priesthood to favor Shiloh or Kiriat Yarim. Bet-El in the Benjamin territory is here, where the holy eternal Shekinah dwells. Moses bestowed his blessing on the Benjamin's to keep the Ark in Bet-El and we are intending to do that."

"Exactly!" spoke a Cohen. "Moses bestowed on you the blessing of having the Ark in your territory and you have the responsibility and obligation to live by the laws of the commandments and to help the tribes enforce them."

The Benjamin continued "We have been abandoned by the priesthood and Judah. We don't want our territory to be passed over. We want to be a destination and benefit from those who come here. Our people feel the anger and bitterness against the priesthood and Judah, and as such, it's true, we did not make the Levite feel welcomed in our territory. We justify our feelings of resentment, which was caused by you, the priesthood." The Benjamin elders went back and sat down.

A Judean elder exclaimed "As to the point that your tribe has been abandoned, it is not true. Times are changing. Our nation is growing. We must allow access to the message of Jehovah and the meaning of the Ten Commandments to the tribes in the north. And that can only be done through the presence of the Ark. Look, the tribe of Dan is looking for guidance for the new the laws of Moses. They have no other means to establish their spiritual connection. Six tribes are already in the north and Shiloh is in the middle of the nation. We must share the time to facilitate access to all the tribes. We must keep the Ark and the Ten Commandments centralized so we all have equal access to the words of Moses, and to make sure we don't get lost in the pagan world. We must unite behind our Priesthood and speak in one voice."

Another elder stood up and brought the group back to the most urgent matter. One thing is clear brothers, no person or tribe can take the law into their own hands. And certainly not to commit a murder. It is the alliances' responsibility to judge murderers, in order to keep peace and unity in the territories of all twelve Tribes."

"The message on the body of the young woman is evident and appears to be directed to all the tribes. We have the right to demand the surrender of the murderers to the tribe's elders because it concerns all the tribes, not solely the tribe of Benjamin."

A Benjamin elder stood up: "We did not bring the accused men with us, but we shall convey to the others, the demand of this forum to surrender the accused. However, we, the tribe elders, and judges of the tribe of Benjamin, take on ourselves the responsibility to achieve justice. We are not of the opinion that the death of Ofra should be judged by an outside court. It is our own internal affair."

A hardliner injected "Our final response will be in three days."

All the members of the Priesthood stood up in unison expecting this opposition but hoping to circumvent their resentment. One elder spoke: "A Levite, a member of the Priesthood in this young tribal nation, was narrowly saved from being sodomized. A young woman, a wife, the Levite's wife was raped, tortured and murdered in a cruel manner, which has not been witnessed since the days of slavery. If this is not a matter of all the tribes, then what is? This is not a matter for the tribe of Benjamin solely, but for all the tribes. We demand the surrender of the murderers."

"We agree! We agree! We agree!" Pandemonium of a thousand men and women erupted.

Chapter 50
"Solidarity"

Three days passed and tens of thousands of people from all over the nation were arriving in Bet-El. It was an amazing display of solidarity and a collective demand for justice for the woman who was murdered and for the honor of the Priesthood. It was the second week since Ofra's murder and the nation was waiting impatiently. The tribal coalition impressed by the magnitude were expecting the Benjamins to bring forth the three men. It was long into the night in the last hours on the third day, but the Benjamins never arrived.

Finally on the fourth day, in the early morning, twenty-six thousand seven hundred Benjamin soldiers were spotted in the distance. The scene of the Benjamin military covering the hill with their shields and swords reflecting the morning sun ready to defend and fight, mingled with the words of the caller, stunned the people.

The caller finally made a declaration.

"The accused men and the undivided tribe of Benjamin speak in one voice. The three men will not be surrendered to Judah and the priesthood."

The Benjamins had no intention of surrendering the accused and when they saw the droves of people descending in their territory in Bet-El supporting the alliance, they perceived this as a threat. Conversely, the coalition was not expecting this kind of response.

The Benjamin leader spoke out. "You don't trust us brother Judah … and you, the rest of our brothers, you don't trust us to bring the murderers to justice here in our territory where the eternal Shekinah dwells."

The Benjamins have not been tolerant of the new Priesthood. They do not want to be ruled by Judah, Simon, or any of these new ways. They will not turn in the three men because they do not want to be told how to conduct their lives. The Benjamins want to uphold the promise of Moses and keep the Ark in their holy territory. They believe this with the strongest of convictions and will not abandon the idea of sustaining Bet-EL as the nation's spiritual center. They feel their hands are forced to defend their position against their brothers and not just because of the murderers. They are ready to die for their cause.

The Benjamin leader continued.

"To those who call themselves our brothers, we are all equal under our creator. He brought us from slavery to freedom and did not appoint a king upon us, as in Egypt. Are we to replace king Pharaoh with a Priest? Or with a Judean king? Moses our liberator gave us his blessing and it is our duty to keep the Ark in our territory were the Shekinah dwells, not in Shiloh or anywhere!" Voices echoed around the camp trying to understand the rage of the Benjamin's words. Speculation was rampant. Some agreed that bringing the murderers would not solve the conflict. Others believed the Benjamins had a right to defend their territory, but their corrupted way of life would infect the rest of the nation. Bringing justice for the surrender of the three men who brutally raped and murdered Ofra became a symbol hoping to putting an end to their sodomizing ways and their moral corruption. But in the eyes of the Benjamin's surrendering the three men meant conceding their way of life and their principles.

On behalf of the entire tribe, the Benjamin caller continues "The tribe of Benjamin is defending the actions of the murderers!"

The council huddles briefly and quickly agree to find out if all the heads of the Benjamin clan and all the heads of the Benjamin families are in accord with this declaration. The speaker responds, "Brothers! Sons of Benjamin! Gives us the permission to approach the head of the families in the whole Benjamin tribe to see if they are all in agreement with your testimony."

The Benjamins needed little time to respond, "We will grant you this permission."

With that said, the Benjamin caller and his small group of advisors rode back to their command center.

The council wasted no time. Judah and the council elders from the tribe of Reuben and Asher promptly agreed on their plan and addressed Eraz, "Assemble a group of twenty-four riders. Two from each tribe and tell them to ride to each city and village in the Benjamin territory. This is what they shall tell the people.

'Surrender the murderers to the tribe's council alliance to face justice'

Carry with you, on your lips, the name of Avidan Ben Gidony and the greatness of this Benjamin leader from the days when we were wandering in the desert."

Eraz carried out the orders and the riders were immediately assembled.

"Twenty-two riders are ready to leave at once," said the officer from the Reuben tribe. "We are missing two riders. ...

from the Benjamin's tent!" "Brother," said one of the elders, look for Boaz in the Benjamin tent. He will be glad to help us."

The officer rode to the tent where the small group of Benjamin's chose to live among the other tribes. "Brother Benjamin, come with us at once, by order of the tribe's council. We need you."

"For what reason, brother Reuben?" "The Benjamin tribe declared that they will not surrender Ofra's murderers. We have been granted permission to verify that the people are of the same opinion as their leaders. And Boaz, go grab another Benjamin to ride with you." Boaz went into the tent as instructed, snatched Dina's husband and returned to the officer.

"Thank you, Boaz, for your great help brother," said the Captain and continued "Brothers, we will start the expedition right now, so let us split into four groups of six riders. Each will cover at least six towns and villages. Boaz, you know this piece of the land better than we do. What do you think?"

"I think it's a good plan, but we cannot split into such small groups. It's dangerous and it would be hard for us to protect ourselves from the people. There is widespread resentment and mistrust. I know. We must go in two groups," said Boaz.

The men assembled in two groups of twelve and departed in opposite directions with Boaz leading one group and Carmi the other.

The first group entered the city of Beeroth. "By the name of the great Avidan Ben Gidony from the days of Moses, surrender the murderers to face justice" the rider proclaimed in a loud voice.

"Traitors! Side up with your brother's the Benjamin's! Don't side up with the house of Judah!" the people shouted.

In the city of Chephirah they were bombarded with stones, and they rushed out of town. In the small villages Boaz was recognized.

"It's our brother Boaz, the hero who is standing with the Levites and the Judeans. Why? The house of Benjamin is not to your taste?"

And so, it went. Children, old men and young, and women, all made sure to step out of their homes, letting the riders know they are in support of their leaders. No one agreed to surrender Ofra's murderers to the hands of the tribes' alliance. It was obvious they were unified in their beliefs. They wanted the murderers to be tried by their elders and judges, not by the Priesthood, and Judah. They were insulted at the insinuation that the justice of the Priesthood was superior to theirs. Lastly and most importantly to the Benjamins, was the resentment over the controversy of the Ark.

"Keep the ark in Bet-EL and not Shiloh' shouted the people from every town and village in the Benjamin territory.

On the third and last day, twenty-four riders returned to Bet-El. The tribe's leaders waited eagerly for their arrival. The exhausted team rode through the night and returned fervently to report to Judah and the council.

"They are all in one agreement, from young to old! Men, women and children. They all speak in one voice."

Several hours later five Benjamin elders could be heard yelling from a distance.

"Those who call themselves our brothers, you are no longer our brothers!" "Are they denouncing the unity of the twelve tribes?" The council members were asking one another.

"Who appointed Judah to be our decision-maker?" the

Benjamin caller shouted. The elder council member spoke. "Matters of the tribes can be solved in council meetings. But now brothers, a murder has been committed. The victim must receive justice. According to the law, you must surrender the murderers!" Word was heard around the nation that the Benjamin's were defying unity and stepping out of the covenant. There was fear that if the Benjamins defected, it could have a chain reaction. "Today the Benjamin's, tomorrow who knows?" The council convened, but only with eleven tribes. As a last effort, word was sent,

"Benjamin, our adversaries are witnessing this feud among us. Why are we giving them a reason to say that we, the Hebrews, are abandoning our God? Benjamin do not create this division in our people. Bring forward the guilty. Let the people go back to their daily lives, and each to their tent and house."

The tribe of Benjamin and the nation were in a deadlock. The people concluded that this conflict will only be resolved through God.

Chapter 51
"Power struggle"

Eight hundred tents were erected around the big tent, the command center. The tents were big and small, square and round, each with their flags, and their tribal symbols flying. Reuben, the eldest tribe, with seventy tents, displayed their red flags with the mandrake flower in the center. Simon, with sixty tents, revealed green flags with a painted topaz stone in its center. The Levite tribe had a black, white, and red flag with the names of the 12 tribes. Judah's flag was sky blue, with a lioness, Issachar, black and blue with the sun and moon. Zebulon had a diamond and a boat; Dan's flag had a sapphire and opal stone and a snake with the justice scales. The Tribe of Gad was black and white with a scene of a camp. Naphtali, had wine-colored flags with a gazelle. Asher with an olive tree, Joseph, with a sheaf of wheat, Ephraim, with the bull and the pyramid and Menasha, his brother, with the wild ox and the pyramid. And Benjamin with the multi-colored flag and a wolf. There were twelve tribes along with the two sons of Joseph, Ephraim and Menasha. There were four hundred thousand willing and able fighters. Some brought their wives and families in solidarity and unity to Judah and the priesthood. They all waited to hear the call of the shofar, the ram's horn, to see if peace or war was eminent. They wanted their voices heard. The Tribes' leaders assembled in the Holy Tent. The question of the day was: "Who will lead this campaign?" Each day that passed, it appeared war was inevitable. The number of animals for the sacrifices of mercy doubled by the hour. The Levites executed their duties in the Holy Tent by sorting out the animals to be sacrificed. They were helped by the Givonite's who made sure the salt and the water supply for the sacrifices were intact. The people anticipated that the next day, when Shemesh the sun god shines, the High Priest would be seen entering the Holy of Holies where the Shekinah dwells. Then they imagined El with all his glory would appear, together with all his divine providence, and show the way, and guide in this time of uncertainty and despair. They knew the High Priest will convey God's will.

They camped in the thousands on the grounds of the Holy Tent, old and young, from the twelve tribes. Some shared memories of the desert crossing, and some even remembered Joshua's great victories. Someone from Dan tribe commented "We did not conquer all the land, and yet we are fighting each other."

He took a pause and in a passionate voice continued. "No tribe can live alone! We must think about what unites us and not what divides us. The pursuit of freedom unites us."

"I agree to that." another man from the Simon tribe commented. "My father told me the story about Joshua and how he saved the Givonites from the Amorites. No way a tribe can live alone. The Benjamins cannot survive alone. We are all in it."

Another man standing by said "This is not the rich land of the Itero in Egypt, my friends. I'm yet to see the milk and honey. But …, … I'm happy to be free." "What do you think is going to happen tomorrow with the Benjamin's? Will they bring the murderers? They always kept themselves apart. Why is that?" said a man from the Asher tribe.

"Well, Joseph was the first prince in the Pharaoh's palace, and Benjamin his young brother enjoyed this preferred status. So here you have it. He grew up to be spoiled."

"And they shared the same mother, who was loved and cherished by her husband Jacob!"

They all laughed and smiled.

"They might surround the murderers, that's what I think is going to happen tomorrow" another man from the Menasha tribe voiced his opinion.

"I hope you're right, brother. But with twenty-six thousand Benjamin elite soldiers in the Givah, across from the Mitzpeh, I don't think so. I doubt they want to bring the murderers to the Priesthood. The Benjamin's want to challenge Judah, and that is what it's all about. They want to build a nation of soldiers. The Benjamin's do not want to be told what to do in their own territory, especially by the priesthood."

"So why do we all have to be dragged into this power struggle?" "It's the price of unity brother. You must agree even when you don't agree." "Oh! And what tribe are you from brother?" asked the man from the Menasha tribe.

"Tribe of Gad, brother."

Bonfires were fading deep into the late hours of the night. The distant jackal howls sporadically shattered the silence.

The young man from the Menasha tribe stared in wonder at the sight of eight hundred tents under the Yareke moonlight and spoke "This is the first time I am witnessing all the tribes so united in this way. One can feel the heartbeat of a young nation in the making."

Chapter 52
"Holy of Holiest"

They all waited with worried impatience for Shemesh to show up at dawn. Butter, milk, bread and olives for breakfast were accompanied by the scent of pine and oak leaves that were ushered in with the breeze and purging the air from bugs. With all the sweet aromas, and the appearance of normalcy, this was anything but a routine morning. Over four hundred thousand eyes focused on the entrance of the holy tent. Finally, after a long wait into the early morning hours, the High Priest walked toward the Holy Tent, tailed by the Cohens and the Levites. The High Priest with a serious look on his face wore a blue robe and tunic, and a colorful belt looped around his body, all assembled in one piece. His head cover was made in the shape of a tower, narrow on top and wide at the bottom. He wore a breastplate of twelve stones with the names of the tribes inscribed on each and the word Justice written in the middle.

Addressing his youngest, a father turned and said, "You see my son. twelve stones. Each represents our twelve tribes. They are placed on the High Priest's breastplate. And we want to keep it that way." The intimation amongst the people was to not let the Benjamins drift away from the coalition, striving for a united federation.

Another man listening to the conversation between the father and his son, expressed his take on it. "And one more thing! The Egyptians have the word truth on their breastplate. We have the word justice because …" the man paused, scratched his head and continued. "… only El possesses truth, we pursue justice!"

The moment arrived. The High Priest walked thoughtfully into the Holy Tent. Soon he would enter the Holy of Holiest where the Ark and the Shekinah dwell. There, God will inspire and put the words in his mouth. The High Priest, the High Cohen, stepped into the domain, slightly trembling from the severity of the moment their young tribal nation was awaiting. His knees buckled, then his hands dropped to the floor, and with his head down, pleaded for direction. His lips mumbled "God almighty. Inspire me with your wisdom to reach the right decision. Our young nation is looking to you for answers. The responsibility is heavy. Should we go to war against a brother, God of Israel?"

The response was sudden, and he was encircled by a glow of enlightenment.

A cloud of white smoke emerged from the Holy Tent. "It's white smoke, it's white smoke!" The roar from hundreds of thousands of people was like thunder in heaven on a summer day and it echoed in the Judean and Ephraim mountains and throughout the land.

"War it will be!" The High Priest delivered the decision. "Judah will go first and will lead." He commanded while stepping out from the Holy Tent.

"Father," said the same young boy, "what happened? Did the Priest see God?"

Before the father could answer, the voices from the people and the high-pitched sounds of the shofar sounded "To the Mitzpeh! to the Mitzpeh."

"Father tell me more about the holy room." The young boy

bombarded his father like rapid fire asking about the shew-bread, the golden table, the Menorah, the candle holder, and most persistently about how the High Priest knew what God wanted the people to do.

"I will my son" he replied while grasping hold of his young boy, and walking swiftly back to their tent so he and his wife can decide the family's next move.

Word was sent and the nation was called to order and in motion. The farmers from all over left their fields, the builders left their bricks, and all that were fit to fight took the road to Bet-El. Every main street in every town and settlement was transformed into meeting points, gathering places. They carried three days of provisions as instructed by the messengers. They came on their horses, donkeys and in wagons which carried their shields, bows, arrows, swords and axes. All the roads led to Mitzpeh, the main gathering point. But in their hearts and minds they all hoped that when the Benjamin's saw this big army, all united and dressed to fight, a war will be avoided. And most importantly, hoping brotherly bloodshed will be averted.

A big, round tent was erected in Mitzpeh and became the command center. From four sides of the tent, each tribe set up their own camps. This became the war of God and his servants, the priesthood, which was advocating and championing the voices for unity, justice, and protecting their image as the sacred and the spiritual divine.

"Judah will go first" circulated the words in the camps. "The High Priest has spoken." Many people voiced their opinion and sided with the High Priest's logic, mainly because Ofra was Judean, and it is the tribe of Judah's responsibility to demand justice.

Close to twenty-seven thousand well prepared and eager Benjamin's soldiers, camped on the Givah, the Hill.

Four hundred thousand soldiers from the twelve tribes, grouped into four formations, and camped downhill in Mitzpeh, on the opposite side of Givah.

"Brothers. as the High Priest has spoken, I am ordered and commanded by his name, our almighty, to lead. I, Judah, shall be the first to face our brother's, the Benjamins! Let them witness how we are all united today, four hundred thousand soldiers strong."

Chapter 53
"Sound the Shofar"

Judah, riding proudly on his beautiful red horse held a sword and a shield engraved with their symbol of the lion. His second in command Eraz, the Judean-born first-generation was strong and solid-looking identical to his master Judah. They rode with eleven riders beside them and formed the cutting edge of their forty thousand Judean soldiers. Behind them, followed four hundred thousand stalwart soldiers, who were fully armed, including archers and slingers.

"Judah! I say let's attack head on from three directions. For a quick victory." Eraz suggested, with full enthusiasm. The anticipation of the upcoming encounter was noticeable all over his young face. It was the first time in his life that he was witnessing unity of the nation in this colossal way, just like the generation before him who witnessed the conquering by the great Joshua.

"My young brother Eraz." Judah responded in a calm voice. "Our brothers, the Benjamin's are from the seeds of our forefathers. They are not our true rivals from across the border. We shall not treat them like enemies." "We shall see brother Judah. I pray you are right." "Who is in charge on the Benjamin side, my young brother Eraz" says Judah mounted on his horse and staring straight ahead. "I think it's Arad, from back at the Goshen meetings." "The one that looked more like an Egyptian soldier? I remember! He's the one that's your age with the curly black hair" Judah turned his head and looked at Eraz. "First generation into the land, like yourself."

"Yes! But we think, we feel, and we act differently, brother Judah." Eraz said with prideful distinction.

Their flag with the symbol of the Judean lion was swaying notably, secured in a leather pouch with a rider on a magnificent white horse. The flags of each tribe prominently preceded their soldiers, all on impressive horses behind Judah's men. "Sound the shofars." Judah gave Eraz the order. Eraz tilted his head back, cupped his right hand over his mouth and gave the signal, screaming "Sound the Shofars!" A coordinated all-encompassing sound of the twelve tribe's one hundred and forty-four shofars resounded. It was followed by silence.

"Benjamin! Benjamin! Come and talk!" Judah stretched his body up on the horse calling in the direction of the hill. His voice echoed in the mountains. And then yelling louder, Judah continued "Let us set a table between us, my young brother Benjamin." The Benjamins heard Judah clearly, but Arad directed his comments to his soldiers.

"Judah wants to trick us." Arad, the Benjamin commanding officer shouted to his men out of Judah's hearing range. "Do not soften your heart, soldiers of Benjamin. Defend your beliefs! Free yourself from those who call themselves our brothers. We shall never be slaves again, not to the Priesthood, nor to Judah. God of Moses is on OUR SIDE! We will defend the blessing of Moses in Bet-El where the Shekinah dwells FOR EVER and EVER!"

There was no audible response heard addressing Judah's plea. Judah knew the Benjamin's superiority in archery but assumed that the Benjamin's might want to make a symbolic show of power toward their brothers, rather than spill blood. Judah allowed his small cavalry of men to go first. He wasn't expecting bloodshed. Sending your small cavalry isn't something that is done in warfare. Judah was in for a big surprise. He was going to realize that Eraz, his young and second in command, was right in his judgment about the Benjamin's.

Before Judah finished his thoughts, the Benjamin's galloping on their horses and sprinting on foot rushed toward the men. By now the Benjamins considered the Judeans not as brothers, but as enemies.

Eraz looked at Judah and said "They made up their minds to fight! ... and to kill us."

Storming and leaving the Hill behind, they showered the men with arrows, spears, and slinger stones. Along with three elite soldiers, Eraz and the men immediately shielded Judah. It all happened so fast. By the time the men emerged from under the barrage of arrows, the Benjamin's were on top of them. The men faced the non-merciful swords, spears, and axes of the well-trained and indomitable Benjamin's. Before they returned back to their hill, which they did quickly, and without hesitation and refrain, the Benjamin's attacked and slaughtered twenty-two thousand brothers, all Judeans.

"They have no mercy" a wounded man lamented. "I lifted my sword" mumbled a wounded soldier full of tears garbling his words faintly. "My hand froze in the air. I couldn't strike but he did. He hit hard and he was cruel. He cut my hand off while aiming for my head. I didn't think I had to fight my brother today" he whispered before he bled to death. A big-bodied soldier murmured on the ground, wallowing in his blood before he died, "And I'm stupid. I ignored my sword, and instead I wrestled the Benjamin with my bare hands! But his sword got both of my hands."

A big cry was heard in the camp on that first day and night. The tribes were in agony and in a state of distress. They gathered the annihilated corpses. In solidarity each tribe sent its wagons, accompanied by the women and the Levites, to help gather the wounded and the dead.

"Don't let the jackals and dogs feast on our Hebrew flesh. Consult with the Levites before deciding if these lifeless bodies are dead or alive. Also ask Boaz to collect his tribal brothers. And give the elderly women everything they need to treat the injured and collect the dead." "Yes, Judah." Eraz responded with sadness while he commanded his officers to arrange the burials and tend to the wounded.

On that fateful day, stories of extreme cruelty and hate reverberated across the nation. Many began questioning the Priesthood and were wondering if this was the way to justice. They were doubting El and fearing the worst. Every member of the Israelite tribes reached deep into their hearts and minds thinking about the coalition's defeat. Especially because it was El who ordered them to go to war against a brother. It was clear that every Israelite faced a challenge of their faith. They recognized that Judah acted mercifully, as a brother, and Benjamin acted like a brutal nemesis. Even though the Priesthood advocated justice for the lack of morality of the Benjamins, still, the Priesthood lost credibility with the loss of the battle. To many it meant defeat, but to others it was a victory for Judah for honoring and elevating his belief and bringing brotherhood to its pinnacle. This realization by the Israelites ignited the first sparks of reason and logic. It laid down the first bricks and it marked the first departure from paganism and mythology which advocates blind belief in Godly intervention.

"El doesn't want us to continue this war against our brothers" many asserted. The morale in the camp was low. The sadness was devastating.

"Why is El the God of Moses not taking sides us? We, who are seeking justice? Why is Benjamin succeeding? Is El with us? We must know."

"We should pray more to the Ashrah and the Baal and not to El?" others questioned.

"Or to the Goddess Anat, the furious fighter! Is she on the side of the Benjamin's?"

Eraz entered the tent and saw Judah flat on his back holding his head between his hands. He was numb, staring at the ceiling in disbelief. "The elders, now more than ever, still believe in you master Judah. The Priesthood as well." Judah heard the low voice of Eraz. "Did you see the hatred in their eyes, my young Eraz. I could not lift my sword, my son." Judah's broken voice was followed by tears. "I saw that, master Judah. We all witnessed it."

Benjamin, the young son, defeated Judah, the moderator, the fourth son, and the lion's heart. Those words traveled around the camp, and around the young tribal nation. It was Judah's naiveté demonstrated in the battlefield, and he paid dearly for his empathy and mercifulness.

The High Priest entered the holy of holiest. Most people believed that God himself was going to come and illuminate the High Priest and provide the guidance just as it happened before.

Will the people continue this battle? That was the question.

The High Priest emerged and addressed Judah "Rise up Judah, meet your brother again. El is with us. Let it be known that Judah was given this order by his holy name, to lead and unite his brothers. To bring justice and defend the covenant. A brotherly war is forced upon us. The Holy name is with us."

This war was clearly a reaffirmation competing for hegemony between Benjamin and Judah and the power struggle between the Benjamin's and the Priesthood. The majority chose to endorse the young emerging Priesthood as the bond that could preserve their unity.

"Eraz, how many soldiers do we have who are willing and able to fight?" "Eighteen thousand master Judah. We lost twenty-two thousand yesterday."

With swollen eyes, tears welled up in Judah's eyes.

"I've never seen tears in your eyes before Master Judah."

"Today, a generation was erased brother Eraz. Young Judeans and young Benjamin's! We never had to fight a brother before. A brother! We walked forty years in the desert and fought shoulder to shoulder so we could live in peace as free men" Judah's devastation was evident in his slumped shoulders, a broken man.

"I saw twenty-two thousand men die today. That's no brother! That's an enemy master Judah! An enemy, a very cruel one, who came to kill us."

"How did my young brother come to possess such hate and retribution?" Judah sobbed into his hands which were covering his face.

This was now a fight for the heart of this young nation.

Chapter 54
"Abhorrence"

Before dawn, the anguish of the previous days' defeat was unmistakable on the faces of the soldiers, but Judah and the entire coalition understood and accepted the order of the High Priest to face the Benjamins who had too much blood on their hands and too much hate in their hearts to be invited to the table for resolution. So, they prepared their weapons and mounted their horses and moved to the observation point where they could see the Benjamin forces ready for battle. But there was still a flicker of hope that the Benjamins would show some sense of brotherhood and some sense of mercy.

In hearing range Judah with a glimmer of humanity addressed Arad the Benjamin top officer and shouted, "Glory to your name brother Benjamin! And to your achievement on the battlefield. Enough blood has been shed. Look behind me brother. What do you see? Four hundred thousand soldiers were all connected by one cause: Justice and Unity! And by the name of the God of Moses."

Silence prevailed and then the voices of the people shouted like thunder from the surrounding hills and mountains.

Benjamin! Benjamin! Benjamin! They continued chanting in unison baffled by the mounting loathing of the Benjamin's until Judah, attempting to grasp the source of the hate continued the proclamation passionately.

"Benjamin, you always regarded yourself as the privileged one. It's true, you were blessed by Moses as a friend to God. And you were unblemished of the brotherly feud of four hundred years ago. Are you renewing the generational grudges of days past? Or is it the new moral code that does not appeal to your taste? Help us understand where this hate killing twenty-two thousand brothers is coming from?

Are you trapped in the past? Is it your ambition to create a rift among the tribes? Do you want divide rather than unite us?" The crowd was ignited as Judah's frustration escalated.

Through the amplified eruption, no response came from the Benjamin's.

From the opposite hill, Arad, the top officer addressed his soldiers. "Benjamin soldiers! The Judeans lost yesterday's battle, and they're back! And they will lose today too because God of Moses is with us and not with the Priesthood! Do not soften your stance now, let us press on to victory! Through this victory we will secure the future of our people. We will never be slaves again. Triumph to the Benjamin's! The future leaders of the young nation!"

With these words the Benjamin army stormed the Judeans head on. They were still intoxicated and enchanted by their victory from the day before. Their hate and brutality was again exposed but magnified. They slaughtered the remaining Judean soldiers and then rushed back to the hill to guard their unprotected city.

The smell of death melted into yesterday's stench. The carnivorous vultures knew the difference decimating the eyes first. It was an easy and quick prey. The wolves and foxes soon followed.

"*God*" Judah lifted his head and with anguished sobs, "Why?

Why? Will it please you, oh God, if I soaked my hands, with my youngest brother's blood?" Judah then fell on the ground in his tent and out of reverence for his fallen soldiers covered himself in mud.

"Judah, Judah!" It was Eraz calling. "Your wife is here." "I cannot see her now brother Eraz; my heart is bleeding; I lost my tongue."

"She insists Master Judah." "Let her in." "My dear husband." His beautiful wife was dressed all in black. She helped Judah stand up from the ground.

"Be assured the people understand. They feel your pain, but they are angry. We all witnessed how a brother turned into an enemy. You fulfilled the Priesthoods order. The people need you, and I need you. Please have this soup to end your fasting. It has been two days since you tasted food."

"Oh, brother Joseph" Judah began pleading up to heaven to his deceased brother. "You raised and nurtured our young brother Benjamin in the Palace of Pharoah, far from Goshen, far from the rest of our brothers. You spoiled him. He became rotten. You taught him the art of war just to end up using it against his brothers. Forgive me, brother Joseph, for what we're about to do. My hands were never blemished from your coat of many colors, now my hands are going to be stained with our brother's blood. We tried to avoid this hour. Oh, Edna my dear wife." continued Judah. "While we were busy building our new homes, Benjamin was busy building an army… just to use it against his brothers." The soup was left untouched.

Chapter 55
"Doubt"

The Benjamins annihilated for the second time. Eraz noticed a large cluster of enraged people gathering around Judah's tent. He abruptly began making his way through the crowd.

"Judah!" a man was shouting as were others in the group "why did you let the Benjamin's slaughter our sons?"

Judah covered in mud, lifted the opening of his tent, walked out and spoke. "We didn't know our brother was so embroiled with hate."

"This is a personal rivalry between you and Benjamin for the tribal leadership. Why do we the people have to pay the price?"

Eraz moved rapidly, pushing Judah and closing the flap of the tent, protecting him from any possible escalating tension.

A Priest was approaching in a colorful two-wheel wooden wagon with two slaves hauling the carriage. "Greetings from the east! Greetings from the land of Nanna and Ningal! The Land of Ur, the Gods of Abraham. Join us brothers and sisters in the name of Nanna. Trust no brother in your day of anguish. Put your trust in Nanna. Your High Priest, the Cohens have no power like the power of Nanna and Ningal."

Another wagon was rolling down the road with a different priest. "I'm Amon, put your child on my knee. I will give you peace and prosperity. Sacrificing your child will stop the bleeding in this brotherly war. Hebrews, your High Priests have no powers like the God Amon."

Further down, children and young girls followed another wagon. "Bring me your gifts, I will give you the holy water. I will multiply your children. Come to me. I will not abandon you the way your God Jehovah is abandoning you now. I'm Baal the master of this land who brings you rain and prosperity, together with my wife Ashrah. She will fertilize your womb and bring you a child." A man scooped water with a wooden spoon and poured it into their open mouths.

"Judah" Eraz called. "Let me silence those priests on wheels who speak against our High Priests and Jehovah. They are spreading confusion among the minds of our people." "No need brother Eraz. Let them speak freely, our faith will prevail."

The people in disbelief began dissipating. Walking with their arms raised and their palms covering their heads, they bellowed "What kind of God is the God of Moses? Which God did we offend?"

Chapter 56
"Covenant"

Early morning at dawn, Judah, and the leaders of the twelve tribes assembled in the commanding tent.

"Judah have you lost your lions roar?" spurted the leader from the Simone tribe and then turned to the others and continued "Judah is our leader! Our unifier! Our moderator! We can no longer witness this ruthlessness. Brother's, we are being torn to pieces. Let us unite our forces and put an end to this torment."

A man from the Naphtali tribe stood up "Benjamin is challenging our brother Judah and the priesthood. They are ignoring our code of ethics and dividing our unity. Benjamin is breaking our alliance."

The leader of the Gad said "Benjamin is not willing to surrender the murderers. They spilled their brother's blood only to defend their depraved people."

Before the meeting officially opened, Boaz and the small group of Benjamin's, who lived amongst the tribes asked to speak next. Boaz was standing on his good foot supported by a crutch made from a large sturdy branch under the opposite arm. His sword was made to fit his measurements, strong and sturdy exactly to his knee, a sign of a professional warrior. They all turned in his direction. "Brothers. They call me Boaz the crippled because I lost my left leg when I fought Nehoshtan the wicked. But with only one leg, I still can fight and so can this small group of Benjamin's who are with me now. We would like our brothers to promise us, that we, the Benjamin's who live amongst the tribes and not in the Benjamin territory, will be trusted and safe. We understand your anger, we see it on the faces of all of you. You are all our fellow tribesmen; we too are outraged. The hatred the Benjamin's demonstrated is reprehensible and unforgiveable." Boaz paused for a moment and continued. "We are not in agreement with Benjamin, nor does our way of life resemble theirs. That's why we chose to live apart." Boaz sat down. Dina s husband, a handsome young man, a fellow Benjamin, stretched his hand and put it on Boaz's shoulder. The leaders noticed his gesture which gave them the reassurance that these Benjamins were all in solidarity.

"Raise your hand if you agree" pronounced the head council. It was unanimous. Boaz stood up quickly "We ask to carry the Benjamin flag." They all agreed. Hands were raised again.

"All have agreed." The councilman responded.

"My name is Menasha, brothers. I am afraid that my heart is heavy; how can I raise the sword while looking in my brother's eye?"

The eldest council member stood up. "Hebrew brothers. Not far from here, twenty-six thousand and seven hundred elite soldiers, fully armed, slaughtered us. You have the right, not only to defend yourself but to kill the one who raises the sword to you."

Another council member stood up. "Fellow brothers. It was not a long time ago since we entered this land. We did not conquer it all. Some of us married the Canaanites, and they married us. Some of us worship their Gods but they find it hard to understand ours. Brothers, the tribe of Benjamin went too far.

They adopted the ways of Sodom and Gomorra. They forced their corrupted ways on their brothers, the ones they inherited from their golden days in Egypt before they were slaves. Now, I don't mind if they want to continue to practice their ways and customs among themselves. Our God has given us the right to choose. But, to force them on others, the way they demanded from the Levite? Now that's unacceptable. Let's not look back brothers. If the tribe of Benjamin chooses to stay in the past, let it be. But Benjamin has no right to drag us into their ways. We do not have to accept their practices which they think are superior to ours."

"They lost themselves to their thirst for power" someone shouted from the back of the tent.

A young council member stood up from the Dan tribe. "Brothers, the Benjamin's adopted the Egyptian slogan: Put no trust in a brother, acknowledge no one as a friend, nothing is to be gained from them, for no man has anyone to defend him on the day of anguish. Brothers, I'm sure some of you are familiar with this slogan but we are free people now. We cherish brotherhood and friendship. Today we lost more than fifty thousand of our brothers. We are united behind Judah and the priesthood, more than ever. We put our trust in a brother and understand Judah's dilemma for treating Benjamin as a brother instead of as an enemy. But NO LONGER!"

Judah stepped forward and proclaimed. "The one who is not with us, is against us. For the next three days and for every one hundred of our men, ten people shall supply food. Every able man must join the ranks." The word went out. Judah's voice gained confidence and momentum. "Is there anyone here, from the town of Yavesh Gilead?"

Eraz responded "Judah, runners were sent to speak to the elders of the Gilead to have them join us as brothers to the covenant. The runners are riding through the night."

"We shall soon know if the Gilead is with us or against us, to serve the covenant and to fight for our brotherly cause."

The head army officers of each tribe remained in the tent. Top officers in the front row, first officers in the second and third row. They all formed a big circle on the sandy ground with their feet folded.

The proclamations began.

"I Judah, with my brother Simon under one command ready to serve the covenant and the Priesthood for unity. We left behind five thousand fighters to guard the boundaries, securing our back to Edom in the south, and protecting us from the sea people, the Philistines, from the west."

"I, Rueben ready to serve the covenant and the Priesthood for unity. We left behind four thousand fighters to secure our boundaries with "Moab" in the south and Ammon to the east. We are ready to unite with Judah and the priesthood."

"I, Gad, with half of the Menasha tribe under one command ready to serve the covenant and the Priesthood for unity. We left five thousand fighters to secure against the Ammonites to the east and the safety of the Jordan passages in the center of the land."

"I, Dan with Asher under one command ready to serve the covenant and the Priesthood for unity. We left four thousand fighters to guard the north passages via the Bashan Mountain top and the big sea to the west."

"I, Zebulon with Naphtali and with Issachar under one command ready to serve the covenant and the Priesthood for unity. We left behind five thousand fighters to secure the northern Jordan passages via the great lake to the east and the great sea to the west."

"I, Ephraim with the eastern half of Menasha, west of the Jordan river under one command ready to serve the covenant and the Priesthood for unity. We left five thousand fighters to secure against the sea people to the west, and with our brothers Gad and the other half of Menasha, to guard the central Jordan passages."

"We are representing the Benjamin tribe under one command ready to serve the covenant and the Priesthood for unity. We are from the seed of Benjamin and ready to fight for justice."

They were all accounted for. Four hundred thousand fighters.

Chapter 57
"The Plan"

Ten experienced runners sent by Judah entered the town of the Gilead just before dawn. The elders were expecting the messengers. Word of their arrival preceded them. They met them at the gate, not far from the statues of Baal, Ashrah, and El, their God's. They heard about Benjamin's great victories.

"Peace be on you, house of Gilead" the runners greeted the elders. "Peace be on you, house of Judah" the Gilead's elders replied. "House of Israel!" The runner commented as a correction to the welcome call, insinuating that there is a covenant among all the tribes.

The horses were given water and feed. They could tell from the unruffled look of the elders that the news traveled faster than a flying arrow.

"I read to you this message from Judah. To the people of Gilead. Peace be on you. Benjamin is unwilling to bring the murderers to justice, and they are challenging the agreement and the unity of the coalition. El has spoken through the High Priest and has appointed Judah to lead in this conflict. We the tribes are united. We will honor the covenant. As brothers, you are hereby called upon to join us in this war. If tomorrow, Ammon and Moab rise against you, we shall unite under the promise to protect you. Today we shall know if you are with us, or against us."

The elders gathered and whispered to each other. Then they proclaimed. "This is what you shall tell Judah. We are not with you nor against you. We shall not join the house of Judah, nor the house of Benjamin in this brotherly war." The ten riders left Yavesh Gilead and rode as quickly as they were capable to bring Judah the reply.

Back in the commanding tent, the Judean officer was briefing the leaders.

"These last two days our Judean mountains and hills have been saturated with the blood of over fifty thousand men. The truth is out! Benjamin lost their moral fiber and became an enemy invader. Today we reclaim our integrity brothers. As the order of the day, place these words into your heart: Ofra is not forgotten but by now we know we are not fighting a brother. We are fighting an enemy whose intentions are to destroy us. Gather your strength. Order your men to avoid the eyes of the enemy. No soft-hearted man shall take part in this battle. Not only will he lose his life, but he will soften his brother's heart who is fighting next to him. To those of you who just became betrothed, or for those who are dedicating a new home, speak to your officer to be relieved, if you want too of course. Let us bring an end to this sad and painful division in our new and young federation's history. The Benjamin's want to create a rift among us, but we will not let them. Brotherhood will not be crushed nor broken."

Eraz stood up and as instructed by Judah announced, "At this moment, I would like to ask all the third in command and below to leave this tent. You will be informed by your superiors shortly."

Half of the members left the commanding tent unsure of what was to come next.

The tent was sealed, and the guards made sure not to let anyone in from both sides. "Brothers" said Eraz, the top Judean officer. He slid aside a curtain and exposed a miniature hill made from sand. It had a hole on the side indicating the cave. Downward from the hill, lines were drawn in the sand that led to a point, marked by a circle, with the name "Mesilot". The lines on the sand continued to another point, with the name "Baal-Tomer". The word "desert" was revealed at the far end of the sand.

"Brothers. It is critical that this plan be kept secret. It will be executed in the battlefield as we go. A selected ten thousand men from the tribes of Naphtali and Zebulon, will gather by the cave. The officer pointed with his stick to the hole in the sand on the side of the hill. Some of you familiar with the cave know that it's too small to contain all ten thousand soldiers. But if we use the bushy area around it, there is a way to congregate together. Its rocky walls will serve as additional places to hide. The Gad tribe suggested securing leafy branches on our bodies to disguise ourselves the same way the Nubian people mask themselves in the land of Kush." Short lived sporadic laughs broke into the air from that briefing. Eraz waited until the steeled seriousness returned before he continued. "At the first sound of the shofar, the remainder of the tribe's fighting force will engage the Benjamin's. When you hear the trumpets, RETREAT! Then immediately retreat in the direction of…" he pointed his stick "… on Mesilot. Benjamin will surely chase us at that time. Our fighting force will continue to retreat to Baal-Tomer right here." He pointed his stick once again. "When the Shofars are again sounded, it will mark the end of the retreat. By that time the Benjamin's will be far enough from their center. The ten thousand men from Naphtali and Zebulon will emerge from the cave and storm the city on the hill. They will burn it to the ground. After they're ambushed, the Benjamin's will turn their horses to go and protect their town and villages. When they realize their territory is going up in smoke, their mouths will get salty, and their morale will be broken. The rest of our forces will close in and trap Benjamin from both sides. The forces from Baal-Tomer will turn and become the chasers. We shall follow them until no Benjamin remains standing. That concludes our order of the day."

A man from the Naphtali tribe stood up "Judah, Eraz! What happens if Benjamin will not chase the fighting tribes?"

"Brother! We think they will. This is exactly what they did, twice, in the last two days. Again, I stress the magnitude for keeping this plan secretive." Eraz instructed an officer to walk on the sand box dismantling the master plan for the demise of the Benjamins.

Chapter 58
"Last Briefing"

Ten thousand selected soldiers from Naphtali and Zebulon tribes secretly maneuvered to the mountain cave and its surrounding vicinity during the night. It was a Judean summer morning and approaching the third battle between the Benjamin's and the alliance. A formal military procession preceded the mission. They all wanted to be a part of this sacred mission. It was a display of shields and horse riders, foot soldiers, archers, slingers, and the Shofar blowers. It was a magnificent display of strength and unity. Each tribe with its own flag heralded the line, with the symbols engraved on the shield of every soldier. With the sounding of the shofar, the four hundred thousand soldiers began a coordinated ceremony. Left and right, up and down, front and back, all were directed by the rhythm of the drums. The shofar resonated in the Judean and distant Moab mountains. Their spirits were lifted. They all knew when the formality concluded, it would be Benjamin's judgment day. Some soldiers didn't realize how significant their fighting was going to impact the future of their young nation. Leaders and officers were told to gather in the big round tent for the last briefing prior to the final assault on the hill. It was an open forum. Judah's words were to be circulated among the tribes. "Brothers! Hebrews! By the end of the day the Benjamin tribe will be eradicated. It is the decision of all the tribe leaders and the priesthood! By sword and by fire the Benjamin territory shall be destroyed and burned to the ground. We will prevent the spread of their disease. This is not a struggle for power between me and my younger brother Benjamin, as some of you may think. No brothers! Their immoral and unrelentless hatred has no boundaries. We lost our young brother to their unwillingness to pursue justice and they betrayed us. If tomorrow there were to be a big war, will we be able to count on them? NO! Their hands are bloody, and their hearts are oozing hatred and they have clouded their capacity to reason. They spilt our blood, and you are the witness. Our people mastered the shield, but now we will use the sword. With the small remaining fighters from our tribe of Judah, we will attack first. Then we will be followed by the others. Engage and kill! It is the order of the day. We will pull back Benjamin to Mesilot and then to Baal-Tomer, and then we strike. And those who manage to run, shall be lost in the desert where they belong. No spoils shall be taken. If you do, you will bring disease to your home. No one shall have the right to accuse us for spilling our young brother Benjamin's blood. Not now, and not in generations to come."

Chapter 59
"The slinger, The Bow, The Ugly"

Before sunrise, and before Shemesh faced the hill, the sound of the shofars signaled the beginning of the battle. The Benjamins too, heard the shofars and thundered down the hill. The attack started. As planned, Judah and his main coalition forces began fighting the hard-core soldiers of the Benjamin's and before starting their retreat, showed just enough resistance and signs of weakness. They were risking the Benjamin's foretelling their strategy. The troops had total assurance knowing the victory of the last two battles, intoxicated, weakened, and clouded the Benjamin's overconfidence and judgment. As prearranged Judah gave Eraz the hand motion and the trumpets blew loud and clear. They all heard the blaring sounds of the united tribes retreating signal. The Benjamin's believing this is yet again a victorious pursuit went into a hunting frenzy. Judah's plan was working perfectly. The Benjamin's with their swords out in front, and their bows spitting arrows were in a killing fury equal to the previous two triumphant rounds. The retreating forces increased their speed and running away fooled the Benjamin's further and further from the hill, in the direction of Mesilot. Benjamin, determined and convinced of their victory continued chasing the tribe's legion. After they reached Mesilot, Baal-Tamar the second post was their next destination. The Benjamin's laughing and cackling in their arrogance were confident the alliance would now be destroyed. They were ready to finish what they started the first and second days of the war. The retreating horsemen positioned the shields on their backs, and shielded themselves from the Benjamin's arrows, while they continued their well-choreographed withdrawal. They waited with anticipation for the sound of the Shofar; the signal for Nephtali and Zebulon to emerge from the cave to burn their cities.

"Oh, brother, why don't I hear the Shofar?" a rider said anxiously. "Hold your breath brother. The Benjamin's are speeding away from their territory exactly as planned. The Almighty El is with us."

The alliance outnumbered the Benjamin's, so watching this huge force running away from the much smaller one seemed absurd.

"Let us stay close together as in the first day" Boaz yelled to Dina's husband Elon, just as the horseman who was carrying the Benjamin flag for the Judean side fell off his horse. He was hit by an arrow and followed by a loud shout. "Traitor! Traitor!" Boaz rushed to pick up the falling flag which distanced himself from Dina's husband. At that moment an arrow appeared from nowhere and flew in the direction of Elon. Boaz, carrying the flag in one hand turned back his horse, saw the bronze arrowhead making its way to his friend and with his good leg lifted his knee onto his horse's back. Still riding, and with his shield upright attempted to intercept the arrow in midair. It clipped his fingers, before landing in Elon's chest. Boaz looked in the direction where the arrow came from and saw a very young boy, maybe fourteen or fifteen years of age, standing frozen. The boy looked at Boaz with regret and guilt, still holding his bow. At that moment, Yoav spotted Boaz looking at his young junior soldier and intercepted before Boaz had a chance to retaliate. Their eyes met. Yoav pointed to his right, in the direction of Ofra's murderers.

"The Bengies" he whispered. "I'm not going to fight you, brother Boaz." Yoav spoke and sped away on his horse.

"And I'm not going to fight you either, brother Yoav" Boaz uttered to himself. Boaz looked in the direction where Yoav indicated. The Bengies, Ofra's killers.

Shouting like blood thirsty assassins, they screamed to each other "There's Boaz! The professed hero! The cripple! The brother who sided with the enemy!" "We're the crazy Bengies" the three men screeched while circling him with their horses.

"Woman Killers! Woman Killers! Woman Killers!" Boaz screamed incessantly, aggressively propelling his horse in their direction.

They fought as a group protecting each other. Boaz remembered Nathaniel words from Givon ... *the slinger is the most dangerous one.* And for some strange reason Ofra's words came to him *Next time do not try to take five men by yourself.* But now looking at her murderers, rage superseded her warning *Heaven be on my side for Ofra's sake, in the name of justice.* He kept repeating this to himself. Of the three, the slinger, rolling his wrist wound his weapon in rapid circles preparing to aim for Boaz's head. The archer loaded his bow while the third murderer moved his horse to protect his two cohorts. Boaz concentrated on the slinger, the more dangerous of the three. He knew that if this slinger was a shepherd, he was good at keeping the wolves away when herding his goats. It meant he mastered the art of the slings which required a high level of accuracy. By now, the slinger was ready to fire so Boaz leaned down and whispered into his horse's ear. His horse whinnied and violently threw up his front legs. The slinger did not calculate this sudden movement and missed his target and instead of hitting Boaz head, the stone landed on his shield. Boaz took advantage of the pause while the slinger was loading another deadly stone. The horseman moved to protect the vulnerable slinger, the ugliest of the three and left the archer exposed. His arrow was now ready to embark on its deadly intention, but Boaz had the special bronze-head arrow Nathaniel gave him when he was searching for these three lowlifes after they murdered Ofra. Already prepared with the arrow in his bow, he said, "This one is for you Ofra" and nailed the archer to the ground. But now the slinger was on it again, and at that very moment an arrow came out from nowhere and landed in the slinger's chest. Boaz turned his head and looked and was shocked to see the young boy who killed Elon, now saved his life. Both looked momentarily at each other while nodding their heads, but their moment was quickly interrupted by the blaring pitch of the shofar. The rams horn reverberated throughout the land and as planned; ten thousand men emerged. They had been hiding in the cave. They joined their fellow soldiers and continued to storm the unprotected Benjamin hill consisting of twenty-four villages in total. They started to burn the towns.

The third crazy Benjie looked up at the city and saw the smoke was climbing up and down the hill. He turned his horse and bolted to the hill, but Boaz raced after him, he was not a match for Boaz.

"This is for Ofra" Boaz declared in a revengeful voice as he imbedded his sword straight through the assassin's heart. Boaz saw the boy who saved his life hesitating for a second, not knowing which direction to go. He noticed the chase was now in the opposite direction. "What is your name, boy?" Boaz asked as he moved closer to see the young boy who had just saved his life.

"Itai," he replied. "Oh! You're the young man with the goat mask from Yoav's training camp," said Boaz. "Run toward the desert, may the almighty be with you." The boy turned his horse away from the hill and rushed enthusiastically in the direction of the desert where he could hide in the Edom mountains.

By now, hundreds of shofars sounded from the hills and valleys and to the mountains and all the way to Baal-Tamar in successive triumphant notes. The Judean fighters lifted their heads up and shouted *Thank you oh God. Thank you, Jehovah.*

Chapter 60
"Revenge"

The Judean soldiers entered the unprotected towns torching every house and every structure. The smoke intensified as the Benjamin forces were rushing back to the hill. Their spirit was broken when they saw their towns filled with the dark smoke going up in flames.

"Have no mercy Judeans! This is no longer a Hebrew town! Burn everything to the ground and eradicate. Their cattle are full of disease, as are their women. They poisoned their children to hate and tomorrow they will be our future enemies. Take none of their possessions. Take no spoils of war! This is the order of the day." "Oh, brother how can I kill a child in their mother's arm? A baby in their mother's bosom?" one of the Judean soldiers said while sobbing. "Brother! The Benjamin's killed forty thousand men and Bethlehem Judea is now a house of husbandless women and fatherless children. Have mercy for our widows and orphans. Here, in the Benjamin territory with no men to feed and protect, hunger and disease will reign. Save the women and the children the agony and send them back to their creator."

Judah looked straight at Eraz and knew exactly what he was contemplating. Judah saw the look of revenge in his eyes "Eraz, do not leave this formation! That's an order!"

"Too much brotherly blood on that man's hands." Eraz pointed his sword in the direction of Arad, the top Benjamin officer. Ignoring his master's order, he instantaneously sprinted after Arad. "Follow him!'" Ordered Judah to his top three officers. Arad rode as fast as he could. He entered the first Benjamin town. It was torched and burning.

Eraz maneuvered among the blaze and saw Arad and his riders disappear into the yard of a big house. It was ablaze. Arad knew he was being followed by Eraz.

"Go protect the towns." Arad ordered his men. They ran off.

Arad yelled "Eraz, I don't wish to kill you." "I have no desire to live after you have murdered forty thousand of my men." Eraz was angry.

Arad shouted "Let me die among my men here, on this Benjamin soil. Have no mercy on me Judean officer! Go ahead! Kill me!"

"Our swords will determine the end brother! It is in God's hands now! Fight me here" Eraz declared. "As you wish, officer Eraz!" They descended from their horses and faced each other.

The three Judean soldiers on horses were circling the burning town looking for Eraz while these two opposing men were fighting among the blazes.

Both Arad the Benjamin and Eraz the Judean, in exhausting combat, were completely depleted and could not lift the sword any longer. Arad was a well-trained professional soldier and Eraz, although lacking in schooling and preparation, was not easy to be defeated. What Eraz lacked in training and experience he made up for in perseverance, grit, and endurance.

"Go ahead Judean, you are using your shield too often! Strike me hard. Do I see mercy in your eyes? You know only hate wins in a battle! Don't fight me with mercy, it degrades me." said Arad while they wrestled each other with their swords dangling from their hands.

"Maybe I don't see enough hate in your eyes either, officer Benjamin!" continued Eraz. "Or maybe I was not taught how to hate a brother. But for the forty thousand brothers you killed, I'm determined to kill you. I owe this to them." "You are using your shield again Judean! They taught us how to win or die. And besides that, we will never surrender to Judah. We will master the sword and will never master the shield. And never again be slaves to anyone, Brother Eraz. We would rather die."

With those last words, Arad hit Eraz' shield formidably and threw Eraz to the ground. Eraz managed to hold Arad's heel and dragged him down.

A mother and her three children witnessed the two men fighting among the blazing fire. They were hiding for fear of being spotted by the Judean soldiers.

"Go Benjamin, kill him, kill him!" said the oldest of the three children. He was no more than thirteen years old. He folded his fingers and punched the air like a boxer. He was cheered on by his younger brother, each time Arad pinned Eraz to the ground. The mother embraced her daughter and the two boys and protected them from the fire.

Arad, laying on his back, saw the log, which supported the wooden roof, engulfed in flames. The wooden plank was about to crash down on the mother and her three children. Arad quickly reached with his sword and inserted it between the floor and the beam. The mother and her three children escaped. Arad was left with no sword, and no protection. Eraz looked in amazement at this heroic and sacrificial act by Arad. Arad still on the ground, forced a smile on his bloody and sweaty face. In an instant this well-trained soldier exposed his humanistic instinct overpowering his duties as a warrior to fight and kill to the end.

Among the blaze the Benjamin riders spotted their officer Arad, but only after a woman blackened with smoke all over her body pointed to the direction of the house. It was almost too late, as an arrow from the Benjamin guard was on its way and directed at Eraz.

"No." shouted Arad with the last trace of strength. He threw his body over Eraz with so much effort for protection. The arrow penetrated Arad's heart.

At that moment, the three Judean officers arrived and saw the Benjamin guards lifting Arad's body. The arrow was protruding from his chest. Eraz was lying beneath the Benjamin. They positioned Arad on the horse, and they took off.

"Let them go" said Eraz ambivalently with tears in his eyes.

Chapter 61
"The Ploy"

"We have been tricked, back to the hill, back to the hill." The last of the Benjamin's forces continued to shout in a state of confusion. By now they were no longer chasing the Judeans and turned their horses toward the hill where they saw a massive infantry burning their towns. The ten thousand Judeans who had been hiding in the cave along with their fellow soldiers were executing the well-orchestrated plan. The defeated army looked left and right, forward and back, but they were trapped. The trailing legion of the Benjamin's had only one option, to head to the desert near the mountains of Edom. Desperately, they continued to run, but many were killed as they were being chased.

"He made me do it!" A young Benjamin soldier cried as he fell on his knees begging for his life. He pointed at his sergeant. His friend pointed at the officer too. Their training officer preferred to fall on his sword after he realized it was too late.

The final verdict was obvious. Many soldiers tried to avoid their bothers eyes and moved their heads away during the slaughter. And although rage and anger overwhelmed the united tribal forces led by Judah, their hearts were broken knowing that this was not only a tragedy but a travesty.

"Itai, Itai" an older Benjamin man shouted, while he rode behind the young boy. "I told you, not to drift away! Stay close to me! They're determined to kill us all." "I heard you, brother

Yoav," Itai answered while they sped away. "Brothers! Benjamin's!" Yoav continued to shout his commanding orders to their small group of escapees.

"Save your life! Head for the mountains! Escape to the selah, the rock and hide."

A Judean soldier emerged perpendicularly chasing Itai. Yoav immediately cut him off and pointing at the dark smoke rising above the Benjamin territory screamed "Save your life Judean! Let the young boy live. It's over! It's over!"

"You dogs! You killed three of my brethren" shouted the Judean with his sword nearly reaching Itai's leg. "I'm no longer your brother! Traitor! You are no longer my brother" the Judean man said in anger.

Yoav jumped and yanked the Judean off his horse and pinned him to the ground. Itai rushed off knowing Yoav would prevail.

"It's over brother! No more killing! Have mercy on the boy." Yoav spoke in a broken voice while forcing his sword away. Leaving the Judean on the ground unscathed, Yoav jumped on his horse and caught up with Itai and the fleeing cluster.

Exhausted, fatigued, and weary, Yoav and the remaining Benjamin's soldiers including the wounded, finally made it to the Edom mountains.

The Judean coalition continued to ride deep into the Benjamin heartland territory burning down the villages. Having ridden through the night with torches, they entered the city of Parah in daylight. One of the riders from Zebulon was startled and said, "This doesn't look like a Hebrew town, it looks more like a Canaanite Town."

"Do not touch any of their belongings! Burn everything! Do not drink their water, or touch their food, nor their cattle! No war spoils!" the Judean officer ordered his soldiers in a serious tone.

The news about the Benjamin defeat had not reached here yet. They caught the people of Parah in the midst of celebrating their victory of the last two battles. At the center of the town, children, women, and men of all ages were gathered around the big statues of the Canaanite God Baal, and the Goddess Ashrah. Naked women, young and old, climbed the Baal from all directions erotically resembling a snake curling on a tree branch. Their tongues were licking every molecule on the body of the stone Baal, all in a dream-like trance. One woman turned to another and said, "Beg him to get you pregnant!" "Oh, Baal God of fertility, make my husband love me and give me a child."

Another woman sat on the lap of the Baal statue and looked around in a hypnotic state.

The soldiers approached the statue of the Ashrah with their swords forward. The naked man who was hanging on the neck of the Goddess jumped down to join his friends who were all put to the sword. After they burned Parah to the ground, they continued to the city of Bet Huron. The further they traveled from the battleground, the more they witnessed the lewd scenes of celebration. Everything they observed in Parah repeated itself in every town throughout the Benjamin region. By the next day in the vast territory every Benjamin met their fate.

Chapter 62
"Sorrow"

"Look at them. They're killing each other. A brother killing another brother" a Canaanite store owner from Jericho was conversing with his friend. The city of Jericho fell into the Benjamin inheritance. When Moses gave each tribe their designated piece of land, Jericho fell under the dominance of the Benjamin territory. Although they lived symbiotically, there was a clear division between the Canaanites living in Jericho and the Hebrew Benjamins living in their twenty-four towns. The Canaanites living in Jericho were wondering what was going to happen now that the Benjamins were annihilated.

"But why?" "Because a woman was raped and murdered."

"A woman? Are they crazy? Was she touched by the Gods?" "She was a priest's wife. I heard that more than fifty thousand soldiers died. Do you think it was revenge?"

"Makes sense to want to redeem her honor."

"This is crazy! Are their Gods vengeful? What a strange God."

"If it's not revenge, why are they killing each other?" "I really don't know. Our priest said that the holy man separated himself from his brothers because he didn't accept their demand 'to know him'. You know, the way we do. Let me tell you something, the Hebrews have no chance of survival in this land. They don't think and act like us. Today they obliterated one of their own tribes! Tomorrow they will all worship our Gods, because our Gods are stronger and now, we're the majority."

"Time will tell."

Another man overhearing their conversation chimed in, "I think their God is stronger. Their God Jehovah helped them conquer all the land. They even settled in the North. They're everywhere."

The merchant replies "I wouldn't worry about them settling on the coast in the north, because the sea people arrived with their vessels, and they rob and steal. And if the Hebrews want to confront them, it's good for us. I never trusted those fair-skinned Philistines from over the great sea, with their God Dagon. Let the Hebrews do our dirty work and protect our land from those filthy thieves."

"Do you think Egypt is going to let the Hebrews take over this land?" said the store owner's friend.

"No! Ramses, the Pharoah, feels more threatened by the sea people, than by the Hebrew slaves who just left his land. They'll make sure they have control of the northern gate. Look, the Egyptians are in Hazur for that reason," said the man who joined their chat.

The store owner, concluding their conversation, became confident with his words. Everyone living in Jericho heard the trumpets and the sounds of the war. "Let them all fight! We love our Jericho! Besides that, the Benjamin's won't be breathing on our necks anymore, trying to take over our cherished oasis. I heard they were all killed by Judah," he stated with conviction. They all concurred and went on their way.

*****

Back in the camp in Bet El, the last briefing was about to take place.

Voices of revenge and anger in the land slowly subsided.

Sadness penetrated every corner of the young nation. People from all around were voicing their opinions. Judah standing in front of thousands of soldiers, stood with his back to the Benjamin territory still in smoke. "Jacob, our father lost his youngest son Benjamin and not to the Egyptians! And we lost a brother! This is not a day of victory. This is not a day for celebrations. It is the first day of our mourning."

Judah paused, lifted his head and continued. "This was the most heartbreaking day for our people. While our brothers were trained to win at any price, we fought with mercy in our hearts and lost forty thousand good honest kindhearted men in two days of fighting. There have been no other wars where so many died because they couldn't bring themselves to kill a brother. Vowing to defeat our warrior brothers, we did not soften our hearts in the last battle, and they shall all be remembered for generations to come." Judah lowered his head respectfully and solemnly and then continued. "Before I let the elderly take over this podium, we must give recognition to the tribes who participated in this struggle. And before we dismantle this camp and go back to our families, let us acknowledge all of those who arrived in Bet El, no matter how early or how late you joined us."

The counting started with Reuben, then Simon, all the way until they reached the Benjamin's. Boaz rising on his good foot hoisted himself proudly. All the officers in the tent stood up with utmost respect.

Boaz addressed the assembly of his fellow soldiers. "I am a Benjamin, son of Jacob. I crossed the desert with you, and fought the serpent Nechushtan, and lost my right leg. Boaz raised his left hand and revealed his dismembered finger that was covered with a bloody cloth. Nine fingers!" Boaz continued, "I am left with only nine fingers. Will we dismantle a house if a wall is broken? Look at me, I'm crippled with one leg and nine fingers. I am a house with a strong foundation, but some of my walls aren't flawless. I am still alive and can challenge any warrior with the strongest knee." Boaz continued articulating clearly. "This is my request to you brothers. In the desert, in the deep south, by the rock, six hundred men are counting on me. I'm their only hope. I am pleading to you, my brothers, we have had enough killings. Hear me oh brothers, please spare them and let them live because the foundation of their house is good, and their walls can be repaired." Applause erupted for quite a long time and the entire assembly were on their feet. It was clear that all would honor his plea.

The tribe elder finally took the stand. "Brothers. When this camp is dismantled, a person must be careful when they meet their families back home. Burn any clothing spotted with blood. Before storing your sword, knives and axes pass them under fire to erase any traces of blood which might carry disease to your home.

Do not boast about your victory in front of the eyes of anyone. There is no victory in a brotherly war. When you are back home, conduct the ceremony of washing your hands, and not only when you come back from this war, or from the field after you attend to your needs, but more often. Additionally, brothers, if you want to show your mark of brotherhood, know your brother according to our new laws. Knowledge of the spoken word is different from knowledge of the body, unless of course, it bears a child. Lastly, store the words of our almighty in a small leather box which represents the Ark of the Covenant. I see some of you are already doing it. Place it on your head to orient your thinking. This will help you to think in the right and just way; to think with your head, and not with your body."

The council elder went back to his seat and Judah took the stand. A soldier approached him and whispered in his ear. Judah made a final announcement. "Brothers, is there anyone here who came face to face with anyone from the Gilead's?" There was silence in the tent.

"Who are the ten runners we sent to the Gilead elders?" Nine men stood up. "As you know Judah, we lost Yechiel in the last battle." He continued. "Judah, we met the Gilad's elders and as instructed, we conveyed the order of the covenant to join the war. We gave you, their response. We fulfilled our mission." "I know, I know. Did anyone from the tribe of Gad, Manasseh or Asher spot anyone from the Gilead on their way through the Jorden passages, to Bet El? Or at any time?" Judah communicated each word clearly. Again, there was silence in the tent.

"As we stated on the first day of this war, those who did not join us are against us. Gilead breached the covenant of our unity. They took sides with the murderers. To us it can only mean they are sympathizers. What will happen, if tomorrow we need them to join us against the Ammonites? … or the Moabites? Will they be here for us? I say, let us send twelve thousand men from all the tribes to burn and cleanse Gilead. Spare only the virgin women. This way a new seed will grow, and we'll witness unity in the future of our nation. They will not know the inherent ways of the past."

"I don't mind being rewarded in this bloody war by getting a beautiful woman from the Gilead's" whispered a soldier to his friend. "Me too." His friend replied unsure if they would really be rewarded.

Judah paused again and cleared his voice and continued. "Unity and the covenant among brothers was not upheld with our adopted brothers and sisters in the Gilead. This is the will of the council. It must be done now."

Eraz prepared the men in advance. "Twelve thousand men are assembled, and ready to go to the Gilead, at your command" said Eraz.

Judah addressed the congregation with his parting words. "God be with you all." He then watched the trove of people lugubriously heading out.

Chapter 63
Four Hundred Virgins

Twelve thousand soldiers rode through the great lake valley, via the north passage of the Jordan River. They crossed through the Manasseh territory. The soldiers were welcomed in every town and provided with bread, water, and honey. The mountainous city of Gilead bordered the Ammonite nation to the south and the west. There were no signs of Ammonite intervention in this Hebrew conflict. The streets of Gilead were deserted. The souk, the stores and their homes were closed. They locked themselves in. The people of Gilead shielded themselves in a deep silence. They realized their leaders were mistaken not joining the war against the Benjamin's.

"It resembles the days of Joshua when they captured Jericho" commented one of Judah's older riders.

The tribe forces entered the towns of Gilead, all resembling the cities in the Benjamin territory. In the street, the Baal and the Ashrah goddess stood tall next to Ammon, the child sacrificing idol. There was no celebration in the streets. By now the truth was out. Benjamin was defeated. The Gilead's broke the covenant and knew they would be confronted by Judah because they betrayed the unity.

"Do not trust this silence. Everyone knows the Gilead's won't go down easily. They'll fight! Our officer was right, they're deeply in fear. We'll go house to house; they'll go down fighting to the last one."

The order was to bring out every young woman who has not known a man and if she lies, twice she will be put to the sword. The Gileads went up in smoke with heartbreaking screams. The girls were rounded up at the town center by the feet of the Baal, the Ashrah, and the Ammon. Some were half-dressed where they were running from their burning homes. Hours passed, and many more women were brought in, from the other towns and villages. Those in fear of their life surrendered, some chaperoned on horseback. It went on and on, day and night. By the time this mission was over, four hundred virgin women scared to their souls were the only ones left standing in Gilead. On the morning of the third day, thirty-eight enclosed wooden wagons were lined up. Before noon the caravan of virgins escorted by the remaining soldiers, were on their way to Bet El as ordered by the council. They passed through the territories of Manasseh and arrived at the Jordan Passage where they were once again welcomed. Messengers from Bet El waited to instruct the caravan.

"It is the decision of the tribe's elders that this caravan will not go to Bet El! You will travel to the city of Shiloh." This was significant because the Benjamin's defeat manifested Shiloh being crowned the central worship center which would now benefit all of the nation. The dissention was over. "This was coming" said one of the soldiers on horseback guiding the mid part of the caravan. His buddy replied smiling, "Reality dictates. Bet El will no longer be the dividing force among us."

In front of the two soldiers, one girl was extremely agitated and screaming. Shaking the wooden enclosure of the wagon she yelled "we're going to be sold to slavery! We are Judah's slaves! I should have thrown myself into the well like my friends. I'm going to be sold to slavery?" She couldn't control her hysteria.

"Shhhh. We're going to be ok" said another girl hugging and quieting her despite the searing anger raging inside her entire body.

The soldier, in an attempt to diffuse the panic, calmly spoke "It is not the Hebrew way to make slaves of our relatives."

Another girl rocking feverishly while holding the wagon bars, shouted, "My grandfather told me they give the most beautiful girls to the best fighters!"

Another girl with a drooping head, shouted "Are we going to be their prize? Are they giving us to the soldiers?" Then she continued sarcastically "… to the victorious heroes of Judah?"

They began recalling their grandfathers' stories about the aftermath of war that prevailed in those days. Soldiers on the winning side were rewarded with beautiful woman, slaves, cattle and land.

The young girls, many who resembled the beauty and age of Ofra, were engulfed in fear and horror. Most were sitting on the wooden floor of the wagons, heads down, with their knees to their chin, hands crossed embracing themselves. Others were hugging each other, but understandably all were in shock.

From the beginning of the trip, one of the thoughtless riders who had been continuously eying a sobbing beautiful young girl spoke "Be happy you are alive girl"

Ignoring him, an older girl put her arms around the crying girl. "I heard we are going to Shiloh. What is your name?"

"Livnat" the young beautiful girl with swollen eyes responded in a soft voice.

"What is your name?" asked Livnat shyly. "Rimona."

"Don't listen to him" commented another girl. She was annoyed and irritated and added "He's stupid." The ignorant rider blurted out jokingly "Hope you are a virgin!" "Stay next to me. You'll be fine," said Rimona to Livnat. With his back to the girls and their distorted faces they snubbed the moronic soldier mouthing curses.

Food and blankets were provided. Over this weeklong journey their tears and screams exhausted and gradually turned into silence. The caravan detoured and continued to climb up the Ephraim mountains. Word spread quickly across the land about the four hundred virgin girls making their way to the city of Shiloh.

*****

In the opposite direction, in the deep south of the country, in the hot steamy Edom caves in the land of Moab, six hundred Benjamin warriors lingered. Fatigued, hungry and wounded, they found refuge and shelter as they waited for their fate to be determined by their brothers. They kept their hopes on Boaz, their goodwill messenger and spokesman. "I hope Boaz convinced the elders of our plea." said Yoav who by now emerged as their leader. His voice was fatigued, and weak, he continued "I say, let us not fight any longer even if they come to kill us. Boaz will ask them to spare our lives and let us put our faith in the hands of our almighty. He will extend his justice and will determine our destiny. I think we can all agree that too many killings have taken place." Dehydrated, starving and broken, they all agreed.

Sadness hovered like a black cloud across the vast federation. The people were in agreement that a resolution to these tragic events must be reached and that an outcome for the remaining Benjamins must be decided immediately. But the elders in the council were conflicted. They were undecided, dithering between eliminating the remainder of the Benjamins or allowing them to live.

No one across the nation was happy with the delay. The people believed that unity could be achieved again. Forty years wandering in the desert certainly surfaced some misunderstandings and disagreements among the twelve tribes but never caused a division, And four hundred years in Egypt, with all its ups and downs never caused a rift among them.

Twenty tents were erected, in a camp in Shiloh. The people awaited the arrival of four hundred virgin daughters of the Gilead's. The long caravan finally entered the town after a long journey. The wooden bars on the wagons which confined the girls were removed. They were sitting next to each other with their feet warily dangling out, like exhausted harvesters returning to camp on wagons after a hard day in the fields.

They entered Virgin City as it would become to be known, to sweeten their poor devastated hearts, Shiloh artists, dancers and musicians brought milk, cookies, blankets and clothing. The girls teamed up into groups of twenty to a tent. Some crashed to the floor trying to sleep away the agony of their losses and the shock and pain of the trauma,

As time passed, the gut-wrenching crying was slowly replaced with random whimpering. Parents were not forgotten, nor brothers, nor sisters, nor friends, nor family animals. Sixty days passed for this group of orphans and each day became slightly easier than the last. Each morning brought hope for the next day. Virgin City slowly transformed into the City of Hope.

By the time ninety days passed, tent city became more challenging for the four hundred young women crowded in their small quarters.

No tents, however, were erected for the six hundred Benjamin refugees constrained in the caves. They were battling nightmares from their losses similar to the girls in captivity. The men, the escapee's, had to combat the anxiety of not knowing if their lives would be spared. Life was miserable in the caves, but Boaz made sure they had food and water. They became more hopeful as the impending threat of death seemed less eminent as the days passed.

Chapter 64
Change

In the south, in the mountains of Edom, the red flamed sun inhaled the sobbing from within the stone caves. It distressingly reached the ears of all the tribes. Throughout the land the people sensed the pain of the six hundred men. Their silent cries penetrated the hearts of every soul. "Almighty in heaven, let no tribe be cut away from his brother. Restore our days as in the past." Boaz' words echoed across the land. "Bring the new, out of the old."

People's voices of forgiveness and rebuilding, grew louder. For the tribe elders, the pressure mounted, especially from the young generation. The youth leadership felt emboldened. *"Elder's! Let us mend the pieces and bring Benjamin back into our fold for the sake of peace, for the house of Jacob, the house of Israel and for our young nation."*

Three more days have passed since the irrevocable heated debates ensued between the young and the elders. "We swore that the Benjamin's will no longer live! Now you're telling us we should keep them alive? You, the voices of youth are ignoring the fact that the Benjamins brutally raped, tortured and killed a young girl in your new young nation. Ofra, a young Judean girl from your generation fell victim to their blindness and their frozen beliefs of the past."

The young leadership stood silent.

The Elder continued, "How will we ever be trusted again if we don't live up to our word? If we breach our vow, they might come after you and then after your children's children tomorrow. You really want us to pardon those six hundred Benjamin murderers and keep them alive? What do you think will happen if one day in the future a man from the Gilead lineage will inquire about his forefathers. He will learn that the Benjamin's refused to surrender the murderers of a young girl and that Gilead's stood by and supported the Benjamin's not living up to their promise of unity with the twelve tribes. And don't you think they will want to know why we kept those Benjamin's alive but not their Gilead ancestors?"

The young leadership remained muted for another few minutes huddled together discussing their innocuous views and chose an articulate young man from Asher to be their spokesman "You accused the Benjamins of not changing with the times and claim they are stuck in their ways. Now look at you? You are just like them. You're doing the same thing." The young councilman received encouragement and pats on the back from his young colleagues.

After listening to the youth and hearing what they had to say, the elders took their time to reply. They realized their young future coalition made a good point. Additionally, they did not forget the plea from Boaz and remembered how this Benjamin warrior not only sided with the twelve tribes but singlehandedly killed Ofra's murderers. So, the commitment of Boaz the Benjamin and his plea to spare his fellow survivors who were suffering in the caves, along with the youth's appeal to change with the times, helped them to reassess their resolve. It looked like a decision was starting to emerge. The elders realized the time was now and replied, "If the High Priest gives his blessing, we will keep the renewed seed of the Benjamin tribe alive through the six hundred men in the caves."

Everyone across the young nation had hope that mercy would emerge victoriously.

Chapter 65
The Benjamin's Fate

The news circulated around the country that the High Priest was dying. The nation held their breath. Time was essential for the six hundred Benjamin's in the south as their fate was in the hands of the High Priest. The torching sun, and the limited water in the desert was their enemy, and if a decision wasn't made rapidly, they all will die.

Leaders of the twelve tribes gathered in Bet El. Boaz was there too. The High Priest, in his dying bed, requested to see Boaz. By now all the nation heard about Boaz and they all agreed that he will be the spokesman, the official representative, of the Benjamin exiles.

The High Priest, almost one hundred years old, was lying on his bed with his eyes wide open, gazing at the ceiling. His long white beard covered his skinny boney chest. Boaz walked into the room, supporting himself with a wooden crutch made perfectly to fit his underarm comfortably. He was fatigued and his bronzed skin was burnt from the scorching sun, traveling back and forth to the six hundred fellow brothers in the caves of Edom.

The High Priest waived his finger to Boaz indicating for him to come closer. He whispered in Boaz ear. "Oh," said Boaz out loud. "You're asking me why I decided to leave my brothers tribe, the Benjamin's? And live apart?" "Yes," signaled the High Priest slightly nodding his head.

In a loud voice resounding beyond the walls of the room Boaz made sure the aging man heard him clearly.

"The Benjamin's wanted to remain, and dwell in the past. I want to live in the present and the future."

The High Priest again beckoned Boaz to come near and whispered another question in an even softer tone than before.

"Did you just ask me about mercy for my brothers?" Boaz wanted to make sure he heard the question clearly. "Yes" The High Priest nodded and blinked his eyes in response. "Definitely, I feel love and mercy for my people." Boaz answered the High Priest.

Boaz thought he saw the Priest's facial muscle move when he heard the word love, but the High Priest closed his eyes, and the meeting was over.

Voices of hope, reconciliation, and mercy for the six hundred Benjamin's was the intense topic from the Dan tribe in the north, to the city of Beersheba down south.

It was finally decided. The High Priest had spoken before he died. "The Benjamin's shall live."

The council sent a message to Judah, to Boaz and the leadership. They needed to make preparations to bring the six hundred men out of the caves. Judah had no idea where to transport the men. The council debated among themselves but once again couldn't agree on an exact location. Some proposed sending them to the Gilead territory, others suggested to head North. This went on for days. Boaz, getting impatient, couldn't wait another day so he went to Eraz to ask for help to gather wagons. Eraz was feeling conflicted about the tremendous cruelty the Benjamins displayed in the battlefield brutally killing their brothers, but at the same time he was having a flashing memory of Arad the heroic Benjamin General who sacrificed his own life and took an arrow to save him. He rubbed his forehead in deep anguish and then finally agreed to help Boaz gather the wagons. Judah would be in charge of sending an army of men to escort them to the "rock" in the deep south.

Back at the meeting, an Elder from the council asked to speak. He said "I know this is going to sound crazy but hear me out. We, the Israelites, swore by the almighty that we will not give our daughters to a Benjamin. But what if we take the Benjamins to Shiloh and unite them with our adopted sisters from the Gilead?"

"Well, that looks like we are truly going to have a marriage made in heaven" said another elder.

"It looks like we are going to have many marriages from heaven" said a third elder. Laughter broke out among the council. They all stared at each other. The solution was obvious. It was a rational decision. Their judgement was logical.

"Go tell Boaz, there is no time to lose."

The council concluded three grueling days finally reaching their decision. They entered the house of peace! The war was over.

Chapter 66
Out of Exile

Malnourished and wounded they waited full of hope. They had no idea what would come next but finally heard voices. "Peace be on you" the messenger called out at the opening of the Edom Mountain caves.

Walking out to greet the runners, the tired, weary Benjamin's approached "Peace be on you our humble and forgiving brothers."

"Peace be on you, sons of Israel." Boaz repeated the greeting along with the messengers sent by the elders. "Benjamin's, cleanse yourselves! Store your sword! But pass it on fire first. Put the words of the almighty in your head, and in your heart."

A big rejoice transpired outside the caves in the camp that night. It was a long four months in the Edom desert waiting for the anticipated news.

"It felt like forty years" said one man with eyes full of tears. "You know I never wanted to go to that war, but we were forced to agree with everyone back then" he turned to his friend.

"Let's not think about it anymore," another man said in a low barely audible voice.

"Let's forget about it!" another man chimed in. "Maybe a lesson can come from this" injected another. "Whatever the almighty does, it's meant to be, brothers." It was early morning and six hundred men, the sole survivors, the exiles of this brotherly war, packed their few belongings; candles, a little water each soldier managed to save and some food they had been rationing. They left the caves with no desire to look back. Half of the men lost their horses to starvation and dehydration. "I hate this place!" said one of the men. They made their way down from the caves forming groups. They were united by brotherly bonds which the war created. Some of the men walked their undernourished horses hoping to keep their steed alive and those without horses marched on foot. The wounded were carried on wagons. They were on a difficult journey with Shiloh approximately one hundred twenty-five miles away. Walking with their compromising wounds and malnutrition it would take them about eight to ten days. They were escorted by the tribe's soldiers. "I did everything to keep him alive," said one man looking at his dying horse only a few hours into the trek.

They passed Baal-Tamar and then took the eastern route via the Dead Sea into Judah territory. They camped and refreshed in En Gedi. After several days of traveling, it was a welcomed oasis.

They all dreamed of a simple hot cooked dinner and something sweet to redeem their bitter tongues. They all needed a good bath. Many of the war survivors were not able to walk any longer. "That wound from the war never healed brother," one man said to his friend with a weak voice. "Anyway, what do I have to live for? I can no longer go on." "Put him on the wagon." said Yoav, just as the man collapsed. "We will make sure he makes it to the final destination. WON'T WE?" Yoav said while he forced his weak vocal cords to make sure everyone was listening.

"Is it true, virgin girls are awaiting us in Shiloh?" "So I heard" responded his friend. "What happens when a virgin girl meets a virgin boy?" asked the young soldier

"Don't worry. You will know what to do when the time comes. But just a little advice my young virgin brother, go easy! Don't bleed the young maiden to death." The man said while he forced a laugh. "No woman can replace the mother of my children," said another man lamenting. His friend responded, "keep your eyes on the future; give life a second chance brother."

"Funny, how the war ended …" one of the men continued "… virgin women awaiting us?" "It is only when the war is among merciful brothers" replied one man forcing a smile. "Brother Yoav" Boaz spoke loudly while they rode slowly next to each other. "What did you say back then in the Benjamin territory in the arena? … about the error a fighter might commit in the battlefield?" "Ah, brother Boaz, you did not forget that conversation …" Yoav continued, and then answered "…it's mercy!"

"Well, brother Yoav, look around you …" said Boaz while he turned his head, and pointed his finger in the direction of the six hundred Benjamin soldiers heading for Shiloh. "… this is the outcome of mercy." Boaz then paused and continued "Mercy my brother Yoav, is hope. In mercy there is birth. In mercy there is a tomorrow. The Egyptians extended us mercy, almost five hundred years ago when we were hungry. That's why we had a tomorrow to live for."

The two men continued the journey heading north.

Chapter 67
Take A Wife

It was now Autumn in the land of Canaan. The early rains forcefully descended on the lowlands. A couple of days later there was a pause giving the fragile floral time to peek out of the ground, to be strong enough to sustain itself against the forthcoming downpours. It was beginning to get colder by the time the war survivors inched closer to the Ephraim mountains. They were exhausted.

The Holy Ark too, was making its way to Shiloh as well. Gershon and three Levites where in charge of accompanying the Ark. Four hundred virgins from Yavesh Gilead have been in Shiloh for months. And the six hundred Benjamin warriors were, on their way, to where else … to Shiloh.

"Child murderers!" came the shouts as the six hundred men passed through the villages. The guards interfered and protected them. "The almighty will punish you for taking my husband," screamed one woman. "They already paid the price …" a guard yelled back "… they have nothing left." But some people in other villages brought food and even honey for a sweeter future. The first group of Benjamin warriors entered Shiloh on a rainy and cold afternoon. Their horses were fed, but no one came to greet them and wash their feet. Tents were built by the coalition before their arrival, not far from the virgin city. Special tents were assigned for the wounded. It had been five months since the war started and they were still recovering. They grouped twenty men to a tent.

The next morning it was dry and beautiful, and the last wagon arrived in Shiloh.

It was as if nature collaborated with their welcoming. It took ten days for this last group of six hundred men to arrive. Butter, milk, honey, fresh bread, hot soup, and even meat was provided. It strengthens their bodies and spirits. They didn't eat a hot meal for a hundred and fifty days. They cleaned and bathed. As days passed, more empathizers came by bringing shirts, tunics, and sandals. Some people were curious about how a man who possessed hate might look. Others wanted to see what a man consumed with cruelty looked like. One guy pushed through the crowd, trying to get closer to the arriving Benjamin's. He stared at their eyes and tried to detect a look of hate.

"Do they look different from others? different from us?" he wondered. "They are like you and me" said one of the guards. "With one exception. Their minds were poisoned by their leaders, and they were manipulated into thinking that they'll be slaved by Judah and the priesthood. Do you blame them for believing that?"

Another man voiced his opinion. "Judah has the Priesthood, the Cohen's, the Levite's and the tribe of Simon on his side. And the Benjamins were concerned that one day they would be overpowered by Judah and the Priesthood."

Another man jumped into the conversation saying that he heard that the Benjamin's truly believed they were protecting the Ark to remain in Beth El as they were promised by the blessing of Moses. The guard responded. "Brothers, open your mind. Believe what your eyes see and what your ears hear. Isn't that what the Levite did after Ofra's murder? He sent her body parts to the twelve tribes for all to see and witness with their eyes. To see what the Benjamin's had done. How else can one convey the truth but with their eyes?"

"I believe Gershon did the right thing" another man stated his opinion. "My wife and I decided to live by the Ten Commandments" he looked at his wife smiling, they both looked happy.

Four days later, on a beautiful Tuesday morning, the tribe elder addressed the Benjamin's at a big open-air meeting.

"Peace be on you my brother Benjamin's. Mercy has engulfed our brothers' hearts. May we never have to come to this again. A brother shall never have to raise a sword on a brother. We did not find it within us to exclude you from our young nation. All of you here, six hundred strong, a big burden rests on your shoulders. From you, there will be a new tribe in Israel."

A subdued pride and joy penetrated throughout the camp.

The elder continued, "The people of the twelve tribes of Israel swear by his almighty name, not to give their daughters to a Benjamin. The Gilead's are not part of the twelve tribes, so, you can take a wife, a virgin wife, from the daughters of the Gilead. When this wife will bear your eldest son or daughter, you will begin to build a family. You will respect the mother of your children. You will go back to your territory and build your homes." The meeting ended and the Benjamins, with a multitude of reactions to this surprisingly wonderful turn of events, dispersed to their tents.

They were, however, unaware of the one lingering problem. There were six hundred men and only four hundred women. The council elders were perplexed not knowing what to do with the remaining two hundred men.

"Let them choose each other." said a young council member. "… and let's rejoice in freedom." They all agreed.

"But we still haven't resolved the problem of the remaining two hundred Benjamin's?" an elder asserted.

"We'll worry about that, when the time comes," another council member responded.

"For now, let us have a celebration of unity and rebirth."

"Did you hear that? I am forced to take a woman from the Gilead!" said a Benjamin.

"One can never satisfy us spoiled Benjamin boys" someone made a counter remark joking and smiling. He then looked at his friend. "Well, you seem to brag a lot about getting the prettiest girl, you now have your chance."

Chapter 68
Fishing Bait

For the first time since Ofra's murder, Boaz was finally able to reflect on the chain of events that had been flying by. He hadn't been able to pause or rest for many months and now taking a deep breath, he sat down under a fig tree in Shiloh. He took out his sword and leaned it on the tree trunk looking at his leg or what was left of it. The healers cut the lower part, but by now it healed, and the pain had finally subsided. He began reflecting on the events of the last five months. A bystander noticed Boaz and while looking at him said, "It's hard to be a hero brother. You always have to live up to it."

Boaz did not know what to make of that comment and said, "You just have to do, what you have to do, it's not a choice brother."

"It's a free man's choice" Boaz whispered to himself afterwards.

It was midday, the sun rays targeted Boaz while he took a nap under the tree. He suddenly jumped and opened his eyes and said to himself, "*Did I just dream about a flowery jasmine bath?*" His horse was reading his owner's mind because they both headed straight to El Sati, the nearby tavern and bath house. Naim the owner, welcomed Boaz and was happy to see him. Smiling, he said "The Egyptian girl is here Boaz, but all the rest of the girls went to look for a Benjamin husband in the love fest. That's why it's quiet around here." "Did you tell them that the Benjamin's are more interested in virgin girls?"

Boaz replied with a long and loud laugh. Naim found that comment funny, and he burst into a hardy chuckle. Hearing the laughter, the Egyptian girl joined them in the reception area.

"I was just dreaming about one of your aromatic baths" Boaz said looking at her. She smiled back and showed him the way, with a welcome gesture. When Boaz was finished, he thanked Naim, and left his coins in the dish. Boaz felt so rejuvenated after that well needed fragrant bath but left hurriedly because his help was always needed back in the camp. While exiting El Sati, he noticed a young man just getting off his donkey. "Brother Alipaz?" said Boaz in surprise. "I'm so happy to see you! Did you have the same dream I had?" he said with a big smile. "Oh brother Boaz, yes I did. All this time in the refuge city, and I always remembered your words and advice. I'm so happy to see you brother Boaz."

"Well, here is another piece of advice my young brother Alipaz. Back home in the Ephraim mountains, at the water well, a young woman was asking about you all this time. I think her name was Tamar. She said that she will wait for you until the day the High Priest dies, and you would be set free. Brother Alipaz," continued Boaz in a fatherly fashion, "Go get your jasmine bath and hurry back home, where true love is waiting."

"I will do that brother Boaz! Thank you." Alipaz ran into the bathhouse and Boaz took off to the camp.

Four hundred young freshly bathed women, some younger than others and many beautiful and some less beautiful, emerged from their tents, walked to the streets and into the delightful, sweet groves of Shiloh. Six hundred young men emerged from their tents. Some young and others not as young, some healthy and several wounded. They flooded the streets mingling with the girls. One person would describe it as the biggest union of orphans ever assembled in that era. "Stay next to me" said Yoav (the much older) to Itai (the much younger and more handsome Benjamin).

"Why? Is this a war?" Itai responded with an amused voice. "I heard that sometimes finding the right woman, a wife, is the biggest challenge in life! They say it's a war up there!" Yoav tittered and continued after a moment. "And how else, will a woman look my way at this old man if I don't have my handsome young friend next to me?" "Oh, I'm being used as fishing bait! That's great!! If that's how it goes, it's worse than a war, my brother Yoav." Itai responded while chuckling.

They all got to meet each other on that first day of the wedding fest. They were all connected with one past, a painful one. They shared their stories and cried on each other's shoulders. One could clearly see and feel the underlining pain extracted from their smiles.

"Livnat, come my daughter, let's go, the men are waiting. Alot of them!" said Rimona with a prolonged gaze. "Oh Rimona, my heart is still heavy. I have nothing left. I cannot think of a boy right now." "It's ok" said Rimona "A boy usually comes to your life, just when you're not thinking about it." Livnat forced a smile. "Let's start by inviting Shemesh, the goddess of light to enter our tent. It is dark and lonely here. Then, let's go and meet the new day. Besides, I don't want to miss meeting the handsome Benjamin men. I heard there are six hundred here." Rimona pointed at the tent entrance and walked to the opening and lifted up the cover. She was giggling and laughing while trying to cheer up young Livnat but she herself was nervously bouncing back and forth. "Come! We must get beautiful first, at least I need to.

The Gods of the Gilead's extended youth and natural beauty to you Livnat."

"Do not say that Rimona! You are beautiful as well!" "Is that why I'm still a virgin? Do you think my virginity is keeping me looking younger?" Rimona said sarcastically. She continued "Men weigh too much on youthful beauty, as if it is eternal. But we all know it is a God given gift. Speaking of the Gods …" she continued " … will we need to believe in the God of the man we marry? The God of Benjamin?"

"Which God is that?" asked Livnat curiously.

"Oh, Livnat, no one can swear they have seen that Hebrew God. They say that the one who sees him dies on the spot. They call him El, Jehovah, not the father of Baal and the Ashrah, but the other El, the God of Moses. Let's not think about it anymore." "Oh," Livnat said. Her eyes glowed with wonder. "Come, sit down right here on this chair, let me comb your beautiful hair. Then I suggest that you put on one of the lovely white dresses the old lady brought to us the other day." Rimona brushed Livnat's hair to a shine and tended to her own primping while Livnat dressed.

After a short time Rimona spoke "Here, I'm done with the bronze mirror. I am ready. The other women will be here soon to borrow this magical mirror." Rimona pulled up the tent cover again and looked outside. "Mmm six hundred men out there, Livnat" Rimona whispered.

Two more women rushed in and asked to borrow the mirror which began circulating around camp. "You both look beautiful," the girls exchanged compliments to each other.

"You look good as well" Rimona responded. "… when you spot a handsome man, do not look straight into his eyes" said Rimona

"I would never do that" Livnat said raising her voice in a higher pitch.

"We have a saying in the town of Gilead," continued Rimona. "... Beauty speaks for itself but provoke the man with your charm." Rimona was speaking nervously as if she was trying to assure herself more than the beautiful maidens. They stepped into a cool sunny day just perfect to start a new life. Many of their friends felt the same excitement in their hearts. The girls from Gilead walked in the enchanting, artsy Shiloh streets and groves. They walked next to each other and mingled with many men from the Benjamin's exchanging looks in all directions. After walking for a while, suddenly Livnat paused and elbowed Rimona. "Look at that cute boy with the big guy" she whispered. Livnat hadn't shown interest in anyone up to this point, so Rimona knew just what to do.

"Benjamin, why are you dragging that handsome boy with you?" Rimona blurted while Livnat blushed.

"To make me look good!!" Yoav laughed heartily. The girls giggled.

"I like an honest answer" Rimona said. Two other men got closer to Livnat. "Brothers, move on, those two are taken." Yoav's stern voice meant it.

"Oh yes?" declared one of the men while he lifted his head, as if he was ready for the challenge. "Oh yes!" Rimona replied and her smile sealed the deal. "What is your name, young boy?" asked Rimona. "Itai," "Aren't you too young to fight a war?" Rimona said while she moved aside and allowed Itai to walk next to Livnat, which placed her at Yoav's side. "I made it through, thanks to him" Itai said while he looked at Yoav.

"My name is Rimona." "And my name is Livnat." Their voices

mingled. "I have a good raisin bread, let's sit, and eat under that tree." Rimona suggested. "I have a good jar of wine" Yoav commented. "I have some honey" Livnat volunteered "And I'm already hungry" said Itai. They all sat under the tree and spent the afternoon sharing stories and getting acquainted.

Chapter 69
The Promise

On the third day, couples emerged, and group weddings were performed. It lasted a week and although Shiloh was known to be the art center of the country, with dancers and musicians, they had never experienced such an extravagant spectacle. It was a love fest of sorts and now husbands and wives paired off to negotiate their compatibility. There wasn't one virgin girl from the Gilead, who didn't find a husband. Some couples rode on their horses while others walked, but all to the Benjamin territory where only traces of recollections were left. Planning their future were the newlyweds' main aspiration for their new lives together.

The love marathon finally exhausted itself, and when it was over, two hundred men were left without a wife to claim for their own. Realizing four hundred of their friends left with their new wives, the unattached men were worried, because they knew the tribes made an oath not to marry their daughters to a Benjamin. The tribe elders from the coalition convened, reality demanded action but a solution for the two hundred men wasn't coming quickly. After two hours, there still wasn't a resolution. An elderly local leader from Shiloh who had been sitting in the rear listening and watching the meeting, was walking slowly to the front and finally approached the podium. "If you allow me to speak?"

The coalition looking skeptical waved him on as if to say ok hurry up, say what you have to say.

The old man spoke slowly. "There was an old mating custom in Shiloh, which can still being practiced today. Our women go to the groves and dance with garlands, bells, and tambourines. The men circle the women, it looks like an ambush, and when they spot the one they want, they snatch her, put her on their horse and take her to be his wife. We can bring that ritual back." The old man said his peace and a younger man helped walk him back to his chair.

Another elder local stood up from the back and said, "I think it would be wise to use that custom now." The locals started vocalizing their support and their experiences and it became quite noisy.

The tribe elder from the coalition stood and began to speak " Ok ok. Settle down everyone. We want to thank you for telling us about this ritual that many of you seem to be familiar with. We did promise not to give our daughters to a Benjamin.

So, if we decide to implement this custom, and the fathers and brothers question us, we shall have to tell them that we acted upon the consequence of war."

"Blame it on the war, brothers!" shouts were heard from the crowd.

"No, blame it on Judah because he didn't bring enough virgins from the war!"

The tribe elder continued while raising his hand to hush the attendees. "Shhh. Yes! When the war ended, we didn't bring enough young women. And now we are incumbent to find wives for the remaining men."

They all agreed because there was no other option.

Chapter 70
The Wounded

Word about the upcoming mating ceremony swept quickly around Shiloh and all the neighboring villages. Many professional dancers and entertainers were elated at the opportunity to marry and start families while others liked their working status, as dancers, and had some internal conflicts. Some fathers disliked the idea of their daughters ending up with a Benjamin, but the renewed use of this custom gave the girls the go-ahead to override their father's objections. The giggles were heard from every home. They merrily packed their bells and tambourines and headed for the groves.

The Shiloh groves were filling up with music and girls with covered faces and garlands on their heads. Their perfumes sweetened the air around the trees and through the fields. The dancers wore their beautiful colorful traditional outfits. White and blue, red and black all with gold and silver linings. It was an enormous hunt. The men always had their eyes on a special girl. When she let him know she was interested, then the chase was on and of course in the end she would let him know if she agreed to join him. The girls would run away and hide behind a tree or large bush if they didn't want to be captured by the man in pursuit, which would leave the man to go and try his luck elsewhere. Sometimes the best dancers weren't the prettiest or the youngest, but their feminine moves and seductive scents grabbed the men's attention.

"What is in a dance?" a shy young Benjamin asked. "Look at the Shiloh girls, and you will know." Answered his older companion. The young boy was still confused but joined the other men for the remainder of the afternoon hoping to select his future sweetheart.

Yoav and Rimona, and Itai and Livnat, went back to the tent to attend to the wounded.

"You know we're not going to leave without you! Our Benjamin Brother's." Yoav said to the wounded soldiers in the tent. "How can I chase a woman dancer in the grove with this broken leg my brother Yoav?"

"Easy! I have an idea," said Itai "Let's see. How many of us are left?" Itai was silently pointing and counting. "Including you, I count … twenty! Ready and willing men to take a second chance on life." "What's your idea my young brother Itai, Let's hear it!" said one of the wounded with some hope.

"Well, first of all, let's start with a bath and a fresh set of clothes," said Rimona reading Itai's mind. "It's a good idea," said Livnat. The enthusiasm was building.

"Everyone get out of the tent" ordered Rimona in a commanding voice, yet with a soft smile. The two women bathed and dressed the wounded Benjamins. Yoav and Itai, carried the first man on a stretcher through the streets and to the grove with loud shouts and laughter. The other nineteen would follow, one at a time. They found a perfect shady spot and left them there, right under a fruit tree.

"The best place for an ambush …" said Yoav with a big smile "… is when you sit and do nothing." In no time, the fruit tree in the grove started to fill with a group of dancers with the sound of bells, tambourines, and clackers, along with the sweet fragrance of oils and perfumes made from tamarisk and coriander. The girls approached the wounded who were laying on their backs and after they selected their man, they sat on the stretcher and began forming conversations.

Two hundred warriors from the Benjamin's, each found a wife and an early evening wedding took place. There was wonderful music and dancing and as the night progressed. Each couple made plans for their departure and for their future.

They packed up their tents and all of their belongings and some teamed up in groups and walked together to the Benjamin territory. Others, just grabbed their woman, put her on a horse, if they had one, and rode away as the custom decreed. Bonfires were spotted all the way from Shiloh to the Benjamin territory.

"Yoav?" Itai questioned, "What are we going to do when we get to our village?"

The towns and villages that existed previously were burnt to the ground. A small lamb was mounted on Yoav's horse.

"We are going to clear the land, raise animals and build farms. We are done with the sword. The curse is gone. The brotherly war is over."

Chapter 71
"Son Of Benjamin"

Shiloh was quiet by the next morning. The last group of newlyweds were on their way and the council members were preparing to return to their territories. There was no unfinished business amongst the twelve tribes and the promise of peace and unity was noticeable everywhere.

Gershon started preparing to leave Shiloh. "Where are you heading Levite?" "To Bethlehem Judea my warrior Benjamin brother Boaz." "Ah, to say farewell to Ofra? "

"Yes."

"May she rest in peace now," said Boaz.

"You probably heard by now brother Boaz, what the elders, and the priesthood proclaimed; to erase all memories of that war and not to speak about it because there is no glory in a brotherly war." "Oh Levite, say those words, to the glorious victims who gave their lives for the name of Brotherhood." Boaz whispered to himself.

"And you brother Boaz the Benjamin, where are you going from here? I don't know why you didn't find a woman and settle down. There were so many beautiful women looking for a good husband. Look how they seduced the men with the music and a dance." Gershon spoke with love and concern for his younger dearest friend.

Boaz looked at Gershon and spoke. "Servant of El. I will let destiny find me the right woman. I can't go and chase a woman up there." Boaz replied. "Destiny doesn't like people waiting around. Go entice destiny a bit. Maybe she will come your way. We are not getting younger, neither you, me, or your horse." Gershon said while he extended his laugh. "I think my horse knows we mentioned him. Look he's kicking the ground with his left foot." Boaz laughed. "He's a lefty like me, as my name implies, whatever that means." said Boaz with a big smile.

"Well, I better leave now brother Boaz, and join the caravan. Rachel is waiting for me in the triangle on the hill. From there we will continue to Bethlehem Judea. She will join me, and we will go to Ofra's father. He offered to have her live in his house, and help him, now that the old lady has passed."

After a moment of silence Boaz spoke. "Gershon, please take with you this small stone, and place it on Ofra's grave."

"I will Brother Boaz. Thank you." That afternoon, Boaz, a man with nine fingers, and one leg, was sitting under a tree by the grove. His beautiful horse was standing next to him. Although the love fest was over, he thought he heard soft bells and a tambourine, so he looked in the direction of the sound and saw a woman approaching. She was dancing towards him to the rhythm of her music but clearly hadn't mastered the art like the girls from Shiloh. Her face was fully covered with a special veil. She danced and walked in a circle around him, and he could tell she was pretty, but definitely not like the professional dancers. "Pretty woman! You didn't find your man yesterday?" "Does this man not like my music and my dance?" "Your voice is sweeter than your music, let me look at your eyes." She dropped her veil.

"Dina? Dina!" Boaz jumped forward staggering.

"Benjamin man …" she said "… five months passed, and my husband is resting in peace. My father and his brothers no longer have a hold on me. Look at me, I can dance." "I can see that, Benjamin daughter." Boaz looked at Dina with a warm and tender gaze. She looked at him with loving eyes and before they embraced, she said "Son of Benjamin, join me, let's go and build a nation."

THE END